SUMMER
ON THE MOON

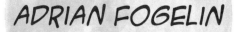

ADRIAN FOGELIN

PEACHTREE
ATLANTA

Published by
PEACHTREE PUBLISHERS
1700 Chattahoochee Avenue
Atlanta, Georgia 30318-2112
www.peachtree-online.com

Text © 2012 by Adrian Fogelin

First trade paperback edition published in 2014

Book design by Maureen Withee
Composition by Melanie McMahon Ives

Printed in February 2014 in Melrose Park, Illinois, by Lake Book Manufacturing in the United States
of America

10 9 8 7 6 5 4 3 2 (hardcover)
10 9 8 7 6 5 4 3 2 1 (trade paperback)

Library of Congress Cataloging-in-Publication Data

Fogelin, Adrian.
   Summer on the moon / written by Adrian Fogelin.
     p. cm.
   Summary: Thirteen-year-old Socko and his mother leave their cramped, unsafe inner city apartment
and move to a house in a new suburban development where they plan to care for Socko's crotchety
great-grandfather, but when they arrive they discover that the rest of the homes are unfinished, they
are the only residents of Moon Ridge Estates, and that trouble has followed them.
   ISBN 978-1-56145-626-0 (hardcover)
   ISBN 978-1-56145-785-4 (trade paperback)

   [1. Great-grandfathers--Fiction. 2. Gangs--Fiction. 3. Suburbs--Fiction.] I. Title.
PZ7.F72635Su 2012
[Fic]--dc23
                2011020467

This one is for you, Matthew.
Hurry up and learn to read!

Big thanks to my friends and critics, the Wednesday Night Writers.
Your support gives me the courage to audaciously commit words to paper.
Your honesty keeps me out of trouble.

Thanks also to my husband Ray, who understands when
I disappear into a world only I can see.

1
SPIDER INVASION

Socko pushed open the front door of their apartment building and instantly noticed—the Temporarily Out of Order sign on the elevator was gone!

"They fixed it!" Damien yelled, leading the charge across the lobby—sometimes Socko thought they shared a brain.

As he skidded to a stop, Damien slapped the Open Door button.

Nothing happened. Socko reached across and popped the button again. The door of their personal amusement park ride was taking its time opening. "Maybe somebody stole the sign." He was ready to walk away when the door slid back with a groan. "After you," he said, then followed Damien into the musty wooden box they called "the Hurtler."

"Don't trust it, boys," called the old guy who always sat in a plastic chair beside the bank of mailboxes. "It's a death trap!"

The boys exchanged glances as the door closed behind them.

Even under normal operation the ancient elevator broke down all the time, trapping people between floors, sometimes for hours—and what Socko and his friend had in mind wasn't "normal operation."

Socko hit the 5 button and the elevator began its wheezy climb to the top floor. He felt tremors through the thin soles of his sneakers, like the "Hurtler" was going to have a heart attack any second—but they had to celebrate somehow.

School had ended less than an hour ago. "Free at last!" Damien had yelled as they ran down the mildew-infested halls of Grover

Cleveland Middle School. If they got trapped joyriding in the "Hurtler," big deal. They had all summer.

The elevator heaved a sigh and stopped on the top floor. "Ya ready?" Socko's thumb hovered over the launch button.

Damien tapped the *S* on his Superman ball cap. "Hit it."

Socko punched the button for the basement.

A flicker of light jumped from one numbered button to the next as the elevator dropped. "Five…four…three…," they chanted.

"Now!" Damien roared.

Socko smacked the Open Door button, triggering an instant malfunction. Like a yo-yo hitting the end of its string, the falling box stopped with a jolt. Socko got a sudden taste of pizza—his last free school lunch of sixth grade.

Damien slapped a hand on top of his cap. "Sweet!"

"*Definitely* sweet."

"Again?" asked Damien.

"Yeah!" Socko hit the 5. Instead of starting the climb to the top, the elevator cable let out a loud *twang*.

Damien scrambled to grab the bar that ran along the walls of the elevator. Socko's breath caught. If the cable snapped, they'd hurtle for real—down the shaft to the basement where the rickety box would explode on impact. But when nothing worse followed the scary *twang*, Damien reached across and popped the 5 button again. This time the box went down instead of up, dropping fast.

"What the heck!" Socko slapped a button. The cable twanged again, louder this time as the elevator lurched to a stop. The box shuddered, then stilled.

In the shivering silence, Socko could hear his own rapid breathing.

"Try it again," said Damien.

"You sure? What if the cable breaks?"

"Wuss."

Socko punched the 5, then slouched against the wall like he hadn't just been a wuss. High overhead, the motor let out a muffled *whirr*. A split second later, the gasp of a dying motor echoed down the shaft.

Socko popped the 5 button half a dozen times, secretly relieved when nothing happened.

"Allow me." Damien tapped the red *S* on his cap again, revving up his superpowers, then thumbed the button. When the magic of the *S* failed, Damien kicked the door.

"You think we broke it?" Socko thought of his mother, Delia, who would have to puff and blow her way up four flights of stairs after a day on her feet at Phat Burger.

"You kidding? It breaks all the time!" Damien tried the Open Door button. The door ground open, revealing the side of the elevator shaft with a space about a foot wide at the top. "Oh, man. Stuck between floors." He grabbed the edge of the floor over his head and pulled himself up. His chest resting on the floor above, he rolled through the opening.

For Socko, who was taller and heavier, getting through the gap was a squeeze.

"Come on, Burger Boy." Damien latched onto his arms and yanked.

Socko was being dragged out of the elevator when he saw the old guy's brown slippers and baggy socks. They were on the ground floor again.

"Need this?" A wrinkled hand held the Temporarily Out of Order sign.

"Thanks, Mr. Marvin." Damien jammed the sign into the crack at the edge of the door that had just closed behind them.

"We didn't bust it," said Socko. "It just sort of happened."

Mr. Marvin turned the newspaper in his lap their way. "Everything's broke." He tapped the headline. "Unemployment Tops 9 Percent." The hardware store where the old guy had worked for twenty-seven years had closed months ago. He crossed his legs. The slipper on his foot jiggled nervously up and down. "The world's a mess, boys."

Socko could tell he was just warming up. "See ya, Mr. Marvin." He started for the stairwell door, then glanced back. "Damien?"

Damien stood, fists stuffed in his back pockets. "Found another one." He stared at the closed elevator door. Gouged into the wood was a crude drawing of a spider. "Rapp," he muttered.

Socko walked back for a closer look. He ran a hand over the scarred wood—which felt strangely cold in the warm lobby. Rapp, the teen who always traveled with a knife in his pocket, lived in 2B—a radioactive danger zone that kept Socko and his friend off the second floor. The danger zone seemed to be growing.

Just the day before they'd found a similar spider painted on the sidewalk in front of Donatelli's, the convenience store across the street from the apartment building.

"Bunch of punks," Mr. Marvin said. "Know why Rapp named his so-called gang the Tarantulas? He had a pet spider when he was a kid." He shook his head. "He's making things up as he goes along. Heck, he's seventeen. What does he know about running anything? Those boys are just playin' at this gang business."

Mr. Marvin picked a speck of lint off the knee of his pants. "Still… Rapp has a temper and don't you ever forget it. My advice to you boys? Steer clear of the whole lot of them."

"Sure thing," said Socko. "Come on, Damien." He pushed open the heavy door to the stairs and listened.

"Nobody," said Damien, listening too. The elevator was dangerous, sure, but the dark stairwell wasn't exactly safe either.

Socko trudged up the steps, breathing through his mouth. This place never smelled good. Today it smelled like a restroom—and not the air freshener part.

"What you wanna do tomorrow?" Damien asked.

Even though it was the first day of summer vacation, Socko couldn't come up with much. "Hang out on the roof and work on our tans?" he joked.

"Genius idea! You turn red like a stoplight, then peel like a banana. And me?" Damien held out one skinny arm. "I'm naturally tan."

"True and true." Socko was what Damien called "beyond white," and although Damien's mom was white, he definitely took after the black dad he'd never met. "*You* got any genius ideas?"

"I'm working on it." Damien loped ahead, his footfalls echoing.

Socko was watching the toes of his sneakers on the gray steps when he bumped into Damien.

"Another one." Damien pointed to the wall.

The spray-painted spider was so new it was still shiny. Socko took a quick look and kept climbing.

"Seriously, man!" Damien caught up to Socko on the second-floor landing. "Mr. Marvin says steer clear. How're we supposed to do that?"

"I don't know. Die young?"

A while back Socko had been flagged to run an errand for Rapp. It was no biggie. He'd delivered a folded piece of paper to a guy on the corner of Baker and Elm. When he reported a successful handoff, Rapp had put a sweaty hand on the back of his neck. "Ya did good, Big Red."

All winter Socko had worn a hoodie to keep his stupid red hair from attracting attention. What he needed was cryptic coloration so he could blend into his surroundings like the moths and lizards he'd seen on the Nature Channel.

Size was Socko's other attention-getting problem—he'd gladly give his short buddy Damien some of the extra inches he had picked up in the last few months. Showing no sign of quitting, his growth spurt was putting him in Rapp's face a little more each day.

"Seriously." Damien slapped Socko's arm. "Sooner or later we're gonna have to join. Probably sooner."

A tingle ran down Socko's spine. "They ask you?"

"Nah."

Socko started climbing again.

"Got any food at your place?" Damien asked.

"Probably." Socko's mom could bring home anything that had been under the heat lamp for more than two hours—one of the few advantages of working at a fast-food place that wasn't a chain.

"Burgers? Fries? How about a couple of those little pie thingies with the greasy crusts?" Damien cut in front of him, climbing the stairs backwards. "I could be a runner for the gang—you know I can really pump on my skateboard."

5

"You want to end up in jail?" Socko heard his mother's words come out of his mouth.

"So? I hear they eat regular in jail."

That morning Socko's mom had stood at their window, looking down on Rapp and his boys loitering on the sidewalk in front of Donatelli's. "Jobs," she'd said. "That's what those punks need."

Jobs. Like *that* was going to happen. Out Of Business signs were taped to windows all over the neighborhood, not just Mr. Marvin's hole-in-the-wall hardware store. The evening news his mom watched spewed reports about people losing jobs like water from a busted pipe.

"Third floor." Damien pushed open the stairwell door. "Gotta drop off my pack." He stuck his head around the door and listened. Apartment 3A was the first on the left. The fight going on inside was coming through loud and clear.

"Or not." Damien pulled his head back and eased the door shut.

"You think your mom's okay?" Socko asked.

"She's fine." Damien jogged up the next flight of stairs. "I'd help her if she was *really* in trouble, but she picks out these guys, not me. This one's really big. I'm not messing with him." He stepped into the fourth-floor hallway.

Socko's apartment was one floor above Damien's—they signaled each other with a broom handle banged against Socko's floor or Damien's ceiling. Socko lifted the key string from around his neck and unlocked the door.

He felt himself unclench as soon as they were locked inside. And double-locked. And chained.

Except for the steady drip in the kitchen sink that had left a rusty bull's-eye on the enamel, the apartment was quiet. Delia wouldn't get off her shift at Phat Burger for another hour.

Socko's backpack hit the floor, then Damien's. They pried off sneakers, peeled off socks. Damien wiggled his toes and sighed, but it was Socko's toes that were celebrating. Delia could get clothes to keep up with his growth spurt out of the Help Yourself closet at St. Ignatius, the Catholic church down the street—you didn't even have to be Catholic to help yourself—but shoes that fit cost money.

Damien padded across the gray linoleum and stuck his head in the fridge. "Pretty empty." He stood on his toes, reached into the cupboard over the sink, then stared at the box of microwave popcorn in his hand. "No butter? This is *so* bogus."

"Delia's trying to lose weight."

"Wish my mom was fat." Damien tore the clear wrapper off a packet of popcorn with his teeth. "Fat moms don't have boyfriends." He opened the microwave door and fell back a step. "Whoa! Mega roach!"

The cockroach faced them, antennae raised.

Socko eyed the can of Raid on the counter, but he didn't want to blast bug killer into the microwave. Plus, he wasn't crazy about killing things, even roaches.

Damien slammed the microwave door and hit the 1-minute button. "Death by laser!" Palms on the edge of the counter, he watched the roach stroll across the rotating tray.

"They're indestructible," said Socko, secretly pulling for the roach. "Been around since the Cretaceous."

The roach stopped in its tracks and began to spark.

Damien gaped at the oven window. "I wasn't expecting that. Were you expecting that?"

Beep.

Damien popped the microwave door. "Dead roach flying!" He flicked the crisp bug across the room.

Socko dodged it. The nuked roach landed legs up and skidded to a stop under a chair.

Damien put the bag in the microwave, selected Popcorn, and hit Start. "Our snack lives!" he said, rubbing his hands together as the popcorn bag began to jiggle.

So Delia wouldn't freak when she saw it, Socko picked up the roach by one stiff leg and dropped it in the trash.

Beep.

They tossed the hot popcorn bag back and forth as they charged the sofa. Damien had possession when they vaulted the sofa back and whumped down on the gray-green cushions. While Damien was ripping the bag open, Socko snagged the remote and hit Power. Instantly a black-and-white face filled the screen.

"Not nature again!" Damien stuffed a humongoid handful of popcorn into his mouth. The panda on the screen did the same with a bunch of bamboo shoots. "I'm so tired of nature!"

"How can you be? You never see any."

"I see plenty of cock-a-roaches." Bits of popcorn sprayed out with his words.

"Roaches don't count." Socko reached into the popcorn bag and stuffed his own mouth. He chewed. The panda chewed.

"Hey, Socko!" Damien pointed at the screen. "That's you, man. You're the panda."

"What're you talking about?"

"The panda's big, but harmless—like you. I mean, a panda's a bear, but all it eats is leaves."

"I don't see you acting like a superpredator."

"Look at me!" Damien spread his arms. They stuck out of his T-shirt sleeves, as skinny as pick-up sticks. "I weigh, like, eighty-seven pounds, so what am I supposed to predate on?"

"I don't know." Socko propped his feet on the coffee table. "Algae?"

"Algae, huh?" Damien dug into the bag, considering. "What does algae taste like?"

2
BURGER QUEEN

A lion pride was circling a baby wildebeest when Socko heard the stairwell door hit the wall. The *bang* was followed by a groan.

"The Burger Queen is in the building." Damien tipped his head back and shook the last few kernels into his mouth.

Socko vaulted off the sofa. He twisted dead bolts, dropped chains, and opened the door. "Yo, Mom."

"Yo, Socko." A wavy strand of black hair hung over one of his mother's eyes. Hands full, Delia stuck out her lower lip and blew. The damp strand lifted, then settled back over her eye.

He tucked the hair behind her ear. "How was your day?"

"Super. A guy threw up on the counter and I had to clean it up—the girls said it was my job since I make the big bucks."

Socko snorted. As day manager she made two dollars over minimum wage. He took the purse clutched to her side.

"And I had to get tough with Rapp. He thinks he's entitled to sit in the booth all day." She held out her arm. "Take this too. How can that elevator be broke again?"

As he lifted the plastic bag of supper from his mom's wrist, he swore to himself, *no more hurtling.*

The arm remained outstretched. The fingers wiggled. "Report card?"

Socko put the purse and the Phat bag on the counter and went to his fallen pack. "Check out math last."

She stared at the paper he put in her hand. "Math's a C+. The rest, all Bs!" She smothered him in a hug that smelled like fries and the cheap rose perfume he'd given her last Christmas. "This place is *not* going to eat *you* alive," she whispered fiercely. "My boy's going to college!"

He hoped the words, hot in his ear, hadn't been heard by his friend on the couch. Who from around here went to college?

Besides, the report card wasn't that great. His mother only thought it was great because she'd never finished high school. He was wishing he had gotten at least one A for her when something crash-landed in the apartment below, followed by muffled yelling.

Delia rested her chin on Socko's shoulder. "You wanna stay for supper?" she asked Damien.

"I wouldn't mind."

"What're we having?" Socko asked, kind of hoping his mom would let go.

He heard Damien cross the room to check out the contents of the Phat Burger bag.

"Specialty of the house," Damien said. "Bun Busters."

Delia gave Socko one last hard hug and turned him loose. "How was *your* report card, Damien?"

Damien grabbed a burger and shrugged. "Mrs. DeLuca liked me so much she's gonna keep me in sixth another year."

"What happened, Damien?" Delia took the Bun Buster out of Damien's hands and put it on a plate. "You're a smart kid!" She handed the plate back to him.

"It's not that big a deal," Socko said. When it came to giving out free advice about "getting an education," his mother didn't know when to quit. "I flunked second, remember?"

"I blame myself for that," she said.

Socko and his mother had camped at a friend's place most of that school year, sleeping on the floor. The only good thing was the apartment was near the Y, so he had learned to swim.

With a mother like Louise, Damien was bound to lose a year here and there. This was the second time he'd been held back—and he couldn't even swim.

"I know it's tough," said Delia as the sound of yelling from the apartment below grew louder. "But you just have to work harder!"

"Why?" Damien asked. "It's not like I'm going anywhere."

She grabbed his shoulders and gave him a little shake. "What are you talking about? Look at the president! His mom's white, like yours. His dad's black, like yours. You're both skinny—both good looking." She tried to catch his eye but he looked away.

"Bet he didn't suck at reading."

"Aw, baby…"

Socko could tell that his mom wanted to hug Damien, but the burger plate was in the way. Instead she rubbed his arms like she was trying to make his blood move faster. "You gonna do summer school?"

"Can't. Summer school got cut. No money."

"It's canceled for real?" Socko was used to things being cut at home, but at school?

"You're going to summer school," Delia said firmly.

"I'm not kidding. There *is* no summer school."

"Sure there is." Delia flattened her palm against the front of her orange and brown smock. "You're looking at her. Starting tomorrow, we work on your reading." She turned Damien around and aimed him at the table. "Don't you dare take a bite of that burger 'til we're all at the table. Socko, grab the napkins."

"I still don't get why we have to sit at the table and mess up three plates," Damien complained.

"Because we're better than this place," Delia said. "We have class."

***

Socko watched Damien wolf down the last bite of the last burger and suck the ketchup off his fingers. "We got the dishes, Mom," he said.

"With paper plates we'd be done already," Damien said, picking up a dish towel.

Delia settled into her taped-up lounge chair. While the boys did the dishes, she read a newspaper left on a table by a customer. Socko's mother read anything and everything that came her way, even if it was just the back of a cereal box.

When the dishes were done, Socko drained the sink. Damien hung the damp dish towel on the handle of the oven and reclaimed the Superman cap Delia had made him take off at the table. "What now?" he asked.

Delia held up her favorite DVD, *Dirty Dancing*. "Movie?"

Damien turned away from Delia and faked a silent gag.

"Uh…no thanks, Mom. Think we'll go up to the roof."

His mother frowned. If it were up to her, Socko would never leave the apartment. She paid for cable she couldn't afford so he'd stay inside. She picked at the tape on the arm of her chair. "You sure Rapp and those losers he calls his gang won't be up there?"

"No, Mom. The roof's ours."

At least until Rapp decides it isn't anymore, Socko added silently.

3
MATH ATTACK

They climbed the metal steps that led from the fifth-floor landing to the roof. "I could use a little help," said Socko, trying to lift the hatch at the top.

"A little help, coming up." They raised the hatch with their shoulders, side by side. "What's *she* doing up here?" Damien asked.

Junebug, the seventeen-year-old who lived two doors down from Socko, had gotten there ahead of them. Wearing her usual tight shorts and tank top, she sat on a beach towel with a book open in her lap, her bare brown legs stretched out in front of her.

"How'd you lift the hatch by yourself?" Socko asked her.

Damien didn't give her a chance to answer. "You never come up here!" he called. "What're you doing up here now?"

She tapped the page with the eraser end of her pencil. "Studying." After Junebug dropped out of high school, Delia had talked her into getting a GED and then enrolling in a nurse's aide program at the community college.

"Give us a break!" Damien said. "The roof is ours. We got stuff to talk about...guy stuff. Can't you study at home?"

She rocked her feet back and forth impatiently on the thick wooden heels of her platform shoes. "I'd like to give you two *men* your space, but I can't study at home. Rapp keeps calling."

"Hate to remind you, but he *is* your boyfriend. Get your aunt to say you're out."

"My Aunt Mavis is so churchy she wouldn't lie if my life depended on it! Am I right or am I right, Socko?"

"You're right." Every time he saw her, Aunt Mavis was either coming or going to the AME church down the street. She'd told Delia she'd taken Junebug in when her mother died because it was her "Christian duty."

Junebug snapped her fingers. "Get over here, Damien. Give me your wrist." The beads on her glossy hair extensions rattled as she tossed them over her shoulders. "Let me take your pulse."

"How much ya gonna pay me?"

"One day soon folks are gonna pay *me* to do this, but I won't charge you this time."

Socko shoved the hatch aside and they climbed onto the roof. Damien sauntered over to Junebug, holding out his arm.

She pressed her fingers to Damien's wrist.

"You pour a whole bottle of perfume on yourself?" Damien asked.

Ignoring him, she kept her eyes on the second hand on the "nurse's watch" she was so proud of. "Pulse, sixty-eight."

"Is that good?" asked Damien.

"Yeah, it's good."

"How good?"

Damien was as starved for compliments as he was for food.

Junebug waved Socko over. "Your turn."

He held out his wrist; he knew the drill. Junebug practiced on him and Delia all the time. Delia's pulse and blood pressure were always too high—and just hearing her numbers sent his vitals soaring too.

While Junebug watched the sweep second hand, Socko checked out her fake eyelashes. They looked heavy enough to sprain her sparkly blue eyelids. Except for the nurse's watch and the fact that she'd cut her dagger fingernails short for the aide program, everything about the way she looked seemed to be going in another direction.

"Pulse, seventy-five," she said.

"Figures!" Damien complained. "He's seven points better."

Junebug released Socko's wrist. "A slow pulse rocks, Damien. You keep that up and you'll never have a heart attack or stroke. A slow pulse means you're an athlete."

Damien knuckled Socko's shoulder. "You hear that, man?" He strutted, scaring the pigeons on the low wall at the roof's edge into a rattling launch. "I'm a ath-uh-lete!"

"Oh yeah! I've seen you on that skateboard." Junebug gave Socko a wink.

Socko grinned. Not that he'd say it out loud, but aside from Damien, she was his best friend in the Kludgeman Arms Apartments. When she used to babysit him, they'd do goofy things together, like making peanut butter pizzas using burger buns and a jar of Jif (once the bubbling-hot peanut butter had peeled all the skin off the roof of Junebug's mouth). Then there was the headstand contest that ended when he fell over and put his sneaker through the TV.

Back then her teeth were too big and she looked as scrawny as Damien. About a year ago she'd filled out in all the right places, turning pretty almost overnight. She'd attracted lots of guys, but they'd disappeared fast when Rapp claimed her.

"You wanna look down my throat or anything?" Damien asked. "I bet I got great tonsils."

"Throats are next week." She went back to studying.

The boys plopped down at the edge of the roof. After checking the low wall for pigeon mess, Socko rested his arms on its warm concrete.

"You think I should wave?" asked Damien.

"Don't," said Socko, even though he knew his friend was kidding. On the street five floors below, Rapp, Meat, and three other guys leaned against Donatelli's storefront.

They didn't look all that scary from here. If his growth spurt kept going, in a couple of months Socko would be taller than Rapp. Even Meat, a slab of a kid with really bad skin, looked more flabby than fierce from this distance.

"Check out the lids," said Damien.

Tonight all the Tarantulas wore their ball caps with the bills turned left, and each left pant leg was rolled. It was like they'd found an out-of-date gangsta handbook, and they'd just gotten to the part about the gangsta dress code.

The cap bills turned, five pairs of eyes tracking Mrs. Arturo as she approached, walking her Chihuahua, Puppy Precious. Most women stared straight ahead when they passed the Tarantulas, but Mrs. A. walked right over and put a hand on Meat's cheek. Socko wondered if she looked at him now and still saw the kid she'd named Freddie. Before walking away, she reached out and patted Rapp's cheek; although they were just second-floor neighbors, she called him her son too.

Hadn't she even noticed how bad her "sons" had turned out? Didn't the knife that fell out of Freddie's pocket when she did the wash give her a clue?

Puppy Precious was piddling his way to the next corner when Rapp slid a cell phone out of his pocket and hit a button. Phone pressed to his ear, he gazed at the brick front of the Kludge.

Damien turned toward Junebug. "Hey. Your boyfriend's calling you."

She pointed a penlight at the page and clicked it on. "I'm not home." The sun was going down.

Rapp dropped the phone back in his pocket. He shoved off the wall of Donatelli's and gripped the waist of his pants with one hand. The four other Tarantulas resting against the wall straightened. Each grabbed the waist of his own pants. As they shuffled away, Socko noticed that hanging from each left back pocket was a red bandanna—it had to be part of the new uniform. Red tails wagging, they hung a left at Baker and disappeared.

Damien opened the flap on his pack and fished out a semester's worth of incomplete math worksheets. "Decimals." He folded the top sheet into an airplane.

Socko watched the math plane's long, slow glide down to the street. It landed on the shiny roof of Rapp's Trans Am. The car, a gift from a dead uncle, was parked in the street in front of the apartment building. "Hope I didn't put my name on it," Damien said.

"That would be a first." Socko snagged the next worksheet in the pile and folded it into a plane of his own.

Damien pulled a cigarette lighter out of his pocket. "Genius idea!" He held the flame under the paper plane in Socko's hand until it caught, then blew on it gently to get the fire going.

When Socko launched the kamikaze plane, it soared with the trailing edge of its wings on fire. His chin resting on the ledge, Socko watched it loop.

"Crap, oh crap!" Damien sat up straight as the plane took a sudden dive and landed on the fabric awning over the door of Donatelli's. "Hide!"

"Whatever you two are doing," called Junebug, "cut it out."

"We're not doing nothing!" Damien protested.

Socko peered over the ledge. Mr. Donatelli, who had just come out to close up for the night, popped the sag of fabric with a broom handle. The plane, now just a blackened scrap, fluttered to the sidewalk. Mr. Donatelli stomped it, then glared up at the roof of the Kludge. Socko ducked.

By the time he looked again, the old man had cranked in the awning and locked the folding metal grate over the storefront.

The fiery math attack resumed.

Fractions burned out in the hedge in front of the apartment building. Numerators smoldered by the curb. Every now and then Socko looked down at the plane on the roof of Rapp's Trans Am, wishing it had landed somewhere else. What if Damien *had* put his name on it?

They had just launched the last worksheet when Rapp, now solo, appeared in the street below. Like a guided missile, the flaming plane hit Rapp's chest. The gang leader slapped the burning paper away. He barely glanced up toward the roof before bolting to the door of the Kludge and letting himself in.

Damien jumped to his feet, the whites around his eyes attracting the last of the daylight. "I'm outta here!"

"What did you do?" Junebug demanded.

"A paper airplane just hit your boyfriend," said Socko. "It was sort of on fire."

Damien grabbed his arm. "Let's go, let's go!"

"Wait!" Junebug closed her textbook. "Rapp'll catch you on the stairs—you know how fast he is. Hide behind the AC box—I'll handle him." As Junebug rearranged herself, leaning back on her arms and crossing her legs at the ankles, the night-light mounted on a metal pole came on, flooding the roof with bluish light.

Damien gave Socko's arm another tug. "Come on!"

Crouched in the shadows behind the box, Socko listened. The only thing he heard at first was Damien, breathing hard.

"Maybe he's not coming," Damien whispered.

Could they get that lucky? Socko heard the ring of boots on metal steps.

He watched with one eye, his cheek pressed against warm metal. *I don't wanna die, I don't wanna die, I don't wanna die.*

Rapp's palms slapped the roof. He boosted himself up and erupted from the hatch opening. Panting, he stood, feet spread. Maybe Rapp wasn't tall or heavy, but he was big like lightning, big like a surge of electricity. Rapp's stare could fry the heart in your chest—and he was staring straight at Junebug.

"Hey, baby," Junebug sassed, but Socko heard the fear underneath.

"So, you're *out?*" said Rapp. Seeing her, he seemed to forget his mission to kill the perpetrators of the flaming plane attack. "And you're *studying?*"

"I *am* out!" she snapped. "And I *am* studying."

Rapp reached her in three strides and clamped one of her skinny arms in his fist. He jerked her to her feet.

"Easy, baby…easy!" She tried to twist out of his grip.

Socko felt Damien's breath on the back of his neck. His friend was watching too.

As Rapp dragged Junebug toward the hatch, she whimpered, "Let go, baby. That hurts!" She turned toward the AC box. Socko pulled back and closed his eyes.

All of a sudden, the breathing on his neck stopped. Socko opened his eyes and looked over his shoulder. No Damien.

When he peered out, his friend was standing in plain sight, both hands in the air like a cop had ordered him to put 'em up. "Listen, man. Sorry about the plane. I was just up here messin'. Didn't mean to hit you. No hard feelings?"

Rapp tossed Junebug's arm away. He strode toward Damien and snatched the front of his T-shirt. Socko heard the air explode out of Damien's lungs as Rapp jerked up on the shirt and shoved him hard. Damien stumbled backwards until the wall at the edge of the roof pressed against the backs of his thighs.

"You still feel like messin'?" Rapp was slowly bending Damien back over the five-story drop.

The blood rushed loudly in Socko's ears. He had to do something!

"You're so interested in airplanes…maybe you'd like to fly." Rapp lowered Damien a little more.

"Come on, man," Damien begged, one hand on his Superman lid, the other feeling behind him for the wall. "I didn't mean nothin'…"

Now, Socko told himself. *Do something now.* He tried to take a step, but his foot wouldn't move. Maybe his sudden paralysis was a sign he should stay put. All that kept Damien from falling was Rapp's grip on his shirt. Surprise him, and he might let go.

Unable to watch, Socko stared up at the muddy gray sky, all the stars snuffed by the lights of the city. He only hoped that dying didn't hurt too much and that Damien would forgive him from wherever kids went when their best friend didn't save them from being dropped off a roof.

He heard the clack of Junebug's platforms. Drawing a sharp breath, he looked again.

"Come on, baby. You're scaring the kid!" She made it sound like she thought Rapp was playing, but she threw her skinny arms around his chest and held on. "He wasn't trying to set you on fire. He was just foolin' around!"

She leaned back hard and Rapp lurched away from the edge, taking Damien with him. Each time Junebug pulled on Rapp, the massive gold cross on the chain around his neck swung, catching the light.

"Rapp, baby?" Her voice was sugary when she turned Rapp loose. "Let's go somewhere, okay? Just you and me."

That seemed to wake Rapp up. He let go of Damien's shirt and shook himself. For a moment he stood absolutely still, staring at his own hands, then he swung around and grasped Junebug's upper arm.

This time she didn't resist. She led Rapp to the open hatch and climbed down through it ahead of him.

The clatter of footsteps on the metal risers died out. Limp with relief and shame, Socko stayed hidden.

"You dead back there, man?" Damien called.

Socko slid out from behind the AC unit. "Sorry. I don't know what happened. It was like I was paralyzed." His voice was a dry whisper. "I can't believe you stood up to Rapp."

"Me neither. Junebug's not even my friend, she's *your* friend." As Damien talked, he paced back and forth, three steps each way, his hands buried deep in his pockets. "Next time he sees me, Rapp's gonna squash me like a bug."

Feeling unsteady, Socko dropped to his knees behind the wall at the roof's edge and stared at the sidewalk below. Nothing happened for a minute, and then he heard the front door of the apartment building open.

Rapp dragged Junebug across the sidewalk and pushed her into the Trans Am. As it squealed away from the curb, Socko saw the pale shape of a paper plane blow off the car roof.

4
THE OFFER

Socko clutched Junebug's nursing book to his chest as they tramped down the stairs. Damien hadn't stopped talking since the gang leader had left the roof. "Was I some kind of crazy taking on Rapp?" The towel Junebug had been sitting on draped his shoulders. "I gotta lie low. Make myself scarce. Go invisible. To kill me he'll have to find me first." Damien gripped the ends of the towel and tugged hard.

"Next time I'll have your back. Promise." Socko was already reimagining the scene on the roof. "I'm big. I can fight him if I have to."

"*You*, fight Rapp? Get real!" Damien jerked the towel from around his neck and tossed it at him. "Never gonna happen. You're the panda man!" Damien's footsteps echoed as he ran down one more flight of stairs to his own floor.

Socko put a shaking hand on the knob that opened the door to the fourth-floor hall. His friend was right: He might be big enough to take on Rapp, but he was nothing but a leaf eater.

"Going through!" Damien called.

They always opened the doors to their separate floors at the same instant so each knew the other was safe—which seemed pathetic to Socko all of a sudden. He'd probably just run away if his friend needed help. "Going through," he mumbled.

He nudged the stairwell door open an inch and scanned the hall on his own floor. Empty. By now Delia would be dozing in her chair, so he let himself into the apartment quietly. He didn't want to talk anyway.

Socko was easing the door shut when his mother yelled, "Guess what?"

He fell against the door, jabbing himself in the back with the lock knob. "Mom! Don't scare me like that!"

"Nancy called!" she yelled again from the recliner.

"So?" His grandmother, who insisted they call her by her first name because "Mom" or "Grandma" made her feel old, ignored them for months at a time. "It isn't your birthday, is it?"

Delia leaned forward in her chair, her eyes bright. "This is way bigger than a lame-o happy birthday. Sit down."

All Socko wanted to do was hole up behind the pull-down classroom map of the thirteen original colonies that walled off the corner of the living room where he slept, but something about the way she was looking at him made his heart beat faster. He fell onto the loveseat he and Damien had rescued off the curb. "Okay, spill."

"Do you remember me telling you about the General?"

Socko scrambled to get his bearings.

"You know, my grandfather on my dad's side."

"You mentioned him a few times. He's a grumpy guy, right? And he's not a real general."

"Nope. Just an army cook in World War II. You never met him. I haven't seen him myself since my parents got divorced all those years ago."

He tried to look interested.

"Remember, he had a store called 'General Starr's General Store'?"

"Yeah. In some touristy place near…somewhere way north."

"Stowe, Vermont." Her eyes were really sparkling now. "And he sold it—which is huge for us."

"Huge?" Socko wondered what Damien was thinking about one floor below. "Huge how?"

"His wife died a few weeks ago." Delia frowned. "I know I should feel bad, but I barely remember her. The last time I saw either one of them I was in second grade."

The General had sold the store…his wife had died…Socko still didn't get it. "And this is huge because…?"

"Luckily the General sold the store before the economy went down the tubes. So he's got money."

"And he wants to give it to us?" Socko asked, trying to hurry things along.

"Yes, well, kind of."

He fell back against the cushions. "You're kidding!" A stupid idea popped into his head, but for one second it seemed reasonable. Money for bodyguards. One for him, one for Damien.

"Nancy says that without his wife around, he's not taking good care of himself." Delia folded her hands in her lap. "He's eighty-eight now, plus he has emphysema."

Socko had seen a gory photo in Junebug's nursing book of a chunk of lung covered with black splotches. The word "emphysema" was printed under it.

"His sons—my dad and his brother—are ready to stick him in a nursing home. He doesn't want to go. So, here's the deal. We take him in and—"

"Wait, whoa!" Socko threw his hands up like a crossing guard stopping a car about to mow down a bunch of kindergarteners. "Take him in?" He eyed the hanging map that was the "wall" of his bedroom. "Where are we gonna put him? In the tub?"

"Would you listen a minute? Here's the deal. We let him live with us, he buys us a house. A house of our own, free and clear once he…" She ran her thumb back and forth over the tape on the arm of the chair. "You know, once he's gone."

For the second time in half an hour Socko felt breathless—this time with relief. A house, away from here. Just like that, no more Rapp— no more tingling at the back of Socko's neck warning that something bad was about to happen.

But the relief burned off fast. If he left, it was just like the roof all over again. How could he do that to Damien? He'd promised—the next time he'd have Damien's back.

He twisted a button on the loveseat's upholstery. "We don't need a house." The button came off in his hand.

"Of course not. Who could leave all this?" Delia spread her arms. The bluish light from the neon sign across the street fluttered on her pale skin.

"It's not so bad here," he bluffed, pushing the all-night neon flicker and the leaky faucet and the nuked roach out of his mind.

"You're *allergic* to here, for Pete's sake!"

"I *used* to be. I'm fine now—I haven't had an asthma attack for years."

"*Please*, Socko." Delia clasped her hands and held them out to him. "No more hairy spiders. No more worries about the rent. No chance you'll end up like Frankie…" She let that one sink in.

Socko had been the first to see Frankie G. lying dead in a pool of blood by the dumpster behind the Kludge. "The guys who did it weren't even from around here," he protested, trying to erase from his mind the picture of Frankie G. with a hole in his chest.

"But it *happened* here! We'll move someplace safe, someplace where no one ends up dead on the ground. You'll go to a new school—a better one."

"I don't want a better one!" Even at GC, where most of the students slept through class, Socko had to bust his butt to get Bs. If the competition was awake, he didn't stand a chance. "Don't *I* get a vote?" he gasped, his outgrown asthma threatening to make a sudden comeback.

"Not this time, Socko. You and me are getting out of here." She slapped the arm of her recliner. "C'mere. Sit."

Hadn't she noticed he was way too big to perch on the arm of her chair like he used to? He walked over, but didn't sit down. He took a breath and pulled out the big guns. "We can't do it, Mom. I gotta stay here for Damien." He couldn't tell her about Rapp and the roof, but he had plenty of other ammunition. "Damien'll starve if we leave!

And you have friends here too. Don't forget Mr. Marvin, and that old lady in 3C. And what about Junebug, your special project?" He couldn't believe she was so ready to dump the people she had come to call family.

"I gotta put us first." She reached up and grabbed his hand. "I've never been able to give you anything. I was fifteen when I had you— just a kid raising a kid." She squeezed his hand hard. "I'm not gonna blow this. This is our one shot, Socko. Our jackpot lottery ticket!" Her voice softened. "Come on!" She squeezed his hand again, more gently this time. "A house of our own. Think about it!"

How was he supposed to think about it? He couldn't even remember the last time he'd been inside a house.

But Delia smiled as if she were standing in front of one. "A house with a lawn...and a hedge... I've always wanted a hedge."

Socko flashed to the burnt plane sticking out of the scruffy bushes hunched between the front of their building and the sidewalk. "We got a hedge."

"That doesn't count. *Our* hedge will be tall and green and at Christmas we'll put white lights all over it." Delia's free hand danced in the air. "The little kind that blink."

5
BIG BIG NEWS

Leaving?" Damien looked stunned, like the birds that sometimes flew into Donatelli's shiny plate glass window thinking it was a piece of sky. "You…leaving?"

"It won't happen for a while." Socko picked a chunk of gravel off the tar roof. "Probably never."

All day Socko had dreaded telling his friend Delia's "good news." He'd nodded dumbly each time Damien had mentioned Rapp and reminded Socko how they had to stick together.

Now Damien slumped against the wall. "I'm dead," he said. "Too bad Rapp didn't drop me off the roof last night. At least it'd be over with."

"It probably won't even happen. Who gives away houses anyway?" Socko tossed and caught the pebble. "And it's gotta take time to buy a house. The old guy might even kick before the deal goes through."

Damien rocked back and forth, hugging his knees. "Man, oh man, oh man," he moaned. "Man, oh man, oh man…"

Socko flicked the piece of gravel at him. "I'll talk her out of it."

The pebble hit Damien's neck, but it didn't catch his attention. "Not gonna happen…not gonna happen."

Socko was afraid Damien was cracking up.

Click…click.

"Crap!" Damien touched the *S* on his cap and his fingers froze there. Someone was climbing the metal steps to the roof.

Socko stared at the dark opening of the hatch, expecting to see Rapp's sideways cap pop through it, but the head that poked up was glossy with cornrows. "Hi, boys."

Socko sighed with double relief. He didn't have to stand up to Rapp, and Junebug was okay. He'd knocked on her apartment door a couple of times earlier that day, but all he'd gotten was a view of half her churchy aunt's face and a curt, "She's not here." He'd been sure something bad had happened to Junebug, and that the something bad was his fault.

She rested her arms on the roof and looked toward the spot where she'd left her stuff.

"It's all at my place," Socko said. "Sorry about—"

"It's okay," she said, cutting him off. "Damien? That superhero move of yours was real dumb, but thanks."

"Ditto," said Damien, hugging his knees.

Socko stared at Junebug. Her eyes were puffy, and a purple bruise darkened the skin on her upper arm. "You all right?" he asked.

"Fine." She looked away. "I need to talk to your mom."

"Go ahead."

"I knocked, but she didn't answer. She working late?" Junebug glanced at her wrist. "It's six fifteen. She got off a couple hours ago."

"Two hours late?" Damien butted in. "Big deal. My mom's a *day* late." Not long after Damien had left Socko's the night before, Louise and her boyfriend had gone out to a bar. She hadn't come home since. But for Louise, being late was normal. Delia was never late. She knew how much Socko worried.

Junebug climbed onto the roof and walked slowly toward them. She stopped when she reached the low wall at the edge of the roof. "Oh, look!" She did a little bounce. "There she is, getting out of a car. Your momma got wheels all of a sudden?"

Socko turned in time to see a shiny, late-model car speed away.

Delia spotted them. "Big news!" she bawled up to them from the street below, waving her arms over her head. "Big! Big! Big! Meet ya at the apartment."

"What do you think it is?" Junebug clicked down the stairs ahead of the boys. "She sure is excited!"

"Socko's out of here." Damien's voice was flat.

"Not yet!" Socko objected. "This stuff takes time."

Junebug stopped on the landing and grabbed his arm. "What're you two talking about?"

"Socko's rich great-grandfather is buying them a house." Damien scraped a wad of gum off the sole of his shoe with the edge of a step. "Socko and Delia are moving."

"Moving?" Junebug's nails bit into Socko's arm. "How far away?"

Socko twisted out of her grip. "Chill, you two. Nothing's happening yet!"

"Big, big news!" squealed Damien. "Something for sure *is* happening. Thought you said you had my back, Socko."

"I told you. I'll work on her!"

When they pushed open the stairwell door, Delia was standing in the hallway. "Ta-da!" The hand she whipped out from behind her back held a glossy brochure. "I was bussing tables—the girls never keep up with 'em the way I like—and I found this card for a real estate agent named Leah Albin from Dream-Come-True Realty!"

"Slow down, Mom. You're hyperventilating!" Socko wanted her to notice the looks on Damien's and Junebug's faces so she'd quit acting all enthusiastic, but she was too excited.

She shoved the apartment door open with her back. "As soon as she heard we'd pay cash, Leah Albin was all over it! So I said, 'Too bad I don't have a car to go see these places,' and she said, 'Not a problem,' and she picked me up and took me to see this place." She opened the brochure on the kitchen table and flattened it with her palms. "Take a look!"

Damien stood blinking. Junebug bit her lip.

"Moon Ridge Estates," Socko read.

"Our new home," Delia added.

Junebug wrapped an arm around Damien's shoulders, but he pulled away.

"Hey, Damien!" Socko called after him as he bolted for the door—but his friend was gone like smoke.

"Wait!" Delia called toward the closing door. "Have supper with us, then we'll work on your reading."

"Work on his reading?" said Socko. "Get real, Mom."

Delia's happy face crumpled.

"Are you *really* going to do this?" Junebug whispered.

Delia took Junebug's face between her hands and stared into her eyes. "You'll be fine. In a few more weeks you'll have your nurse's aide certificate, you'll get a good job. You're on your way!"

Junebug bit her lip hard and nodded once. "I'm happy for you." She vanished as quietly as Damien.

"Did you see that bruise on her arm?" asked Socko. "Rapp's been whaling on her again."

Delia blinked. "What can I do about it?" Her eyes were shiny, but her voice was tough. "I've told her to dump that sorry loser a hundred times. I can't do it for her."

"She's scared, Mom, but she listens to you. You're the one who got her to go back to school."

"She's seventeen! At her age I was supporting a kid all by myself. I can't save the world." Delia stared at the brochure on the table. "Just us."

"Mom, stop and think about this. What about the old guy we have to take along with the house? If he's like Mr. Marvin, he'll talk our ears off. And you always say we don't need a man, but if this deal goes through we'll have one—a really old one!"

"This isn't just any old man. The General is family and he's giving us a house. We need the house—and we could use some family too." When she said the word "family," she looked as wishful as she had when she'd mentioned the hedge.

"*I'm* your family! And you said he was a big grouch!"

"So he won't be a bed of roses. We're not either." She pushed the glossy paper toward him. "Would ya at least take a look?"

He put one hand on either side of the brochure and gazed at the drawing of a two-story house. The artist had gone heavy on the hedges, and the sky was pure blue with puffy white clouds, like the weather was always perfect at Moon Ridge Estates.

"Oh, Socko, the house is even prettier than the picture! Wait 'til you see the inside. It's so big and clean and new." His mother put her arm around his shoulders. "You'll go to a brand-new school, and you'll have your own room. A real one with walls." She ran a finger down the list of amenities. "There's a clubhouse, an Olympic-size swimming pool, a nine-hole golf course. And look at this!" Her finger stabbed the last item on the list. "A wildlife area!"

For a second, leaving looked easy. It wasn't his fault if his mom made them disappear from this place. Even Damien couldn't blame him for going.

But suddenly it was the roof all over again. Could he really leave his best friend to face Rapp on his own?

"I can't do this, Mom," he said softly. "I can't." The arm around his shoulders tightened.

"I'm scared too," she said. "But we can do it together, like always."

6

THE CHECK IS
IN THE CHEX

In Socko's experience, nothing that cost money happened fast. He was used to waiting for new shoes, school supplies, even milk. One year they'd celebrated Christmas in February. He figured he'd have plenty of time to convince his mom to forget the whole moving idea.

But just five days after Delia found her dream home, someone knocked loudly on the door of 4A.

He and Damien were on the sofa spooning Marshmallow Fluff straight out of the jar. Mouths full, they looked at the door, then at each other. It was a little after three and Delia was still at work.

"Express Mail," barked a voice outside the door.

"Just leave it," Socko yelled back. He wasn't opening up. Anybody could say "Express Mail."

"I need a signature."

Socko raised his eyebrows at Damien.

His friend shook his head and dug his spoon into the fluff.

"Who's it from?" Socko called.

"Some law firm," said the voice.

Law firm? mouthed Damien.

"Which one?" Socko asked. Anyone could also say "law firm."

"Do you want the letter or not?"

"Just a sec." Socko put his fluff spoon down on the arm of the sofa and walked slowly to the door. Keeping the chain on, he opened it a crack. The front of a blue postal worker's shirt filled the gap.

"Can *I* sign for it?" asked Socko.

"You got a hand?" A clipboard slid edgewise through the gap. "Line four."

Socko signed line four with the pen attached to the board, then passed the clipboard back. The mailman thrust a cardboard envelope at him. Staring at it, Socko closed the door. Between the blue eagle printed on it and the words "EXPRESS MAIL" in all capital letters, it looked pretty official.

"Open it!" Damien jumped off the couch and sprinted over. "It's gotta be about the house."

"It's addressed to my mom."

"So? The house is our business too. Mine especially. I wanna know how long I have to live."

Socko slid his thumb under the flap and tore it open. Inside was another envelope—a thick one with an embossed return address. "Sweeney, Marcum, Jarvis, & Petty, Attorneys at Law."

Damien snatched the envelope and ripped it open. He pulled out a sheaf of folded papers. Clipped to the top sheet was a check. Damien let the other papers fall to the floor. He held the pale blue rectangle in both hands. "You are *rich*, man!" Resting his back against the door, he slid to the floor. As soon as his butt touched down, he twisted around and slapped the door with his palm. "Is this thing all-the-way locked?"

Socko threw the extra bolts, and then slid down beside him. Reading the figure on the check for the first time, he thought he might pass out.

"Look at all the zeroes!" Damien breathed. "With this I could live easy the rest of my life." He surveyed his torn jeans and the baggy T-shirt left behind by one of his mother's boyfriends. "First I'd buy me some nice threads, then a car…" He was grinning so big, Socko could see the Marshmallow Fluff between his teeth. "Don't worry, my man. I'd buy you one too."

"Don't drool on it!" The check was making Socko nervous, and the check in Damien's hand was driving him right to the edge of crazy. "We gotta hide it good!"

"I'm on it!" Damien scrambled to his feet.

They looked everywhere, Socko trailing Damien as he waved the check around, but no place seemed really safe.

"Genius idea!" Damien folded the check and stuck it under his Superman lid. "Super protection!"

"No!" Socko jerked the hat off his friend's head and caught the check before it fluttered to the floor.

"Don't get so jumpy! I'm just messin' with you."

"Why'd you go and fold it?" Socko had zero experience with checks. Folding one seemed risky.

"Wait—genius idea number two!" Damien plucked the check from Socko's hand. "No one'll look in here." He stashed it in the oven, leaned casually against the oven door, and began to whistle.

"What if someone accidentally bumps the dial and turns it on? Your butt is right next to it!" Socko grabbed his friend's arm and jerked him away from the oven door.

They tried to pry the back off Socko's baby picture frame to sandwich the check between the photo and the board—but there was too much tape.

Damien came up with genius idea number three. He pulled a box of Corn Chex cereal out of a cabinet and hid the valuable piece of paper inside. "Chex...check. Get it?"

Socko was still uneasy. What if they accidentally ate the check? Okay, okay. That was stupid, and he didn't have a better idea.

When they finally heard Delia in the hall, they rushed the door and fumbled the locks open. "It came!" they said together.

"My gosh...oh my gosh!" Delia triple-locked the door behind her before letting them retrieve the check from the cereal box.

"Great god in heaven!" She kissed the check, and then tested the locks. "Put it back in the cereal!"

Damien looked as if someone had slapped him. "You got the check, next you get the house. And after that—you're gone." He turned to Socko, like Socko could make it not happen.

Ever since he'd told Damien about the offer, Socko had assured his friend he was working on his mom. And he was. He hadn't made any progress, but until the check arrived Socko had really believed there was a chance to convince her. Now he knew there wasn't. Not with all those zeroes.

***

"I wish he didn't know about the check," Delia said after an unexpected knock from below had summoned Damien home.

"Come on, Mom. He won't steal it! He's my best friend!"

"No, but he'll talk. You know the way that kid runs his mouth!"

She was right. Even when he had nothing to talk about, Damien suffered from diarrhea of the mouth.

Delia took the cereal box down and teased the check out and held it in both hands. "This is our new life, Socko." She hid the check under the plastic tray in the silverware drawer, then picked up the papers scattered on the floor. "And this is what we have to do to live it."

She sat down at the table and put on the drugstore reading glasses she wore, not because she needed them but because she said they made her feel smarter. Peering over the tops of the glasses, she read the contract that outlined the General's "terms and conditions" three times before signing.

Socko didn't sleep much that night. He woke up once from a brief stretch of unconsciousness and heard his mother humming. When he came out from behind the thirteen original colonies, Delia was standing at the window, silhouetted by the flickering blue from the neon sign across the street.

"Mom?"

"I moved the check again," she whispered. "So don't freak when you open that drawer and it's gone."

"Where to?"

"Don't worry about it. You can't spill what you don't know."

"You don't trust me?"

"I don't even trust *me*. This is too big."

7
MESSAGE FOR
THE BLIMP

ocko and Damien were hanging around the apartment hiding out from Rapp just like they had for the last few days. But today was different. Today Delia was there too, driving them crazy singing about "house-buying day!"

When they couldn't stand it anymore, they decided to take a chance. "We gotta be safe by daylight on a busy street," said Damien as they carried their skateboards into the elevator—it was temporarily working.

They didn't see Rapp until they skated around a corner and almost ran into him. He didn't say a word, just narrowed his eyes and pointed a finger at Damien.

Stepping on the tail of his skateboard, Damien did a fast kick turn and jetted away. Socko did his own clumsy version of the maneuver and lit out after his friend.

"It was like he was holding a gun!" Damien gasped when they were back in the elevator at the Kludge. He punched the button for his own floor. "I can't take all the happy-happy at your place."

"Just in time," said Delia as Socko walked in. She pointed at the side zipper on her black dress pants. "I could use a little help here."

He jerked the zipper pull but it didn't budge. "You won't even be able to breathe if I get this closed."

"Who needs to breathe? I'm buying a house!"

Socko gave the zipper one last hard tug and it closed. "Mom, I'm begging you not to do this."

"Beg all you want. I'm doing this if it kills me."

"What if it kills Damien?"

"Enough drama! Now, do I have everything?" She twanged a bra strap through her shirt. "I got the check right here."

"The check's in your bra? Gross!"

"Gross, maybe, but safe."

Not knowing where the check was hidden, Socko had spent the past week afraid he might accidentally destroy it. Now he almost wished he had.

His mother went to the window to watch for the real estate agent's car. Leah Albin was picking her up—along with the cashier's check—and driving both to the closing. "You sure you don't want to come?" Delia asked.

"Positive." Socko walked behind his hanging "wall" and threw himself down on his cot.

"Wait 'til you see the washer and dryer at the new place, the walk-in pantry!"

Tuning her out, Socko stared up at the stained ceiling. When they'd moved in, he'd been sure the stain over his bed was blood that had seeped through from the apartment above. His mom had assured him it came from a plumbing leak. She'd pointed out that it looked like a clown. After encountering the word "demented" on a vocabulary list, he'd always called the stain "the demented clown."

In a couple more days he'd never see the demented clown again. It wasn't just his best friend he'd be leaving behind, it was his home, his neighborhood—his life.

Delia's tube of lipstick opened with a *pop*. She was probably slathering it on, staring out the window. "You're going to like our new place, Socko. No more squishing together for us! You, me, and the General each get a real bedroom, with one extra left over."

Socko bolted upright on his cot. "An extra bedroom?" He rolled off the cot, rattling the thirteen original colonies as he barged out from behind them. "Genius idea, Mom!" In his excitement he borrowed Damien's favorite phrase—but it *was* a genius idea. "Damien can come with us. Louise won't care."

His mother never lost eye contact with the street. "There are a lot of people in this building who deserve to get out, like Junebug and Mr. Marvin—he's about to be evicted, you know. But there are only two people here I can save. You and me."

Delia stuck her head out the window and waved both arms. "Be right down!"

Socko followed her out of their apartment and into the elevator. "Can we at least *talk* about it?" His mother stared at the floor numbers as the elevator dropped. "Mom?" The door opened.

She hurried out of the elevator with Socko right behind. "Sorry, Socko, I can't do it!" She shoved open the front door of the apartment building with her hip.

Rapp was leaning against the outside wall smoking. Socko should have paid more attention when Rapp cut his eyes their way, but convincing his mother about Damien was all that mattered at that moment.

He stood on the sidewalk watching her wobble across the cracked concrete in her high heels. "Tell me you'll at least think about it."

She climbed in the car, then waved at him through the window as the car pulled away.

Socko smelled the smoke from Rapp's cigarette first. When he turned, the gang leader was so close it made his skin prickle.

"Got a little job for you," Rapp said, but his eyes never left the shiny car rolling slowly away. "Where's *she* going?"

"My mom's buying a house—so—we'll be out of here soon." Socko threw the news about the house in Rapp's path, hoping he might forget about the little job he wanted him to do.

Rapp's head swiveled like a hawk's. "You lie."

The alertness in Rapp's voice scared Socko. *Never look a predator in the eye.* He stared at the cigarette butt Rapp had just dropped on the sidewalk. In addition to the smoldering butt, he could see Rapp's combat boots, each tied with a different color lace, and the turned-up cuff of his left pant leg. *Gangsta handbook*, he thought. He almost smiled, but his lips felt numb.

"I said…" The right combat boot lunged toward him and in a

37

flash, a fist held the front of his T-shirt twisted tight against his chest. "…you lie."

"No, for real! My great-grandfather's buying it for us." When Socko tried to meet Rapp's gaze to prove he was sincere, he inhaled sharply. Riddled with the dead craters of a million acne scars, Rapp's face looked like the surface of the losing planet in some intergalactic war.

"What're you lookin' at?" The T-shirt twisted another half turn.

"Nothing." Socko turned his head, and over Rapp's hard-muscled shoulder he saw Damien peering through the glass door of the Kludge.

Terrified, he wanted his friend to come out and help him—but he knew if Damien showed his face, Rapp would kill him…twice. Damien must have figured that out too. A second later he vanished back inside the building.

The hand on his shirt jerked hard. "So, you and the Blimp are going uptown. Fine. But first you do something for me."

"Could you get someone else? We're getting ready to move, and, you know, my mom needs help." Socko could only talk back to Rapp because he was avoiding his eyes, watching the gold cross twist on its chain.

"You can deliver this message while you put all your sorry-ass crap in boxes. Tell your momma to stay outta my business with Junebug. Junebug's mine 'til *I* say she ain't."

Socko's gaze dropped to the ground. "Yeah, okay."

The fist that was latched to the front of his shirt gave him a shake. "Hey! Eyes here!" When Socko looked up, Rapp pronged the first and second fingers on his free hand and pointed first at his own eyes, then at Socko's, almost jabbing them. "Tell her I ain't playin'. Tell her she better leave Junebug alone."

Rapp let go and pushed Socko away with stiff fingers. Apparently losing interest, he studied the gray face of the apartment building. As Rapp cracked his knuckles one at a time, Socko saw a tattooed spider on the pale web of skin between his thumb and index finger.

Socko edged toward the building.

"Freeze! You don't go 'til I say go." Rapp swung an arm out like he was going to smack him. Instead he gave Socko's cheek a light slap. "Go." He let Socko take one step. "Stop. Repeat my message for the Blimp."

All Socko had to do was parrot back what Rapp had said. Was that so hard? But in his head he saw Junebug rescuing Damien—something he'd been too chicken to do himself.

His voice came out high and shrill, like a little kid's. "Why don't you just leave Junebug alone?"

***

Delia reached over and grasped Socko's chin. "You're sure you can see okay?" She turned his battered eye toward the light.

"Yes, Mom." He wrapped another dish in newspaper and handed it to Damien, who added it to the box they were packing.

She released his chin, then stood straight. "Now hear this!" she announced, as if demanding the whole apartment building's attention. "My son has taken his last punch. As of tomorrow we start our new life. As of tomorrow, Delia and Socko Starr are outta here!"

She picked up a stack of newspaper and thrust it at Socko. "Here. Wrap that platter good. I don't want it to break."

Damien shoved his fists into his pockets. "You have a box big enough to pack me in?"

Delia shook her head sadly.

"Please, you gotta get me out of here! I'm a homicide waiting to happen!"

Socko stuck the wrapped platter into a box. "Please!" Damien pressed his hands together like he was praying. "Rapp's gotta know I went and got Junebug to break up the fight."

It hadn't occurred to Socko to wonder why Junebug had showed up just in time to save him. Rapp would figure it out fast. Damien's panic was contagious. "Let Damien hide out with us for a few days, Mom! Louise wouldn't care."

"Care?" Damien looked desperate. "She wouldn't even notice."

"You're breaking my heart, Damien, but I just can't bring you along! It's part of the deal with my grandfather. I don't dare do anything that might mess things up."

"Please, Mrs. S, I'm beggin'!" Damien's bony knees hit the floor. "I *have* to get out of here!"

Delia wrung her hands. "I can't. I just can't. Do good in school, Damien. You'll get yourself out of here."

Damien choked out a ragged breath. "Like I'll live that long!"

Socko dropped to his knees beside Damien. "Mom? Please?" Delia's "someday" advice didn't help. At the Kludge, "right now" was all there was—and right now could be over in a heartbeat.

Tears in her eyes, Delia turned away and started pulling dish towels out of a drawer.

8
REARVIEW MIRROR

It was barely light when Delia shook him awake. "Wyman can't drive us. His kid's sick!" Socko's heart leapt. No transportation. Did that mean no move?

But when he stumbled out of bed, his mother was at the window staring down on the puke green roof of a scabby SUV with an open metal trailer hitched behind it. Wyman, the night manager at Phat Burger, must have brought it over after his shift.

"Surprise!" Delia said with a desperate smile. "I'm the driver!"

"Really? You?"

"Why not? Wyman came by about an hour ago and I drove it around the block a couple times. He showed me how to handle the trailer. I'll be fine, right?"

Socko knew it was his job to reassure her, but this whole thing was *her* idea. He didn't even want to go.

"I'll do fine," she said, answering her own question. "You think it's too early to get Damien up to help us load?"

It was, but Socko couldn't lug their stuff down to the trailer by himself, and Delia got short of breath whenever she had to lift anything. Besides, unless his mom changed her mind, this might be his last chance to hang with his friend.

Socko rapped the floor beside his bed with the broom handle. *Thump, thump, thump.*

In a minute, Socko heard the secret knock.

Damien slipped through the door wearing yesterday's clothes and his hat of invincibility.

"You okay?" Socko asked.

"My mom's gone again and my best friend is about to disappear. Why wouldn't I be?" Damien's hands beat a nervous rhythm on the back of a chair. "You have a leftover burger around? We're down to a jar of relish and a six-pack at home."

While Delia zapped him a burger, Damien sat down in front of the Moon Ridge Estates brochure, which lay open on the table. "So this is where you'll be." Resting his weight on his elbows, he studied the little map on the back.

"It's not far. The Kludge is over here, Moon Ridge is here." Delia traced the route with a finger. The microwave beeped. "Would you like fries with that, sir?"

Damien snatched the burger off the plate she held out. "I'll take whatever you got. I'm eating for a lifetime."

"*Mom?*" Socko was pleading.

His mother held up a hand before he could say more. "I'll still be at the Phat, Damien. You get hungry, you come see me. And bring a book. We'll work on your reading during my break."

While Damien scarfed down fries, Socko and Delia loaded the dolly they'd borrowed from Mr. Marvin. Delia shoved it across the hall and into the elevator.

After Damien's meal of a lifetime, the boys moved furniture. The loveseat they'd rescued from the curb went back where they'd found it; the trailer would only hold so much.

Even though they didn't have that much stuff, it was hot and heavy work. Damien raided the refrigerator each time they made the round trip, taking advantage of the fact that Delia was camped out by the Suburban, guarding their stuff and saying long, teary good-byes to the neighbors she knew so well.

Getting the sofa down the stairs nearly killed them—it was too big for the elevator. It got away from them once, bumping down the steps until it smacked the wall on the second-floor landing.

"Gotta rest." Damien fell onto the slanting sofa, one end three steps higher than the other. Noticing a stain on the sofa's arm, he grinned. "Hey, I did that! You dared me to stomp a ketchup packet, remember?" He shook his head. "Good times, good times."

"I'm only gonna be eleven miles away."

"And how am I gonna get there? Fly?"

Damien's mom had no car. Sometimes one of her boyfriends did, but they didn't exactly line up to drive Damien places.

"I'll come see you," Socko said.

"You heard your mom. Once you're outta here, you're gone." He rested his neck on the back of the sofa and stared at the gray plaster overhead. "Listen, if something, you know, *serious* happens to me, you gotta promise to come say good-bye."

"Nothing's gonna happen." Socko's throat felt thick.

When they forced the sofa out the front doors of the Kludge, they saw Rapp standing slouched against the outside wall, Meat beside him. Even though it was early afternoon, both looked like they'd just gotten up. Damien scuttled sideways, almost dropping his end of the sofa.

Delia stood at the curb by the Suburban, the dolly loaded with cartons beside her. She wiped her damp forehead with the back of her wrist, then rested her knuckles on her wide hips and stared at Rapp.

Whatever you're thinking, Mom, don't say it, Socko pled silently.

"Anything wrong, Mrs. S?" asked Rapp with mock politeness.

"Not for long," she said. "In half an hour I won't even be able to see you boys in my rearview mirror."

Damien wilted against the couch they had just set down.

For a moment, the air around "the boys" seemed to crackle. Then Rapp waved off the insult. "The way I see it," he said, like he was talking to Meat, "they're just taking out the trash."

Socko turned away but felt their eyes watching as he and Damien talked about how to load the couch. Damien tapped the *S* on his hat. "Super strength, don't fail me now."

Together they lifted one end and rested it on the tailgate. They picked up the other end and shoved. Nothing happened.

43

Delia hitched up the waist of her sweatpants, then turned and pressed her back against the end of the sofa.

"No, Mom!" Junebug's blood pressure cuff always registered high on Delia.

"I am *not* going to be beat by a couch." Her rubber flip-flops gripped the pavement. "One...two...three."

The sofa stuttered across the metal grate of the trailer floor and hit the back wall. Delia's eyes were closed, her arms limp. "I'm fine," she panted, as if reading Socko's mind.

"We'll do the rest, Mom." While Delia sat in the driver's seat, directing them through the open window, Socko and Damien piled the boxes and other pieces of furniture around the couch. When the kitchen table had been wedged in and everything bungeed, they raised the tailgate.

"Go back upstairs, boys. Take one last look. Make sure we didn't forget anything."

***

Apartment 4A looked sad with nothing in it but the radiators, the stains on the ceiling, and a few gouges in the floor.

Socko pushed the window open and leaned out, studying the gray cursive letters of Donatelli's unlit sign. The jittery light from the convenience store sign would be eleven miles away when he lay in bed tonight. Feeling sad and stupid, he gave the demented clown on the ceiling over his corner of the room a quick wave. "See ya around."

Damien picked up the worn-out broom Delia had left standing in the corner and thumped the floor three times with the handle. "Guess I won't hear that anymore." Holding the broom like a spear, he hurled it out the open window.

Socko rushed after Damien to see where it would land.

It flipped, then plummeted into the scrawny hedge in front of the building. Damien leaned his back against the wall and slid down to a sitting position.

"I got something for you," Socko said, joining Damien on the floor. He hooked the string around his neck with a finger and lifted it over his head. "Here." He dropped the key string over Damien's head. "It'll give you a place to go."

Blaaaaat… Down in the street Delia leaned on the car horn.

"Yeah, yeah," Socko said under his breath, shoving to his feet. He listened to the *click* as he closed the door behind him for the last time. "Gotta do one more thing," he said, pointing at the door to Junebug's apartment.

He knocked, but her aunt answered. Socko caught a whiff of litter box and frying chicken.

"Junebug's at the nursing home cutting old people's toenails."

"She's gotta go to school to do that?" said Damien under his breath.

Socko was kind of relieved Junebug wasn't home. "Just tell her good-bye for me…and thanks."

Junebug's aunt pushed the door shut.

***

"After you," said Damien as the elevator door opened.

"No, after you."

Damien grabbed his arm and they stepped in together. They rode the elevator to the top and then straight down, taking one last hurtle before walking out the front door of the Kludge.

Neither one of them looked at Rapp.

"Move it, Socko!" Delia leaned across the seat and opened the car door. "We have to pick up the General at the airport at 3:30!"

But Socko had stalled out. "This isn't right."

Damien gave Socko the shove that propelled him through the open door of the Suburban. "Do it, Socko. Get it over with." Damien closed the door behind him. "I'll be okay."

Delia spread a Phat bag with a map penciled on it in Socko's lap. "You're the navigator." But Socko barely noticed. Damien was on the other side of the closed door, his fists in his pockets, his gaze on the sidewalk.

Socko rolled the window down and held up his palm. "See ya later—seriously." Damien's hand came out of his pocket. Forearm to forearm, they locked hands.

When Delia touched the gas pedal, their hands were jerked apart. The Suburban jackrabbited forward and took a crazy tilt as two tires climbed the curb. Looking back, Socko saw that the trailer's tires were still on the road, squealing along the curb.

Damien called after them through cupped hands. "You're gonna die, man!"

Delia jerked the steering wheel left. *Whump*, the tires bounced down off the curb. Socko hung out the window. "I'll call you!"

Wind whipping his hair, Socko kept his friend in sight for as long as he could. He held onto the window frame with one hand and waved with the other. Damien didn't wave back. Instead he stood, fingers riveted to the *S* on his hat. But Damien was shrinking fast.

Although they were further away, Rapp and Meat seemed to shrink much more slowly.

9
THE OLD FART

Delia gripped the steering wheel, perspiration glistening on her forehead and upper lip. "You sure you know how to drive?" Socko asked. She didn't look exactly comfortable.

"I'm fine. Just keep us from getting lost, okay?"

Too late. They rolled past a convenience store called the Quick Stop. If the store had been Donatelli's, the old guy coming out with a ribbon of scratch-off tickets in his hand would have been easy to name. But this was someone else's neighborhood, someone else's old guy.

"Right or left here, Socko?"

Socko turned the burger bag on his lap ninety degrees. It didn't help. When it came to being a navigator, Socko stunk.

His mother sent him into two fast-food places for directions before they even got out of the city—she seemed to think they could trust anyone who flipped burgers.

As soon as they found the freeway—speed limit 70—Socko was sure Damien's prediction was going to come true. Delia drove a car the way he and Damien piloted the Hurtler.

Socko twisted in his seat and watched the load. He didn't trust the bungee cord job they'd done. With each lurching lane change he expected the sofa to go rogue and fly out of the trailer.

"Why are ya slowing down?" Delia yelped.

Socko whipped around. They'd be sitting in the backseat of the car in front of them if they got any closer—and they *were* getting closer!

At the last second, Delia swung the Suburban into the next lane. Socko swiveled in his seat as the sofa careened right.

"Wide turns, wide turns," Delia chanted. "Don't roll the trailer."

They'd been going along fine for a few minutes—Delia had just said she was getting the hang of towing a trailer—when Socko caught sight of the airport sign coming up fast on the right. "Exit! Exit!"

His mom cut across three lanes, hitting the exit just inches shy of the barrier. They were celebrating still being alive when the next set of signs appeared.

Arrivals.

Departures.

Terminal Parking.

"Which lane?" White-knuckled, Delia strangled the wheel.

"Parking! Go for parking!"

She swerved hard. They plunged into the dark hole called Parking. Just before hitting a wooden arm, Delia stomped the brake. "How can I park with *that* in the way?"

"Ticket, Mom."

"Oh." The machine next to her window spat out a ticket and she grabbed it.

When they abandoned the car and trailer, the rig sat diagonally across four spaces.

***

"My gosh, who knew an airport was so big?" Delia whispered as they walked from the glass-enclosed tube into the terminal.

Unsure what to do next, they stalled. "How will we even find him?" Socko asked, watching a swarm of impatient travelers rush by.

Delia threw herself on the mercy of a woman in a crisp white shirt at the Delta service desk. The woman leaned across the counter and pointed down the concourse. "You can meet your party at baggage claim, carousel six."

"I don't think meeting an old man's gonna be much of a party," Socko mumbled as they walked away.

"Don't be such a smart-mouth. It *will* be a party. A family reunion!"

Delia chewed off the last of her lipstick while they stood by the silent baggage carousel. "I was way younger than you last time I saw the General. It's been so long." She pulled a little mirror out of her purse. "Sheesh! Why didn't you tell me my hair was going crazy?" She tried to pat down a hairdo that had been whipped by wind blasting through the open windows of the SUV but quickly gave up. "What if I don't recognize him?" she asked, staring down the concourse.

"What did he look like then?"

"Big. And scary."

Socko surveyed his enormous mother. No matter how big General Starr was, she had to outweigh him. And no matter how scary he was, his mother had stood up to worse—dealing with the landlord when she didn't have the rent, for instance, or convincing Mr. Donatelli to give them credit until she got paid.

"Hopefully he's mellowed," she said softly. "Anyway, he's old now. How scary can an eighty-eight-year-old man be?" Suddenly she pinched his arm. "You don't think that's him, do you? Nancy didn't mention a wheelchair."

A skycap was pushing a shiny chrome wheelchair that made the shriveled old man who sat in it look like a prune served on a fancy plate. The skin on the top of his bald head was splotched with brown. His fingernails were long and yellow and his legs so thin they looked like they'd knife through the legs of his pants if he crossed them.

"Don't let it be him, don't let it be him," Delia breathed.

The old man viewed his surroundings with just one eye. The left. The right one was covered by a black patch. The lone eye ranged over the crowd gathered around the baggage carousel.

Socko avoided the searchlight eye by stepping behind his mother and bending his knees, but the eye found her with no trouble. "Delia Marie Starr," the old man wheezed. Though there was barely any real voice in the sound, it carried like a strong wind. "My, how you've grown."

Socko saw his mother flinch—and right away he wanted to punch the guy. Was the old man starting right out with a fat joke?

Delia squared her shoulders. "Thanks for the house. We really appreciate it."

She took one step toward the General, but he held up his hand. "No phony display of affection is necessary. What we have is a simple business arrangement. You get a house plus one old fart. It's a package deal."

"I was hoping my boy and me were getting a little more family too." Delia paused, giving the old man a chance to say something nice, but he didn't.

"Sir, what are we looking for?" asked the skycap as carousel six rumbled to life.

"One wheelchair. One valise. One footlocker." The General scanned the first half dozen bags quickly, and then turned back to Delia. "Tell the kid hiding behind you to step out and show himself."

"I'm not hiding." Socko edged into view.

Delia put an arm around his shoulders. "This is your great-grandson."

The old man squeezed the arms of the chair. "Where'd you get that red hair?" he demanded, as if Socko had shoplifted it.

"No place in particular."

"No place in particular?" The answer seemed to anger the old man. "Well, you got too much of it. Makes you look like a sissy. You need to get those girl-curls buzzed."

Socko almost commented about the General's long, girly nails, but if he was going to talk him into letting Damien live in their extra bedroom, he had to be nice.

The old man's single eye zeroed in on Socko's shiner. "And if you can't defend yourself, kid, don't get in a fight." The roving eye focused on the conveyor belt, assessing the latest additions to the luggage parade, then snapped back to Socko. "Name?"

"Socko."

"Socko, sir," the old man corrected. Then the name itself seemed to catch his attention. "Sock-o?" His laugh was just a shaking of his shoulders. "What are you, kid? Some kind of punching bag?" His shoulders shook again.

"His name is Socrates," said Delia.

"Boy, oh boy, did you ever draw the short straw, kid! Might as well hang a Kick Me sign on him, Delia Marie."

Socko had to agree. Some librarian had suggested Socrates when Delia had asked for help finding a "smart" name.

"I thought Nancy was pulling my leg when she said we had a dead philosopher in the family." The General turned away. Frowning, he watched the emerging luggage shove the plastic strips aside. "That's the chair," he snapped.

The skycap retrieved and opened the wheelchair, then transferred the General to it.

"The boy can get my valise and footlocker."

Shaking his head at the quarter the General slapped into his hand, the skycap hurried away, pushing the polished chrome chair ahead of him.

The General's wheelchair looked as battered as the old man himself. Plastered to its vinyl back was a bumper sticker that read: VETERAN—I FOUGHT FOR YOUR SORRY HIDE. Tattered American flags were attached to the chair's handles with gummy wads of duct tape. But Socko thought the General didn't look as bad in his own chair. They kind of matched.

"The green one." The General stabbed a yellowed nail at the latest suitcase to hit the belt. "Get it, boy."

Socko got it. It wasn't big or heavy, and it had wheels, although they squealed when he dragged it over to the wheelchair.

"And that."

The footlocker that had just shouldered the hanging plastic strips aside almost pulled Socko's arm out of the socket when he dragged it off the belt. "No wheels?" he gasped.

"Manufactured before the invention of the wheel," the General croaked. "Suck it up, kid."

10
WELCOME TO
MOON RIDGE

The General shrugged off their hands when they tried to help him climb into the car. "What do I look like, a cripple?" he asked, holding onto the doorframe.

"As a matter of fact, yeah," Socko muttered as he rolled the wheelchair back to the trailer.

"Socko…" His mother gave him a don't-blow-it look.

Socko rolled his eyes at her.

Although Socko and Delia had seen the skycap open the wheelchair, they had no idea how to fold it up again. They jiggled knobs and bars; they flipped it on its side. As Socko sat down on it hard, the chair collapsing under him, the Suburban's horn blasted.

"Mercy!" Delia slapped her hands over her ears as the sound ricocheted around the garage. The General, moving at the speed of an advancing glacier, had managed to climb into the car with enough time left over to get mad.

"Great new life so far!" Socko shouted as his great-grandfather smacked the horn again.

"Wait 'til you see the house!" Delia shouted back.

They wrestled the chair into the trailer, and Socko pushed the footlocker up the dropped tailgate.

On the way out, Delia grazed one of the parking garage's concrete pillars. Metal squealed.

The old man glared. "Someone gave you a license?"

Delia climbed out to inspect the damage. "Lucky accident!" she reported with a big fake smile. "We hit the car door that already had a dent."

When they reached the little booth, another bar blocked their exit. "They don't want us to *leave* either?" Delia asked.

A hand reached out of the booth's window. "Ticket?"

Socko leaned over Delia's shoulder from the backseat and grabbed the ticket off the dashboard.

The woman fed the card into a machine. Out came the hand again. "Four dollars."

Delia pulled out three bills, and then stared into her empty wallet. "Who knew it cost so much to park?"

"Have you ever been anywhere?" the General asked as Socko made up the difference using the change in the cupholder.

"Sure." Delia steered the SUV out of the garage. "A few places."

She was exaggerating. Socko knew she'd been nowhere. He'd gone there with her.

"Hitler took care of that for me," the General wheezed. "Raised so much ruckus Uncle Sam shipped me over to Europe to straighten him out."

While Socko waited, hoping for a war story, he studied the leathery skin on the old man's neck and the fringe of white hair that stood out above his collar like feathers.

"My advice?" The General turned his head toward Delia, the wrinkled skin on his neck twisting like strands of rope. "Enlist the kid. Of course he'll have to get a little older, but the U.S. Army'll teach Sacko in the backseat there what to do when someone throws a punch." He raised his voice to a loud whisper. "You know about Sad Sack, kid? Sad Sack was a comic strip character in the Army newspaper, the *Stars and Stripes*. That poor old soak was one sorry excuse for a soldier."

Socko didn't know what he'd expected from a newly acquired great-grandfather, but name-calling wasn't it. He stared into his lap and imagined it was a regular day. He and Damien were skating—

"Holy moly!" the General yelped.

The shoulder strap cut into Socko's neck, and he was instantly back in the Suburban.

Delia was in the middle of another sudden lane change.

"Delia Marie Starr, pull over right *now*," the General ordered. "I'm driving."

Socko gripped the seat, knowing that wasn't going to happen. His mother didn't like being told what to do.

Delia pulled over immediately. For a minute, they sat, the passing traffic sending shudders through the car.

"I just remembered," Delia said, eyeing the General. "Nancy said you lost your license for being half-blind."

"Desperate times call for desperate measures. Change seats."

With the General at the helm, the needle on the speedometer never wavered, glued to the 45 mph mark. Cars veered wildly around them. The General stared straight ahead.

"You drive like the lead car in a funeral," Socko blurted out.

The old man flinched and Socko remembered the reason they suddenly had a house and an old guy to share it with. "Sorry...I didn't mean...sorry about..." Socko didn't know what to call his dead great-grandmother.

The old man waved his sympathy away. "Let's just find that fool house."

Delia managed to interpret the directions the fry cook had drawn on the back of the Phat Burger bag, shouting them at the General over the squeal of locking brakes, honking horns, and screeching tires. Socko kept a death grip on the seat until they pulled off the freeway.

It was getting dark when they finally passed the entry to the first subdivision on the main road to Moon Ridge Estates. Hot, dry air blew Socko's long hair around as he hung out the window to read the gold-edged letters on the sign: Quail Roost Acres. The subdivision was guarded by a man in a booth. It looked like a pretty cushy job.

Colonial Park. Heritage Oak Manor. Lorelei Meadows. Socko read each of the signs that rose from elaborate beds of flowers. Every one of the subdivisions had its own guarded booth. Were they expecting an invasion or something?

"Stop!" yelled Delia.

The General pulled over.

"Look! That's my bus stop."

"Not anymore it isn't," said the General.

"Oh, sugar!" Delia stared at the little bus shelter with its three plastic seats. A large notice had been taped to the schedule sign: Route Cancelled Due to Budget Cuts.

"Mom, how are you going to get to work?"

Delia stared at the sign a moment longer, then turned away. "Don't be such a worrywart, Socko. I'll think of something. I am *not* going to let this spoil things!" She waved the General forward. Within a few yards, another sign, this one leaning as if it were about to fall on its face, passed by the window.

"Stop!" Delia yelled again.

The General tapped the brake. Going as slow as they were, that was all it took to bring the SUV and trailer to a creaking halt.

Delia took off her seatbelt and hung out the window too. "Turn here! This is it!"

"Shoulda warned me," the General complained. "Now I have to back up the whole wagon train. Hope nobody's behind me 'cause I can't see worth spit."

Socko looked back over his shoulder. "You're clear."

They moved so slowly, Socko felt the trailer resist before beginning to roll. The subdivision's sign inched past Socko's window, giving him plenty of time to read it.

Welcome to Moon Ridge Estates—A Golf Course Community
Buy now! Units going fast!
Another "Holmes Homes" Project

Where are the flowers from the brochure? Socko wondered. *And why is the sign falling over?*

The guard booth behind the Welcome sign had a sign on it too—Nonresidents Check in with Guard—but the booth was empty. The bar meant to keep out nonresidents pointed at the sky.

"Our house is right near the entrance." Delia held her hair back with one hand. "Take your first right…"

"Where are the hedges?" Socko pressed his palms to the warm outside of the car door.

"Hedges, lawns, and trees come later. They're Phase 2."

"What's Phase 1? Dirt?" the General wheezed. "Tarnation, Delia Marie. A man could get lost and die out here. It's just the same house over and over."

"Because they're perfect," said Delia.

To Socko the perfect houses looked creepy. Wasn't it a little early for every window to be dark?

Delia pointed. "There it is! That's it!"

"You're sure?" The General hesitated before turning into a driveway that looked like all the other driveways, at the end of which sat a house that looked like every other house.

"Positive. I recognize the coffee cup on the step." In the dimming light the white cup glowed.

"That's not a coffee cup, Delia Marie." He set the brake and turned off the ignition. "It's trash."

Delia opened the door and climbed out. Socko did the same. He expected her to rush up the walk, but she stood, one hand clasped inside the other, looking the way he imagined people did in church. "Come on, Socko." She put a warm hand on the back of his neck.

"Don't you dare leave me in this car!" the General yelled in a loud whisper.

"We'll be back in a sec." Delia gave Socko's neck a squeeze and they walked up the path to the front door together.

The cup on the step was Styrofoam, and it would have blown away except it still had coffee in it. Delia picked it up and dumped it. "There'll be no litter in our yard." She covered her mouth with a hand. "Oh, Socko, we have a yard!"

Socko took a long, hard look. Did she see what he saw? Like the General said, the yard was dirt.

"The inside is even better!"

Socko hoped so.

Delia wore the key to the new house on her good gold chain, the one she hocked when they really needed money, and got back again as soon as she could repay the loan. She unhooked it from around her neck and handed the key to Socko. "You do the honors."

The General leaned on the horn. *Blaaaat!*

"We'll be right back," Delia called to him.

Socko turned the key.

Holding her breath, his mother pushed the door open. They stepped inside and she flipped a light switch. "Welcome home."

Socko had never seen anyplace this white before. Nothing had ever dripped or spilled here. It was like he was inside a gift box that had never been opened. He wrinkled his nose. "What's that smell?"

"Paint, carpet. Breathe deep, Socko; this is what *new* smells like."

He breathed in a lungful of new, then coughed.

"Is this perfect, or is this perfect?"

He was just about to ask if there was a choice C when an engine roared to life in the driveway.

Delia's penciled eyebrows shot up. "You don't think he'd drive off, do you?"

Socko rushed the door and jumped from the top step to the ground. Headlights came on, blinding him. He stumbled toward the light and threw his arms across the hood of the SUV. "Where are you going?"

The headlights went out. The warm hood stopped vibrating under Socko's chest. He heard the driver's door unlatch. When he lifted his head, the dome light in the SUV was illuminating the old man's shiny scalp. "For future reference, I don't like being left in the driveway." Socko detected what could have almost passed for a smile as the old man looked at him. "You make a fine hood ornament, Sacko."

11
THE GREAT WHITE

As soon as they carried Delia's recliner inside, the General deserted his wheelchair, scuffed over to it, and took possession.

Socko thought he looked like a scrawny king seated in the overstuffed chair—and he acted like one too. "It's hot as blazes in here," he proclaimed. "Crank up the AC."

"I'm the one paying the electric bill!" said Delia. Shaking her head, she turned on the air-conditioner as commanded.

Socko didn't like his mother doing heavy lifting, but it took both of them to get everything inside.

"Table over there," the General ordered. "Chair over here. And while you're up and around, lower the thermostat."

Although the house was turning into a walk-in freezer, the sweat stains under Delia's arms were as big as dinner plates by the time they brought in the couch.

"Over there." The General waved toward a distant wall.

Delia dropped her end of the couch with a groan and fell onto it.

"You okay?" Socko asked.

"None of this broke-down junk is worth dying over," observed the General. "Fini-kaput, every last bit of it."

"Yeah? Well, it's still gotta get moved," Delia puffed.

Socko put a hand on the shoulder of her damp T-shirt. "I'll get the rest."

"I'll be," the General remarked, watching Socko carry his folded metal and canvas bed into the house. "It's a goll-durn army cot."

"Your room's the first one on the left," Delia called as Socko carried his bed up the stairs.

He reached into his new room, felt for the switch, and flipped it. Light flooded the huge white cavern. "Whoa!" he whispered. He crossed the floor, his footsteps muffled by the oatmeal colored carpet, and set the cot down in the middle of the room. It seemed to float in a sea of nothing.

After he'd carried the rest of his stuff up the stairs, Socko took a look at everything he owned. It had seemed like a lot when it was crowded into his skinny corner of the living room, but in a room this big, three milk crates of clothes, a backpack, a stop sign with a bullet hole through the *O*, and a skateboard didn't add up to much.

He wondered what the kids who lived in the houses around here had in their rooms.

He flipped the switch in each of the other three bedrooms and tried to decide which one would be Damien's.

Not the one with its own bathroom. That one would probably be the General's. He knew from the way old guys at the Kludge sometimes used the stairwell like it was a bathroom that people the General's age needed easy access to a toilet.

The second-biggest room would be Delia's. That left the third empty bedroom, which was smaller than his—but Damien was smaller too, so it would work fine. Plus, the room was right next to his. They could signal through the wall, no problem.

In a place this big, the General wouldn't even notice Damien.

***

"He smells," Socko whispered, putting plates and dented pots in the kitchen cupboard.

"Of course he smells. He's past his pull date." Delia slid a stack of plates to the back of a shelf.

"And what about the names he calls us? Sacko and Delia Marie?" His mother's middle name was Ann.

"Still, he's family. He'll grow on us."

"Like mold," Socko whispered back.

"He's family," she repeated. "And just look at what we have because of him!" She pointed out the side-by-side washer and dryer in the laundry room off the kitchen. "No more going down to the basement."

Socko had to admit the washer and dryer were pretty sweet. He was the one who had always done the laundry in the basement. He wouldn't miss the musty damp that made his chest tight or the stress of listening for the sound of footsteps on the stairs, wondering who was about to catch him alone in a soundproof room.

"And how about this?" Delia slapped the humongous refrigerator, an extra she had bargained hard for. It was so big that, with the shelves out, Socko could have climbed inside.

He was emptying the zip-up cooler that contained the contents of their old refrigerator into the new one when he noticed something.

Or the absence of something.

Unlike the fridge at the Kludge, which panted like an old dog, this one was absolutely silent.

He listened harder, straining to hear something, but the silence didn't stop at the refrigerator. There was no *beep beep* of trucks backing up in the street, no one yelling in the apartment below, no gut-thud bass from a car stereo, no wheeze when the temporarily working elevator door opened.

Trying to bring the old place back in his mind, he closed his eyes, but the silence of the new house wrapped around him like cotton. When he opened his eyes again it got worse. What he could see was a kind of silence too: the white interior of the refrigerator, the white kitchen walls and ceiling, and the inky square of sky in the window.

Missing the neon flicker of Donatelli's sign, he walked to the window. Up close, the simple black square was flecked with dots of light. His forehead pressed the glass. He had always wanted to see a starry sky someplace other than TV. But now, gazing into a sea of stars, he felt like he was falling up. Suddenly he didn't know where he was. Or who he was. Or what he was.

His heart was racing in a panic of not-knowing when a voice he barely recognized broke the silence. "Sacko? Sacko! Hustle me up some grub. My belly button is shaking hands with my backbone."

12
GI PAJAMAS

His mother's voice ripped though his sleep like it was a school morning. "Rise and shine!"

Groggy and confused, he opened his eyes.

"I gotta go." She stood over him, already dressed in her ugly brown and orange Phat Burger uniform. "Feed the General, okay?"

"Go away!" Socko moaned.

"As soon as you get your butt out of that bed."

"Ten minutes." He closed his eyes.

"Five." She thumped back down the stairs.

"I don't even want to be here!" he called after her. He covered his head with the pillow and rolled up on his side, the stretched canvas of the cot giving under him with a strained *creak*.

He slid back into sleep.

Thud...thud...thud. He woke to the sound of Delia rocking up the stairs again.

"The General's getting antsy! Get *up*, Socko. I have to leave!"

Today he would be babysitting a cranky old man. Tomorrow and the next day too. Every day, all summer. Great. Just great.

His mother fiddled with a button on the front of her blouse. "There's a little problem with food. There's only one burger left, and some dry cereal, no milk. Who knew a skinny old guy could eat so much supper?"

Socko didn't mention all the food Damien had scarfed before they even hit the road.

"I'm on from seven to three. Tell him lunch will be late but plentiful." She walked out the door.

He pushed up on his elbows. "How are you going to get home? There's no bus!"

She stuck her head back in the room. "I'm working on it! Just make sure the General puts on some clothes. I've seen more old man than I can take before my first cup of coffee."

"What?" Was she leaving him with a naked old guy?

"You can call Damien," she added as she started down the stairs. "The phone's on the kitchen counter. Just don't talk too long." Delia paid for minutes, or as she called them, "emergency minutes."

Giving him permission to call Damien had to be her way of saying sorry I screwed up your entire life.

Was it too early to call? Yeah, probably—plus, the phone was downstairs with a naked old guy.

Socko heard the car start in the driveway, but he didn't get to hear it drive off because downstairs the General started hacking like he was trying to get rid of a lung.

Socko stared at the white, white ceiling over his bed and the metal air-conditioner vent. No demented clown here.

"Hey, Sacko!"

Only a demented great-grandfather.

Could the old guy be all-the-way naked?

When Socko had gone to bed, Delia and the General were arguing. "I give you a house and what do I get? A vinyl chair instead of a bed!" Delia said she kind of thought he'd bring his own—and she didn't know about the wheelchair when she'd picked a house with the bedrooms upstairs.

Had the General gotten so mad he'd taken his clothes off?

"Hey!" the voice scraped again. "Roll out, private!"

"Okay, okay. I'm up." Socko stepped into the shorts he'd dropped by the bed and scuffed his feet into his sneakers.

Wary of what he was getting into, he crept down the stairs. He leaned over the railing to check out Delia's recliner. A snot green afghan he'd never seen before spilled out of its seat and onto the floor, but the General wasn't in it.

Socko slid into the living room. The old man sat turned away, his wheelchair facing the picture window. Above the chair, Socko could see bare shoulders and the knobby bones of the old man's neck. Below, a pair of skinny bare calves. All the General seemed to be wearing was a pair of dingy crew socks. Was he flashing their new neighbors?

Socko wanted to snatch up the green afghan and drop it over the old man, but tangling with the General would probably be like picking up a stray cat.

The chair whipped around. "There you are!"

Socko drew a relieved breath—not that the view wasn't scary. It definitely was. The hair the old man didn't have on the top of his head grew white and wiry on his shoulders and chest. It waved in the breeze from the air-conditioner.

The good news was the General had on plaid boxers.

"What're you looking at?" his great-grandfather demanded. "GIs always sleep in their drawers!"

Socko read the tattoo on the old man's skinny shoulder and grinned.

"What?" snapped the General.

"Is your tattoo supposed to say 'MOHTER'?"

"Only if you're lit and so is the guy giving you the tattoo. Now, where in the Sam Hill did Delia Marie hide my valise?"

"You going somewhere?" A bubble of hope rose in Socko's chest.

"I'll be going after *you* if you don't bring me my clothes so I can get dressed."

"Oh. Yeah. Good idea." Socko had carried the suitcase upstairs to the room Delia had set aside for the General. But it looked like they'd have to rethink that. The General was never going to be able to make it up the stairs.

Which meant there was one whole floor of the house that was General-proof. And *two* extra bedrooms.

Picking up the suitcase, he imagined letting Junebug have the room the General would never use. She'd be safe from Rapp here. But how many miracles did one guy get? In his experience it was usually less than one.

***

"Did your 'mohter' like your tattoo?" Socko called as he slid the last burger out of the microwave.

"Does your 'mohter' serve this pickled monkey all the time?" the General shot back, glaring at the plate Socko set on his knees.

"Pretty much."

"Doesn't she know about fruits? Vegetables?"

"She knows, but they're expensive."

"Another meal or two like this is going to stop up my plumbing." The single eye glared at Socko. "And I'm not my usual sweet self when I'm plugged up." He took a bite and chewed in silence.

Socko sat down and ate a handful of Lucky Charms straight out of the box. He wished there was a second burger, but he got less and less hungry watching the General chew. With each bite the old man's face seemed to collapse.

The General stopped after the third bite. "You always watch people eat this closely?"

"No." Socko stuffed a handful of cereal in his mouth.

"No, *sir*. Great breakfast you're having. Is milk too expensive too?"

"We're just out right now, okay?"

The General thrust the gnawed Bun Buster at him. "You eat it. I can feel my guts locking up."

Socko hesitated. Finger-shaped depressions dented the damp bun.

The General whapped Socko's hand with it. "Take it!"

Socko took it, but he wasn't eager to eat it.

"Chow down," the General ordered. "I suggest you keep your strength up. You're going to need it."

"For what?" Socko took a bite out of the unchewed edge of the burger.

"For later."

13
RECON MISSION

Socko was scoring major points against alien invaders when the General's wheelchair rammed the sofa he was lying on. "What?" He kept his eyes on the screen of his Nintendo DS.

"You plan to kill little green men all day?" the General demanded.

Maybe it *looked* like he was killing little green men. What he was really killing was time. Unless wondering about a best friend who wasn't answering the phone, worrying about how his mom would get home, or watching an old man stare out a window counted, there was nothing to do here.

A hand blocked Socko's view of the small screen. "Show me how to work that fool thing."

"Aren't you kind of old for video games?"

"I could say the same of you." The old man took the DS.

For the next hour they took turns killing little green men. Socko always had the higher score, which miffed the old man and made Socko as close to happy as he'd been since leaving the neighborhood.

"Winning's easy for you, you have quick young hands." The General made it sound like being young was a form of cheating. "Give it time. Arthritis will get you too." He frowned at his own hands.

Seeing the long yellow nails, Socko tried to banish the word "talons" from his mind. Why didn't the old guy cut them? He wasn't exactly too busy. "Your turn." He tried to hand the General the DS, but he waved it away.

"Enough thumb exercise! It's *my* turn to pick the game, and I say it's time for a little real-world action."

"Like what?"

"Like what, *sir!*"

"Yeah, whatever, sir."

The General glared, but let it pass. "This little game is called Recon Mission."

"What would that be...sir?"

"Recon. Reconnaissance." The General looked around as if he was appraising the living room. "This is Central Command—that's CENTCOM in the lingo—and I'm the commanding general."

"Who am I?"

"You're the buck private who reports back."

"Back from where?" Socko's gaze followed the line of the old man's gnarled finger.

Outside the window, the sun beat down on the dry dirt that was their yard.

"You kidding?"

"I know modern kids are delicate indoor creatures," the General said. "But too bad. It is your mission to scope out the territory."

That made Socko mad. He was an outdoor creature, just one who had been caged in a small apartment most of his life. He'd never had any outdoors to explore—but the little bit of the outdoors he'd seen driving into Moon Ridge was a dead zone. "What, exactly, am I looking for?"

"Figure out the lay of the land. Check on the rest of the troops."

"The rest of what troops, sir?"

"The other inhabitants of the moon! Find out who the heck else lives in this godforsaken desert." He slapped the arm of his chair. "Now get your lazy patoot off that couch and deploy!"

Socko thought about pretending to need a drink so he could go to the kitchen and try Damien again. He had just opened his mouth to say he was thirsty when the General roared, "Why are you still here, private?"

***

66

Socko stood on the concrete steps of his new house in a downpour of sunlight, squinting against the glare bouncing back at him from the blistered white dirt of the yard. Heat radiated through the soles of his shoes.

He remembered a show about desert lizards that stood on two feet at a time, raising and lowering them so no foot was on the sand long enough to burn. All *he* could do was walk fast.

As he approached the house next door, he wondered what he would tell the neighbors if he got caught looking through their windows. I'm on a recon mission? That might work if he was five years old. At thirteen it could get him arrested.

He peered through a picture window into a living room identical to his own. "Definitely no troops here." Except for a box of nails and a roll of masking tape on the floor, the house was empty.

Socko crossed the road at a sprint. The house opposite his was even emptier. No nails, no tape, just trapped air and slanting light that tagged window shapes on the floor.

He shaded his eyes and stared at the house one lot over. No signs of life there either. It was too hot to walk that far. But he didn't want to go home.

Instead he squatted in the skinny strip of shade next to the house and checked out the street. It was wide, with zero cracks. The only skateboarding hazard would be the deltas of sandy soil that flared out at the end of each driveway. Without Phase 2 lawns, wind and rain were gradually moving the yards into the street. But the sandbars would be easy to avoid; they might even add a little interest. Especially for a pro skater like Damien.

In the old neighborhood Damien worked the curbs and railings. He skated fakie, apologizing to anyone he almost knocked over. With so many obstacles, he rarely achieved what he called "warp speed." Now, his eyes half closed, Socko could almost see Damien flash down the street in front of him.

It took a while for him to even notice a faint, persistent tapping. Across an expanse of dirt and tar that shimmered in the heat, an old man in a wheelchair was rapping his knuckles against the glass of a

picture window. An impatient arm movement summoned Socko
inside.

***

Sweat dripped off his bangs as he made his report. "I saw four houses,
sir. Three were empty."

"One was occupied?"

"Yeah. Ours."

The General snorted. "Look at all those big boxes out there. You did
a fast check of four and then you sat on your keister! I gave you a job."

"You call that a job? I call it sunstroke, *sir*."

The General thumped a knuckle on a paper bag that had held
kitchen towels. "Draw me a map."

Of what? he thought. But Socko drew four quick squares. "The
houses." He scribbled a pair of parallel lines. "The road."

"Which one of these boxes is us?"

Socko added a star.

"The name of the road?"

"How should I know?"

"Are the houses exactly opposite each other like you drew them?
And what's past the four houses?" The rapid-fire questions pelted
Socko. "And where's your compass rose?"

Compass rose? Socko didn't answer. Copping an attitude was better
than looking stupid.

"Ask or stay ignorant." When Socko kept his mouth shut, the General stabbed the paper on the far side of one of the boxes. "What's
behind the houses?"

"*Behind* the houses?" Socko didn't really want to go there.
Although he knew it wasn't true, this new neighborhood felt fake to
him, like a movie set—like it might really just be walls with nothing
behind them. "You want me to trespass?" Being old, the General probably respected private property.

"Not trespass," the General snapped. "Reconnoiter. And while
you're out there, note the location of the sun. You'll need it for that
compass rose you don't know a blame thing about."

68

Socko took a long, slow drink of water. He chewed the ice. He excused himself to go to the bathroom. But in the end, he stomped back out into the withering heat to reconnoiter. This was the dumbest game ever!

He stood in the middle of the street and looked right, then left. Okay, the houses *were* exactly opposite, so perfectly opposite that their vacant windows stared across the street at each other, as if each house were daring the other to blink first.

Past the four houses he had drawn on the map, the road turned into a lollipop. On the brochure these streets to nowhere were called "cul-de-sacs." They were supposed to be "highly desirable" because there was "no through traffic."

To Socko, it looked like the place you'd get caught if you were running from somebody.

Burning sand sifted into his sneaker through a hole in the toe as he walked around to the back of one of the five houses that ringed the cul-de-sac. He put his face up to a kitchen window. Counters and appliances had been installed, but a large cardboard box with the words "Base Cabinet" printed on it sat in the middle of the room. It looked as if the job had been finished in a hurry. In the second house, a spackle knife lay on the counter. Socko tried the door, but it was locked.

On the back patio of the third house, something caught his eye. He approached the metal lunch box cautiously. Before trying the latch, he looked over both shoulders.

Slick move, he thought. Who did he think was watching? The old neighborhood had a million eyes. This one was blind.

Socko tried to flip the rusty latch, but it wouldn't budge. He sat down and clamped the box between his knees. It took both thumbs to creak the latch open—all that "thumb exercise" was paying off. The stiff hinge squealed when he forced the lid open.

"Oh, gag!" He jumped to his feet. The box tumbled to the ground, spewing out a black banana and a Baggie full of greenish fuzz.

Socko held his breath and knelt for a closer look. Best guess? Tuna sandwich.

Without Damien to share the gross-out, finding the lunch box was a waste. Unless... Socko thought about toeing the sandwich back into the box and springing it on the General, but maybe it was a dumb idea to prank him now. Sooner or later Socko was going to ask him to let Damien "visit" (and then forget to leave). For that to happen he had to stay on the old man's good side. Make that *get* on the old man's good side.

Wondering if there was anything else in it, he rolled the lunch box over with his foot. As it righted itself, it dumped two more things. "Cool!" Leaving the banana and the sack of fuzz on the ground, Socko nudged the other two items back into the box and picked it up.

Socko was almost home when he remembered: the General had asked him to reconnoiter the name of the street.

He walked past his own house, waving at the old guy in the window (a get-on-his-good-side move) but didn't get a return wave. Did the General *have* a good side?

He pushed his sweaty bangs off his forehead and peered up at the street sign. The General was right about one thing—he needed a haircut bad. Tranquility Way. It sounded like a name made up by an English teacher. He checked out the other street name on the pole. Full Moon Circle. Not much better.

Lunch box under his arm, Socko walked back to the house. Before going inside he located the sun, not because he cared about the compass rose—whatever that was. He just didn't want to get sent back out into the heat.

"Report?" the General demanded as soon as he stepped inside.

"Gotta chill first." Socko threw open the refrigerator door. Holding onto a side with each hand, he stuck his head and shoulders between the shelves.

In the next room, the General muttered something about "a lack of discipline."

His face damp but cool, Socko reported to the living room. "I found something." He held up the lunch box.

"Map first. That's the protocol." The old man stabbed at the paper bag with a long nail. "Where was the sun?"

70

Socko pointed at the back wall. "Over there."

With painfully slow movements, the old man drew two crossed lines that looked nothing like a rose. At the end of each one he printed a letter—*N, S, E, W*—then handed the pencil to Socko.

"I've seen those plenty of times." He'd spent hours staring at the map beside his cot, those same little crossed lines right at eye level. "I just didn't know what they were called."

"Now you do." The General pushed the paper bag toward Socko.

Socko added the cul-de-sac with its five houses, the four houses on the other side of theirs, and the street names. He expected another volley of questions. Is our road really that straight? You only looked at two streets? What's over here?

Instead the General frowned at the lunch box, then looked away.

Socko grinned. The old man wanted to see what was inside it—but wasn't going to ask. And Socko wasn't going to offer to show him. The General wasn't the only one who could come up with a dumb game.

"Okay!" the General finally sputtered. "What's in the dad-blamed lunch box?"

"Stuff."

The old man folded his hands over his small potbelly. "Whatever it is, it's mighty ripe."

"I got rid of that part."

"So what *didn't* you get rid of?"

"A couple of things." Watching the General twitch with curiosity, Socko felt kind of bad about building up the suspense—the stuff in the box wasn't all that cool.

When the hinge creaked, the General leaned forward. "Playing cards…"

Socko slid the deck out of the box and fanned the cards. They were old-school—numbers, kings with curly beards, queens dressed like the nuns at St. Ignatius—but Socko could tell the General liked them. He was old-school too.

"And Camels." The old man licked his lips. "Unfiltered." He reached for the cigarette pack.

Socko pulled the lunch box back. "You sure you should smoke?"

"Do I look like I need your permission?"

When Socko gave him the cigarettes, the General ran his thumb along the cellophane that covered the pack, pushing out a book of matches. He rapped the pack sharply against his knuckle. The top of one cigarette popped out.

"Gross. Those things have been next to a rotten sandwich for, like, eons!"

The General pulled the cigarette the rest of the way out of the pack with wrinkled lips.

"And what about that health issue with your lungs?"

"Huh!" The cigarette bobbed, the sound leaking out around it. "If you're not breathing, then you have a health issue. Do I look like I'm dead?"

Socko didn't answer.

"Been around too long anyway," the old man mumbled. "And what's it matter to you? The sooner I croak, the sooner this house is all yours."

"I didn't want this house in the first place. I was fine where I was."

"Sure you were, getting knocked around by the local punks." The General thumbed the cover of the matchbook open and bent down a match, then closed the cover behind it. With a flick of his thumb, the match blazed.

"Hey, do that again."

The General lit the cigarette in his mouth, and then flipped the matchbook at Socko. "You figure it out."

The General took a deep drag...then choked. "Out of practice." He thumped his chest with a fist. "I quit when Mary O'Malley got sick."

"Who's Mary O'Malley?" Socko fiddled with the match.

"What do you mean, 'Who's Mary O'Malley?'" The old man whipped the matches out of Socko's hand and bent a match down with his thumb. In a heartbeat a tiny blue flame wavered above the closed matchbook.

"I mean, who's Mary O'Malley?" Socko figured she was the General's dead wife, but who used a last name when talking about their wife?

The old man stared at the flame. "You hear that, honey? The boy doesn't even know who you are." He blew the flame out with a damp puff and watched the smoke rise. "Mary O'Malley was my wife of fifty-four years—also your great-grandmother. Doesn't anyone care about family in this family?"

"I don't. Not unless that family cares about mom and me."

"Caring goes two ways!" The General's cold blue eye stared at him. "Never heard a peep from your mother until I had a house to offer, not even when her grandmother died."

"We didn't even know she'd died! Nancy doesn't talk about you guys, so it's not our fault."

The old man crossed his legs and jiggled his foot. He took a drag on his cigarette, then coughed.

"You think Mary O'Malley would want you to smoke?" Socko asked.

"Don't know why she would. She never did before." He took another drag. "I picked up the habit when I was in the army. GIs smoke when they're bored. They smoke when they're scared. Between bored and scared, that about covers army life." The General shook his head. "I don't get scared anymore, but with Mary O'Malley gone, I sure do get bored. If I smoke and die sooner? Good."

"Come on, nobody wants to die."

"What do I have to live for?" The General pulled a cloth handkerchief out of his pocket and coughed into it. "Your mother's cooking?" He tossed the matchbook at Socko. "Here. Play with fire while I go to the john."

Socko thumb-popped the match head against the striker. He wasted four matches before the General rolled back into the room. He never did get the trick to work.

14
ONE SWEET RIDE

Day one of the new life dragged on forever. The General constantly ordered him around. "Get me a drink of water!" "Put my valise behind the goll-durn sofa!" The cell phone in Socko's pocket bumped against his leg with each step, reminding him, *call Damien, call Damien.* When the General dozed off in his chair, Socko snuck upstairs and hit redial. He counted five rings before someone picked up.

"Yeah?"

"Can I speak to Damien?"

"Dunno where heezat." Damien's mom sounded skunk drunk.

Maybe his friend was safe, hanging out one floor above in their old apartment. But what if he wasn't? "Tell him to call me, okay?"

"Who're you?"

"Socko."

"Socko z'gone."

"I'm calling from my new place. Tell him—" Socko heard the phone clatter against something hard—probably the floor. "Hello, hello?" Two of Delia's precious emergency minutes passed while he listened to dead air.

***

"I eat lunch at twelve o'clock sharp. That was four hours ago," the General complained. "My stomach sounds like John Philip Sousa and his whole dad-blamed marching band."

Socko didn't care about the General's musical stomach—his stomach was making music too—he was worried about his mom. Delia had been off shift for an hour, but without a car, how was she supposed to get home?

Now when the cell phone bumped his leg, he willed it to ring and be his mom, even if she was just calling to say she was stranded at the Phat. He didn't want to call her because of the "emergency minutes" thing, but in ten more minutes he would.

Nine.

Eight.

The General was grumbling about "breach of contract" when the bright blast of a car horn sounded in the front yard.

Socko ran outside. "You borrowed Manuel's car?"

"Sort of." Delia grabbed the overloaded Phat sack from the seat beside her. When she hugged him, Socko smelled fryer grease. It always got in her clothes, her hair, everything. "How's himself?" she asked.

"Complaining."

"So what else is new?"

They went into the kitchen where the General had already positioned his wheelchair beside the microwave.

"Lunch." Delia put the bag on his knees. "And supper."

The General lifted out burgers one by one, handing them to Socko, then glared into the bag. He popped the lid on a Styrofoam box. "What in the Sam Hill is this?"

"Crispy Fried Salad," Delia said. "It's a new Phat Burger special."

Socko opened the microwave door. "You said you wanted vegetables." He stuck in three burgers.

The General poked at the contents of the box. "These aren't vegetables!" He slung the Crispy Fried Salad, bag and all, into the trash.

Socko reached into the can to rescue it. The chicken nuggety things on top of the salad had looked pretty good.

"Two questions, Delia Marie," the General rumbled. "Number one: do you cook at all? Because our arrangement included room *and* board."

Socko held the Styrofoam box in his hand. What part of "free food" did the General not get?

"I cook sometimes," said Delia.

The General glared up at her through a forest of eyebrow hairs. "Define sometimes."

"You know, now and then." She could cook if she had to, although not too well. "What was the second question?"

"Where'd you get the jalopy?"

"It's a loaner from Manuel," said Socko. "He works at Phat Burger too."

"It is Manuel's," said Delia, "but it's not a loaner. Here's the good news!" She clapped her hands. "For just five hundred dollars—that's five hundred—it's all yours, General!" She smiled, but Socko knew the smile covered the way she really felt—which was desperate.

"Five hundred's a steal!" said Socko, hoping the General wouldn't take a good look at what he was buying. Delia had to have that car to get to work, and Socko needed a ride back to the old neighborhood.

The General rolled to the window. "Great car. It would look right at home in a junkyard." He crossed his arms over his stained sweater-vest. "What would I need with a car, Delia Marie? You said it yourself—being as old as dirt, I am no longer qualified to drive."

"*I* can drive *you* around. Like a chauffeur. It's a sweet ride. Please say yes." She walked over to him, her palms pressed together. "Pretty please?"

The General stared at the sweet ride. "Orange and turquoise. I guess for five hundred it's asking too much to have the paint on the doors match."

"It's festive…like a party on wheels!" said Delia.

"It runs good and it's cheap," Socko added. Who cared about the paint job? With wheels, Socko could check on Damien tomorrow. Even slaves must've had a day off now and then.

"The way *you* drive, you have no business taking a car out on the highway in the first place," said the General.

Delia stood over the wheelchair. "There is no bus out here. I was told there was, but there isn't. Without this car I can't get to work."

The General drummed his fingers on the arm of his wheelchair. "I'll *lend* you the money. With interest."

"Interest? Come on, General. We're family!"

"Really? You never even told Sacko here about Mary O'Malley."

"What would I have told him? That I once had a grandmother who made great sugar cookies? That's about all I remember. I was seven the last time I saw her. You two just disappeared from my life!"

The old man let his breath out slowly. "Maybe you should ask *Nancy* about that!" He winced as he slid a knobby, arthritic hand into his pants pocket and brought out a checkbook. He opened the checkbook's plastic cover. "Five hundred at 12 percent is my best offer," he declared. "Take it or leave it."

Delia clenched her fists. "Forget it! I'll get a loan from Insta-Cash."

Socko put a hand on his mother's arm. "Remember the time you got money for asthma medicine there?" Delia had taken an Insta-Cash payday loan just once, and only because Socko needed to breathe. "It cost you twenty to borrow a hundred for a week." It didn't take a math whiz to know that was more than 12 percent.

Delia sat down slowly on a kitchen chair. One by one she pulled out the bobby pins that held her hat in place. "You win, old man." She looked as limp as the paper hat in her hands. "Make the check out to Manuel Garcia."

The General clicked the pen point in and out. "On one condition. Tomorrow you get me something with roughage before my plumbing clogs up."

Socko let out an exasperated sigh. In one day he had heard enough about his great-grandfather's "plumbing" to last a lifetime, but he was sure the subject would come up again. And again.

He was gazing out the window at their new three-tone car when a familiar voice inside his head said, *Genius idea! Jack the car and come home.*

15
DRIVE-BY

Socko didn't even get to make his case for catching a ride back to the old neighborhood. Delia had already left for work the next morning when the old man rammed his wheelchair into the bottom step. "Rise and shine, private. It's way past O-dark thirty."

O-dark thirty? It was probably more army lingo. Socko didn't open his eyes. One day in, and he was already sick of being the grunt in an army of two.

"Get your sorry keister down here, private. Right now."

Socko put the pillow over his head. But the General's weak and windy voice was like a brain worm. (No urban myth, brain worms. Socko had seen them on the Discovery Channel.) "Suit yourself," the brain worm whispered. "But it isn't getting any cooler out there."

Socko shoved the pillow aside. The chilled air pumping out of the AC vent in the ceiling over his bed settled over him like a clean sheet. But when he squinted toward the window, a no-mercy sun was beating down on Moon Ridge Estates.

He threw the pillow as hard as he could and rolled off his cot. He pulled on shorts, a T-shirt, and socks, then stomped his feet into his sneakers. It was time to straighten a few things out.

The General was waiting in his wheelchair, the incomplete map of the neighborhood spread across his bony knees. The situation was an improvement over yesterday. The old guy was dressed and he had obviously fed himself—a fresh grease stain splotched the front of his shirt.

"What're you looking at?" The General pulled his shirt front out and took a look too. "It's nothing but a canteen badge. Your mission today is to go farther afield and check out the Big Empty," he wheezed. "See if we really *are* alone in this godforsaken place. Compree?"

"Don't I even get to eat first?"

"You slept through breakfast."

Socko shoved a pencil stub and an envelope into his pocket. Making notes during the mission would be easier than trying to remember things. He charged back upstairs and grabbed his skateboard.

While the old man went off about kids these days being soft, Socko detoured into the kitchen and slipped the cell phone into his pocket.

Outside, he dropped the skateboard onto the road and turned left. Kicking the board down Tranquility Way, he created his own hot wind. When he reached the street sign, he dragged a foot, slid to a stop, and looked back. No way the General could see him from here.

He slid the phone out of his pocket. He had tried to call his friend again the night before, letting the phone ring and ring. Someone had finally picked up, but hit the End button without saying a word. Delia had said it had to be Louise's latest boyfriend, so it was no big deal, but Socko was worried.

He hit redial. As it rang, he imagined the phone in Damien's apartment, buried somewhere in the mess, or sloshing around in Louise's purse. "Come on...come on..." But no one picked up, not even the fake British voice that said, "You have reached voice mailbox two-three-seven-nine..."

"Don't worry. Everything's fine." He flipped the phone shut and dropped it in his pocket. Great, now he was talking to himself.

He looked right, then left, trying to decide which way to go. If it *was* a circle, it didn't matter which way he turned.

But he didn't trust the signs around here. The big one out front said "Units Going Fast!" So far, the known census of Moon Ridge Estates was three. Make that two, in real time. His mom got to spend most of every day back in the old neighborhood.

It looked pretty much the same in both directions. Socko turned left. As he rolled along, he became aware of the slap of his sneaker hitting the road, the swish of the wheels. At the old place, those sounds would have been buried under a pile of noise. Moon Ridge was so silent it was like the world had died.

Since no one was watching, he tried out a trick.

He'd never mastered an ollie on the cracked streets and sidewalks of his old neighborhood. Now he snapped the tail of the board down, slid his front foot forward, and jumped. For a second the board rose with him like it was glued to his feet, but he didn't get much air. Landing was going to be a crash-and-burn, so he bailed, jumping off the board before he fell.

Damien was the one who could skate.

Keeping it simple, Socko carved down the street. He stopped at each corner to jot down the street name. Then he'd look back the way he'd come and forward in the direction he was going. Even though he knew turning around would take him back to Tranquility Way, he couldn't shake the feeling he was going to get lost.

He continued to list the streets that radiated like spokes off the hub of Full Moon Circle—checking each driveway along the edge of the road for a car, each window for curtains or a face looking out. The houses, at least on the left side of the street, were getting more and more skeletal.

When he came to a house with no walls at all, he dragged his foot and stopped. Bare studs framed rectangles of sky. He stepped on the tail of his skateboard and picked it up. Board under his arm, he trotted up the front steps and through the gaping door frame.

The house must have been standing unfinished for a long time. The warped floorboards creaked under his feet.

Stairs to the second story had been roughed in, but there was no railing, just a pair of holes at the outside edge of each riser where the spindles of the railings would go. He tested a step with one foot. It felt solid.

When he reached the landing, he stopped and listened. Somewhere in Moon Ridge Estates there had to be a crew hammering, running saws, mixing concrete.

All Socko heard was his own breathing.

He peered through the gaps between beams that ran from future wall to future wall. His skateboard looked awfully small on the floor below.

If he were here, Damien would dare him to tightrope-walk across a beam—then Delia's voice in his head drowned out the dare. "No disasters, Socko. We got no medical."

If there was a place as cool as this at the Kludge, it would have been Tarantula territory.

Then Socko remembered, there *was* a place this cool at the Kludge—a fire escape chute a tenant could jump into from any floor. The official warnings about "emergency use only" and the unofficial spray-painted silhouette of a tarantula on the entry doors had stopped Socko and Damien from trying the chute until one day they were so bored, they'd dared each other. Deciding to go for the maximum ride, they wrenched open the door on the roof. The air inside the tube smelled hot and metallic. Damien sat, legs in the tube. Socko climbed in behind him, one leg on either side of his skinny friend.

"*Ahhhhhh...*" Screaming, they careened through the dark. But when their feet smacked the lever at the bottom of the escape tube, the door did not pop open and dump them in the alley behind the Kludge. Instead they heard an evil laugh from outside the door, followed by a too-familiar voice. "Good luck getting out, suckas."

After numerous back-slides during their crawl up the slick tube, they emerged on the second floor sweat-drenched and dehydrated, but they had learned a lesson. The chute, like every other inch of the neighborhood, was claimed territory.

But the house with no walls wasn't. In fact, as far as he could tell, none of Moon Ridge had been claimed.

He took in the view from his perch with new eyes. The vacant houses, roads, and dirt yards that went on all the way to the horizon—Rapp couldn't even *imagine* a territory as big as this—and all of it could be Socko's.

But he needed to *do* something to stake his claim. His stomach clenched, because he knew what it was. He had to walk across the not-yet-there second floor and he had to do it the way Damien would. Anyone could balance with their feet on two separate beams and waddle across. This situation called for a little tightrope walking.

Through the joists he spied a two-by-four lying on the floor below.

The board flexed with each step as he carried it up the stairs on one shoulder. He tested the weight of it as it rested in both hands; he slid one sneaker onto the beam, then slid his foot back again.

He put down the board and pried off his sneakers, then peeled his sweaty tube socks off too, tossing shoes and socks down through an opening between the beams for easy access later.

It was weird to be barefoot outside—or sort of outside. In the city he never went barefoot except in the apartment. He'd heard too many warnings from his mom about rusty nails and lockjaw. But by walking the beam barefoot, he could get a grip with his toes, which meant he would be safer—Delia would like that.

With the extra weight of the board in his hands and the hot beam testing his will, he walked, step by step, away from the staircase and out over absolutely nothing.

When he reached the middle of the beam, he looked down—the brochure hadn't lied about the "cathedral ceilings." The distance to the floor was so spectacular he felt a little dizzy.

He was trying to figure out just how far he'd fall if his foot slipped when he heard the distant growl of a car engine approaching from behind. He whipped around. Because he didn't take into account that he was at the center of the turn and that the ends of the two-by-four would be moving much faster, the force of momentum took him by surprise. His felt his feet slide out from under him, but he couldn't do a thing.

His balance pole sliced through the gap between two beams and he went down with it, whacking his arm on an adjacent beam before smashing into the floor. The air left his lungs with a rush. Could lungs deflate like punctured tires? If so, he was dead. It would be weeks before anyone found him. He'd lie there and dry up like a fly on a windowsill.

The sound of the engine that had spooked him got louder and louder. He took a jagged breath and rolled up on his side. The toothy chrome grille of a black car rounded the curve in Full Moon Circle. The tinted windows were so dark Socko couldn't see who was inside. He couldn't even tell how many people were in there. He *could* tell by the speed, which was very slow, that whoever was in there was looking for something.

He was partly hidden by beams, and his brown T-shirt might blend in with the floor. But what about his red hair? He tried to reassure himself: this wasn't the old neighborhood; he was safe here.

Traveling at a crawl, the car pulled even with the house.

Then it stopped.

Fear prickled Socko's scalp. Whoever was in that car, they weren't looking for him. They couldn't be. Still, if the doors opened, he'd forget about being dead and run.

The engine idled and the car sat.

Taking shallow breaths, Socko smelled the warm plywood of the subfloor.

He heard a *tick* as the brake pedal released. The car began to roll slowly forward.

It seemed to take forever for the sound of the engine to die to a whisper and vanish.

As he sat up, starry explosions shot off like bottle rockets inside his head. He dropped his forehead to his knees.

He didn't know how long he'd been sitting like that when he heard the engine again. Now he was sure—they'd seen him the last time. They were just messing with his head! Ignoring the rushing sound in his ears, he pushed himself to his feet and snatched up his shoes and skateboard. He ditched his crumpled socks and jumped through a gap between the studs of the house's back wall, then hesitated.

He had come a long way on Full Moon Circle. Should he go back the way he had come, or continue on the Circle? The decision was critical. In such a flat landscape, a kid breaking for home would be visible from a long way off.

Taking a chance, he continued to follow the circle, but he didn't use the road. Instead he darted from house to house, stopping behind each to listen, his sneakers dangling from one hand, his skateboard under his arm. The bare dirt burned his feet and he worried about rusty nails, but he didn't stop to put his shoes on.

He was flattened against the side wall of a house trying to breathe when something red in the driveway caught his eye. *Hey*, thought the small corner of his brain that wasn't in a panic, *a ripstick!* Even crazy scared, he was about to check out the figure-eight-shaped skateboard when he heard the car again. He took off running.

He couldn't believe it! Just ahead was the sign for Tranquility Way. He'd only been five streets away from where he'd started.

He dropped the skateboard and jetted down his own street. Desperate to get inside, he abandoned the board outside the door, turned the doorknob, and fell into the cool. Letting the sneakers tucked under his arm drop, he twisted the knob lock, then put the chain across. It was so flimsy one good kick would bust it.

The General's voice wavered from the kitchen. "That you, Sacko?"

"Yeah, it's me." When he walked into the kitchen, the General was filling a water glass at the sink.

"Listen," Socko said, trying to catch his breath, "we...we gotta keep the door locked."

The General twisted the tap shut and stared for a long moment at Socko's dirty bare feet. "Let me guess. Our neighbors are Mafia. And they stole your shoes."

"No, but there was this black car with tinted windows cruising real slow on Full Moon Circle."

"Imagine that. A car on a road. You need to grow a spine, Sacko." The paper bag map crackled as the General flattened it against the kitchen counter. "Report." He pushed the bag toward Socko.

The old man didn't get it. He'd probably never lived in a tough neighborhood. Socko scribbled a loopy circle, then added a few spidery lines and began copying the names of the streets that radiated from the circle, but his mind was on the dark car. His danger sensors had gone wild when it had slowed down—and it had circled three times that he knew of. Something was definitely up with that car.

"And these?" The General's yellow nail unerringly targeted the five unlabeled streets.

Socko shrugged. Running from the car, he hadn't taken a lot of notes.

"Slipshod. Well, there'll be time enough to find out tomorrow."

Socko turned away, ready to retreat to his room to try calling Damien again, but the General pulled rank.

"Park it, soldier. You and me are going to play us a little poker." The old man slid the deck of cards Socko had found out of its box. The cards became a waterfall of blurred white as the deck flew from one gnarled hand to the other. Although clumsy on the Nintendo DS, the General's hands were lightning when it came to shuffling cards— as quick as they had been with the matchbook.

The General snapped the cards back into a tidy stack and slapped it down in front of Socko. "Cut."

Socko sat there.

"Don't tell me you've never played cards before? Not even a sissy-girl game like Old Maid?"

The only card game Socko had ever played was one he and Damien had made up called "Go Spit." You couldn't play it inside. Right now he wasn't exactly in the mood to learn a new game. "They're just stupid pieces of cardboard."

"Famous last words, son. Famous last words." The General lifted the top half of the stack, thumped it down on the counter, then picked up the bottom half of the stack and set it on top. "You try."

"That looked really hard."

"Get your laughs in now, because I'm gonna take you to the cleaners, Mr. Wet Behind the Ears. This is a little game called Seven-Card Stud. I suggest you quit moping and pay attention." He began dealing cards off the deck. *Flick. Flick. Flick. Flick.* Two cards landed in front of each of them with the pictures hidden. "The first two—which are your hole cards—are down and dirty."

The next card hit the piles face up. "Lesson number one," said the General. "The poker face. Never let your opponent know what kind of cards you have. Whether you have the best or worst cards in the world, you keep a straight face. Show me." The old man glared at Socko. "That is *the* worst poker face I've ever seen. What's the matter with you, boy?"

Normally Socko had no trouble looking blank—he wore the blank face every day in school—but the feeling that he had to reach Damien had just swept over him. In the same way he knew the black car was trouble, he knew something had happened to his friend. He dropped his cards on the table. "Be right back."

"I thought only old guys like me got sudden urges!" the General shouted after him.

Socko sped up the stairs to his room and closed the door behind him. With his back against the door, he punched redial. After half a ring he heard a click—someone was picking up!

But the voice that answered wasn't Damien's.

It wasn't even human.

"The number you are trying to reach is no longer in service."

16
THE MIGHTY ANT

"Mom, did you hear what I said?" Early morning wasn't the best time to try to get his mother's attention. "Mom! You gotta do it!"

"We'll talk about it later. I'm kinda busy right now." Delia reached into the refrigerator and snatched a Phat Burger bag off the top shelf. She was about to bustle past him. Instead she grabbed his arm, zeroing in on a fall-off-the-beam injury. "Where'd you get this big old ugly bruise?"

"Forget the bruise. You gotta check on Damien. I can't reach him. His phone's disconnected."

"Seems like you're getting in enough trouble all by yourself without Damien," she said, frowning at his bruised arm. "Breakfast!" she sang out, opening the bag in her hand.

The General grimaced at the cold Hot Apple Tart Delia dropped in front of him. "When I said room and board"—he picked up the box and gave it a shake—"I didn't think you'd give me a *real* board."

"You wanted fruit?" She jabbed the word "Apple" on the box with a finger. "You got fruit." She took the box out of his hands and tossed it to Socko. "Nuke this for your great-grandfather. And here's one for yourself." She tossed him a second box.

Socko put both in the microwave and hit the 1-minute button. "Mom?"

"I don't have time for this, Socko! I gotta get to work. They're disconnected because Louise didn't pay the bill. End of story."

The General put a hand on his belly. "Tonight there'd better be *real* food, because my pipes—"

"I get the message!"

Beep. Socko took the pie boxes out of the oven and dropped one on the table.

The General unfolded the cardboard flaps and winked back the steam. He snapped the flaps shut again. "Delia Marie, this is unacceptable. I repeat. Real food tonight, or I call my lawyer."

"Mom, about Damien?"

Delia rested her knuckles on her wide hips. "Hello? I'm kinda in a rush right now! You two may have time to complain, but I don't have time to listen!"

The General cleared his throat loudly and spat in the garbage can beside his chair.

Delia had just slung her purse over her shoulder but she stopped. "Was that a comment?"

"Darn straight it was a comment!"

"Well, it was gross! I won't allow it in my house!"

"*Your* house? It's not *your* house 'til I'm six feet under, which is probably what you're hoping for, feeding me all this heart-stopping—"

Socko stuffed his box of hot apple breakfast in the pocket of his cargo shorts and opened the front door.

Delia and the General turned. "Where do you think you're going, private?" the General demanded.

"Somewhere else."

"It's barely light out, baby," said Delia.

"At least it's quiet." Socko stepped outside and closed the door. His house was beginning to sound like Damien's apartment.

Still holding onto the knob, he took a slow breath.

It *was* barely light out.

Lying in bed last night, he'd admitted to himself he'd probably freaked about nothing. The black car was probably just a car on a road, like the General said. Still...he had learned to trust the tingle on the back of his neck. It had saved him too many times. But even if the car

88

was bad news he wouldn't see it now. He'd learned in the old neighborhood that if there was a safe time it was early morning. Although they might cruise all night, bad guys—like vampires—disappeared with the first rays of light.

He took a few steps away from the house and listened, just in case. But there were no sounds outside, and none from inside either. Delia and the General had probably moved to the scorching-glare stage.

The silence was creepy. While he didn't miss the sounds of fighting coming through the floor in the old place, he did miss the everyday noise of people doing stuff, like Junebug practicing in the hall when she'd heard *American Idol* was coming to town. Turned out it wasn't true, but everyone on the fourth floor learned the words to her audition number before she got the bad news.

Maybe today he'd find someone here. Moon Ridge Estates was a big place. Some part of the subdivision had to be populated.

Socko was about to set out on foot when he saw his skateboard lying in the dirt in front of the house. He couldn't believe he'd ditched it, and that it was still right where he'd left it. Even though it was a piece of crap, at the old place it would have gone missing within ten minutes.

He remembered the ripstick. It was *not* a piece of crap, yet it had lain abandoned and untouched too. Maybe he'd read the house wrong. Maybe it wasn't empty. But it sure looked empty. And if it was, he'd have himself a ripstick. If it wasn't? His mom would say, "Then you'll have a new friend!"

As he kicked down the street he stared at the board under his foot. The grip tape was peeling and the scars and dings on the deck were glaring. But the ripstick was mint. If the kid who went with that ripstick was around, he wasn't sure he wanted to meet him.

When he got to the house he peered through a window. Empty.

No kid, but no ripstick anymore either. With one foot on his skateboard, he looked left, then right, scanning the street. He wondered which way the kid had gone, and why he'd been there in the first place.

He thought about going back to the house. His mom had left for work by now, and the General would bust him if he didn't get his "patoot" home pretty soon. But today Socko didn't feel like playing his great-grandfather's games.

Instead, he decided to follow each of the streets off the circle. Maybe he'd find a different phase of Moon Ridge, one where people lived.

Harvest Moon. He stared down the street, which still seemed to be waiting for Phase 1. The road was there. Sidewalks and curbs were in place. On each lot pipes stuck up out of the ground like periscopes, but the lots were vacant.

Socko was about to give the road a pass when, at the back of the first yard-to-be, he spotted giant sections of pipe lying on their sides. He thought about tucking his board under his arm for the trek to the tubes, but left it at the curb. There weren't even houses on this street, so who was going to steal his cruddy board?

He stepped over the curb and into a dirt yard. Here and there a weed grew out of the parched ground. "Nature's Phase 2," he muttered. Even if the developer never planted a thing, weeds, like the ones that muscled up through the cracked sidewalks around the Kludge, were planting themselves.

Watching the toes of his shoes sink as he walked forward, he spotted a tiny black hole in the ground. Ants wandered in and out of it, probably looking for food.

Socko felt the heat from the apple tart box in his pocket. He fished it out and opened the flaps, then broke off a corner of the pastry and dropped it a few inches from the hole.

Antennae tapping, a dozen ants approached the chunk of crust cautiously. Deciding it was food, they mobbed the crust and began to drag it toward the hole.

Socko lay down on his stomach and propped his chin on his hands.

The sugary chunk jammed the hole. Ant frenzy! The ants shoved it back out, turned it, then tried again, breaking off a few crumbs. When the ant gang and their prize finally went subterranean, Socko dropped a piece of apple.

Damien would think he was nuts watching a bunch of ants—Damien always said he was allergic to nature. But Damien wasn't here, so Socko monitored the activity closely, every now and then dropping another chunk of pie. He'd seen leafcutter ants on TV, carrying the giant green sails of cut leaves, but this was real, and real was better.

He only realized how long he'd been there when the backs of his legs sent him a message, *hey, we're burning back here!* He ignored the message for a few more minutes. In some weird way the ants felt like company.

Before getting back to his feet, he slid the rest of the tart out of the box and set it a few inches from the hole. The half apple tart, sitting like a colossus in the dust, would assure him a place in ant legend.

He would have liked to see how they stuffed the giant pie down the midget hole, but the sun's heat felt like a weight on his back. He turned his head on his arms. From the ground the tubes looked ant's-eye-view big.

When he stood up, the ants became ants again, the tubes less gigantic, but they did look shady.

***

He sat inside a concrete tube, legs crossed. Slumped into its curve, he felt the cool through his T-shirt. He'd never seen concrete so clean and white.

One time he and Damien had found a nearly empty can of spray paint in the dumpster. They had sprayed Socko and Damien rule! on the concrete wall of the stairwell. When Delia confronted them, Socko claimed someone else had tagged it. "Who, besides the two of you, thinks you and Damien rule?" she had demanded. Socko was grounded for a week.

But Delia would never sit in this tube. No one but Socko ever would. He could write whatever he wanted. He pulled the pencil out of a pocket, then remembered—his best friend was the one who could draw. Socko's tag, whatever it was, would have to be simple.

Circle… The pencil scraped across the concrete. Circle. Circle. He began adding lines. How many? Six? Yeah, they always have six. Plus two antennae.

He leaned back and looked at his symbol. It was—an ant. Compared to a hairy tarantula? Pretty lame. But then he remembered the ants bench-pressing several times their own weight.

THE MIGHTY ANT, he wrote. Jagged lightning bolts zigged away from the stick-figure ant. The lead wore down to a nub before he finished the third lightning bolt, but the idea came across. This was no ordinary ant.

This ant was indestructible.

Radioactive.

Glow-in-the-dark.

Telekinetic.

Kick-ass.

Out of the corner of his eye, Socko caught a flash of movement. The dark car! But it wasn't cruising this time—it was speeding. He heard a grinding sound, then saw his skateboard porpoising through the air; the car had somehow caught and tossed it as it drove by.

He waited a full minute before sidling over to assess the damage. The board lay wheels up, the front edge of the deck cracked. Socko kicked it over. Stood on it. It still rolled. He pushed it back and forth under his foot.

Should he break for home? Although the prickling sensation at the back of his neck was warning him big-time, he decided to hang tough and go right on making his survey.

As he sped down Harvest Moon, the neck-prickle stung like a thousand needles.

Mighty Ant, he thought, *Mighty Ant.* He heard words in the hum of the wheels. *Indestructable. Radioactive. Glow-in-the-dark. Telekinetic. Kick-ass.*

He looked over his shoulder. The dark car was behind him somewhere, prowling.

It's just a car on a road, he reminded himself. *Just a car on a road.*

When he hit the cul-de-sac at the end of Harvest Moon, he sped back, flew the short distance on Full Moon that would take him to the next spoke on the wheel, and hung another left.

Again, no houses.

Again, a cul-de-sac. He made a fast 180. His wheels screamed on Full Moon. *Mighty ant. Just a car. Mighty ant. Just a car.* He careened onto Blue Moon Drive.

Suddenly houses as finished as his own lined both sides of the street.

There were still no cars in the driveways, no lawns, no scattered toys, but no cul-de-sac either. This road came to a different conclusion.

17
A COMMUNITY OF ONE

The sprawling brick building was so new, the mortar between the bricks was toothpaste white. In the middle of a flowerless flower bed stood a sign: MOON RIDGE ESTATES COMMUNITY CENTER AND CLUBHOUSE.

Socko peered through a louvered window into a huge room with lines painted on the floor. It had to be a gym. Walking along the front of the building, he saw a kitchen, and what would probably be a game room, although so far all it had in it was a lone foosball table. He turned the corner and looked into more empty rooms. Offices, maybe. He couldn't tell.

When he went around the back of the building he almost ran into a large sign:

MOON RIDGE ESTATES COMMUNITY GOLF COURSE
ANOTHER HOLMES HOMES PROJECT

But he barely noticed the sign. Behind it towered a heap of dead trees twice as tall as he was.

Socko had never seen anything like this in the city. Street trees got distorted when the city's bucket trucks lopped off limbs that grew too close to power lines, but the trees were always left standing.

Dead leaves whispered in the hot wind as he walked around the enormous pile. He turned away, only to discover that this pile was just one of many. Broken trees littered acres and acres of bare dirt. It looked like the scenes of rain forest devastation he'd seen on National Geographic. He wished he could change the channel.

He watched the ground as he walked, not even noticing that the dirt beneath his feet had turned to concrete until he stepped out over nothing. He wheeled his arms and threw his weight back. He had barely escaped falling into the deep end of the Olympic-size swimming pool promised on the brochure, which would've hurt, big-time. The pool was as dry as the dirt of Moon Ridge.

He jogged along one side of the pool and jumped in at the shallow end. Dry leaves crunched under his feet as he ran down the slope.

His back against the wall at the deep end, he slid down to a squat. Now he couldn't see anything but the turquoise concrete of the pool and the lid of sky overhead. He felt like a specimen in a tank.

For a place that put the word "community" on every sign, Moon Ridge sure was lifeless. He was about to feel sorry for himself, a community of one, when he happened to look up the long blue slope of the pool floor. His jaw dropped. "Genius idea!" The floor of the pool was a ramp, and the floor and walls curved where they met. All he had to do was get rid of the leaves and dirt.

He found a piece of plywood behind the clubhouse. First he scraped the dry leaves into piles, then used the board as a dustpan. Sweat was dripping off his bangs by the time he got rid of the leaves and twigs that littered the floor. All that was left on that long smooth ramp was a fine layer of dust.

He stood on the skateboard on the edge at the shallow end.

Before he could lose his nerve, he stepped on the tail of the board, put his other foot on the front, and dropped in.

***

The chilled air in the house iced his sweaty skin.

"When you am-scray, you don't mess around." The old man closed the book in his lap.

In Socko's absence the General had put on a sweater. Just looking at him made Socko hot.

The old man straightened the position of the book on his knees, as if the alignment were critical. "Sorry I was fighting with your mom."

"That's okay." Socko fell into a chair. "I was sort of fighting with her myself."

"True. Who in the Sam Hill is Damien?"

It took a good twenty minutes to explain his best friend, but the General held his tongue for once and listened. Socko talked about how the Tarantulas were after Damien, and about how he hadn't been able to reach him.

The General sat quiet, staring at the cover of the book in his lap.

Socko took a chance. "He could ride home with Mom, hide out here a while."

"*Two* boys? Here?" The book slid to the floor. "Now there's a recipe for noise and foolishness!"

"That stuff about Rapp almost dropping him off the roof? I wasn't making it up! Damien could die if he stays there."

The General squinted up at him with his one eye. "Listen, Sacko, there's such a thing as being too old for this life, and I am. All I want anymore is peace and quiet. I've done my part."

"But Damien's just a kid and he's in trouble!"

"I appreciate that, son, but he's somebody else's problem."

"Whose? Nobody cares about him but me."

"Guess that makes him your problem, doesn't it?" He turned the chair toward the window.

The old guy was useless! Socko left him staring into the bone-dry yard and went up to his room, where he lay on his cot. That didn't help. He went back downstairs to try again.

"Sir?" The General was still staring out the window.

"About time you came back. I'm bored."

"Whose problem is *that?*"

The General turned and spat in the garbage can. "Yours." He fished the deck of cards out of the pocket of his sweater, but stopped as he zeroed in on the bruise on Socko's arm. "How *did* you get that bruise Delia Marie was all over you about? It's getting pretty ripe."

"I walked across a beam in one of the houses."

"And fell, I assume. You could've busted your gourd." He took another look at the bruise. "You got more guts than I gave you credit for. I'm a little worried about your brains, though." He slid the cards out of the box. "You ready to lose a few hands of gin rummy?"

***

Socko lost—and won—more hands of gin rummy than he could keep track of. The afternoon faded.

"The bag of used burgers is late," the General announced.

"Delia Marie is late," Socko corrected him. Maybe she was checking on Damien. Or maybe not. "I hope Manuel's car didn't crap out on her."

"Me too. If the car crapped out she'll be *really* late. Then we'll have to reheat the burgers in the microwave from dead-cold. Makes the buns all rubbery."

Socko lowered his cards. "Is that all you care about?"

"Get older and you realize, it's the simple pleasures. Eating. Sleeping—even if it's just eating greasy burgers and sleeping sitting up."

"What about caring about other people? Something might've happened to her." Socko was playing a losing hand and imagining an eighteen-wheeler plowing into Delia's multicolored car when the multicolored car pulled into the driveway, tailpipe smoking. He tossed his cards down on the table.

By the time he made it to at the car, he was panting. "How's Damien?"

Delia climbed out and unstuck her polyester pants from the backs of her thighs. "I tried to check on him, but I couldn't get into our old building. I turned in the key, remember?"

"What about Mr. Marvin?"

She waved a hand. "He got a job, or got evicted, I don't know. Anyway, there was no one to let me in." She hung her purse over her shoulder, picked up a couple of plastic sacks, and trudged up the walk.

"Mom?" Socko danced around her until he was between her and the front door. "You gotta take me to work with you tomorrow! I'll find a way in."

She planted her feet wide. "That is one thing I am *not* doing, ever. I have enough to worry about with the way Rapp is treating Junebug. You are never going to be anywhere near that thug again." She reached up and put her hand on his cheek. "When school starts you'll make another best friend."

He pulled away from the hand on his cheek. "I don't want another best friend."

As soon as they got inside, the General lifted the Phat sack off her arm and peered into it gloomily. "Bun Busters. Cold." He balanced the sack of burgers in his lap and began to roll toward the microwave.

"Wait! See what else?" Delia dug in her purse. "Apples!"

"Why are they individually wrapped?" the General asked as she set them in his lap.

"Mr. Donatelli always wraps them. They're more sanitary."

"What did you pay for these two sanitary apples?"

"Seventy-five cents each."

"Either you're a fool or he's a thief—or both. Find a real grocery store, Delia Marie." The General shook his head and rolled toward the kitchen. Halfway there one of Mr. Donatelli's sanitary apples fell out of his lap and bounced across the floor. The General didn't even slow down.

"That's the last time I buy you fruit! And I don't want to hear another word about your plumbing!"

"You better hope that *hearing* about it is the worst that happens!" he shouted back.

Delia watched until he disappeared into the kitchen. "Socko!" she said softly, opening the second bag that hung heavily on her arm. "Take a look!"

As she held the bag out to him she broke into a big smile. "What is it?" He looked, but all he could see was the top of another bag.

"Grass seed! I also got a rake. This Home Depot place is unbelievable! They have everything for your house and yard."

"Mom, did you really try to check on Damien?"

"Of course I did, Socko. I wouldn't lie to you. But come on, what do you say?" She shook the bag of grass seed. "You want to help me plant a lawn?"

"What about Phase 2?" asked Socko. "They're going to *give* us a lawn."

"And Santy Claus is going to bring you a pony!" the old man called from the kitchen.

18
THE HOUSE ACROSS THE STREET

Delia stood in the middle of the dirt lawn, gripping the handle of a rake so new the white bar code label glowed in the dim light. "You didn't wake up you-know-who, did you?"

"Nope." Socko sat on the front step to put on the shoes he'd carried down the stairs so he wouldn't wake up you-know-who. A wasted effort. "If his own snoring didn't wake him up, nothing can."

Delia waved a hand. "I'm thinking flower beds along the driveway."

It was so dark out, Socko could barely see the driveway.

"And my hedge right about here." She scratched a line in the dirt with the rake handle. "Everything else is going to be lawn."

"Do you know how to plant a lawn?" he asked.

"The bag's got instructions."

Socko read the print on the back of the bag by the light over the front door. "We don't have a spreader or a roller, and it's summer. It says right here, 'plant in late spring.'"

"It is what it is." Delia handed him the rake. "Here. Fluff up the dirt."

"Fluff up the dirt," he mumbled. But he figured helping her might convince her to do something more than "try" to check on Damien, so he scrabbled the tines of the rake across the ground. The dust rose. He sneezed.

Delia followed him, flinging seeds into the air. "See? Who needs a spreader?"

When all the seeds had been flung, Socko consulted the bag again.

"To 'ensure good contact between seed and soil,' we need a roller filled with water to make it heavy."

"We're heavy," said Delia. "We'll *stomp* the seed in." They took baby steps back and forth across the yard, stomping the seed in.

"Are you gonna find out about Damien today?" Socko asked, mincing toward the road.

"Yeah, yeah. Keep stomping."

Delia and Socko were heading in opposite directions on their stomping mission, so at first only Socko saw the truck.

"Why are you not stomping?" she called over her shoulder.

"Mom?"

Delia turned and was caught in the truck's headlights. "Take a look at that!" She came and stood behind him, her hands on his shoulders. "That moving van is huge. No one owns that much stuff!"

The behemoth moving van stopped right in front of their house. Socko remembered the General's comment about Santa Claus. But with a series of high-pitched beeps, the truck backed into the driveway of the house across the street.

The man in the passenger seat got out, unfolded a piece of paper, and smoothed it against the side of the van.

"They've got so much stuff they need a map to show where to put it," Delia whispered.

The first thing the men pushed down the ramp was huge and wrapped in padded blankets. It had three thin black legs. Although the men moved it carefully, when it hit the hard surface of the driveway, it boomed a hollow note. "You think it's a grand piano?" Delia breathed.

A china cabinet followed the piano down the ramp, then a cushy leather chair, then a dozen cartons so big a couple of homeless guys could have slept in them with room to spare.

"So they have a lot of stuff." His mother squeezed his shoulders. "We'll have a lawn before they do. Keep stomping."

Socko continued to stomp, but not with the same vigor. The parade of stuff kept him distracted. And stomping seed in front of the moving guys was embarrassing.

"Sweet," said Socko, watching the men carry a flat screen TV as big as their picture window down the ramp.

"Study," said Delia, still stomping. Delia's recommended route to everything he wanted had been reduced to that single word.

He threw up his hands. "What's wrong with 'win the lottery'?"

"Hey," said Delia as the men carried a Ping-Pong table into the house. "Maybe these people got a kid your age."

Yeah, a kid with tons of stuff. All Socko had was a stop sign with a bullet hole through the *O*. Impressive.

Computers...a hutch...three more armchairs...

A sound from inside his own mostly empty house caught his attention. The General was at the window, slapping the glass with his palm.

"I'll see what he wants." Socko let himself into the house.

The General pointed at the thick king-size mattress the moving men were carrying. "I want to live over there."

"Me too."

"What are you and Delia Marie doing out there, anyway? An Indian rain dance?"

"Gardening." Socko nuked a mug of water, added coffee crystals, and stirred. He handed it to his great-grandfather. "You want something to eat?" He was in no hurry to go back to looking stupid in front of the moving van guys.

"No, but if you get me my electric razor I'll cut off those girl curls of yours, give you a GI haircut."

"Thought you were a cook, not a barber."

"In the armed services you do a little bit of everything."

A GI haircut would drive Delia nuts. A shaved head or a buzz cut so short it was more scalp than hair was popular with Rapp's gang. "I better let Mom cut my hair."

"If she doesn't do it soon, we'll have to change your name to Betty."

Socko went back outside.

"Take over." Delia pumped the front of her blouse in and out with one hand. "I'm running late and I'm sweaty as a fry cook."

Great. Now he got to look stupid all by himself.

The last thing to come out of the truck was a basketball hoop. It took both guys twisting it back and forth on its heavy base to walk it up the driveway. They looked over the papers on a clipboard, then locked the house. "Keep up the good work," the driver called to Socko as he swung himself up into the cab.

"Whatever it is you're doing," added the second mover as he hopped in on the passenger side.

The van pulled into the street and turned right.

Socko listened until the engine's growl became silence, then sprinted across the street to get a better look at the new people's stuff. The sun was fully up now. He shaded his eyes with one hand and peered up at the basketball hoop. It had a glass backboard and a shot clock welded to the pole. It was easy to see that a street-bunged basketball had never swished through its white net.

Socko was a city kid, and he knew he should be slick at shooting hoops. But he wasn't. The court at the park was Tarantula territory, so he didn't go anywhere near it if he could help it.

He pictured the scene in his near future when the kid who owned the hoop challenged him to a game of H-O-R-S-E and he embarrassed himself completely.

Man, he hated this place.

19
NOT A SUSPECT

Socko knew he was going dangerously fast. He didn't care. He rode the skateboard up the short wall at the shallow end of the pool, catching some air before doing a 180.

He was ticked. His mom got him out of bed way before O-dark thirty to stomp grass seed, and he rolled right out, didn't even complain. But when he begged for a ride back to the old neighborhood to check on Damien, her answer was to gun the car engine and point at the basketball hoop as she drove away. "Looks like you'll make a new friend soon!"

Steaming mad, Socko had marched inside and asked the old man where he kept his electric razor, and the "girl curls" had hit the floor.

Delia would have a fit when she saw him—he did look a little like Meat now—but too bad. The air felt good on his freshly exposed scalp as he carved his way across the pool.

He slalomed back and forth, going higher and higher up the pool walls. He'd wiped out a couple of times already, but no one was watching and he hadn't gotten hurt much. This was solo skating—no fault, no glory. His wheels touched down with a clatter.

He charged to the top of one of the side walls near the deep end and cleared it. "And the Mighty Ant totally airs the pool!" The board hovered above the wall. In that breath-held millisecond, he 180ed and jammed the wheels back down with both feet.

After executing a sweeping turn at the shallow end, he was plunging toward the deep end when a voice yelled, "Hey! Mighty Ant! This is a pool, not a skate park."

He whipped his head around. Standing on the edge at the shallow end was a lanky long-haired girl with one hand on her hip, a cell phone in the other.

"Who the h—" The rest of the sentence was smacked out of him. He slid down the wall. Sprawled on his back, he listened to the *tick, tick* of the wheels on the flipped skateboard. He was trying to get the double-image of the girl to focus into a single person when she leapt off the wall.

Maybe he was hallucinating—a side effect of the crash—because she didn't jump like a normal person. Even for a girl. This girl hovered, her ghost-blonde hair floating around her head, her iridescent phone catching the light like a laser sword. He closed his eyes.

He didn't hear her land. He didn't hear anything. He had definitely made her up.

"Ohmygosh!" someone whispered.

He opened his eyes and gasped. His breath riffled her long hair. It brushed his cheek. He'd never seen hair that color. Dazed, he almost reached up and touched it.

She pulled her hair back with one hand and watched him intently. "Are you okay?" When he didn't answer, she punched a button on her cell phone.

"What're you doing?" he moaned.

"Calling 911."

"No, don't!" He flailed an arm and the cell phone skated across the pool floor. "My mom'll kill me."

"Okay...so...you get hurt...I call 911...and your mom kills you?" She crawled after the phone. "That makes sense!"

"Trust me, it does." He pushed himself up and leaned against the wall of the pool.

She sat down cross-legged at a safe distance and studied him.

He wasn't used to being looked at by a girl, and this one was really looking him over. "Do you have to be so...yellow?" he asked. In the bright sunlight her yellow shirt and shorts were almost blinding.

She fingered the hem of her T-shirt. "The outfit? Not my choice. Mother bought it. Everything's in boxes and I can't find any of my real clothes." She leveled her gaze on him again. "Where are your helmet and kneepads?"

"Don't have any." Suddenly the yellow of her outfit and the colors of everything around her looked runny, like an ice pop melting on a hot sidewalk. He rested his forehead on his bent knees.

Hearing a quiet *tap-tap,* he looked up. The girl was typing something on the phone's keypad—but there were way too many numbers for it to be 911. "Who are you calling?"

"Not calling. Texting." Her thumbs never slowed as they punched the tiny keys. Then the tapping stopped. "How'd you get the black eye?"

"Black eye? Oh." The shiner Rapp had given him had ripened. The dull purple was surrounded by a sick greenish yellow. "A fight."

She leaned toward him. "A fight? You mean, like, a real fight? Did you win?"

"Close enough." He wasn't about to say, "The other guy pulverized me."

She turned the phone toward him and clicked.

"Wait...did you just take my picture?"

"Yup"—he heard another small click—"and sent it."

He had to get out of here, but he felt too woozy.

With a jingle of little bells, a message came back. The girl read it and her cheeks turned pink.

"What?"

She slumped forward so her face was hidden by her hair. "My friend Izzy thinks you're cute. BFN," she said, typing the letters. She slid the cell into the pocket of her shorts and stretched her legs out in front of her. Her thighs were skinny; her shorts ballooned around them. But she had muscles, like she ran or something.

"Did you sneak over here from Lorelei or Colonial Park?" she asked.

Socko was just putting it together—she thought he came from one of the other subdivisions—when she answered her own question.

"No. You're not from around here."

"I *live* here," he said. He could hear the attitude in his voice, like he was imitating Rapp, but he guessed he needed a little attitude to talk to a girl. "What are *you* doing here? You're in my territory."

"Your *territory?*" Her eyes flitted from his cropped hair to the shiner to his T-shirt. "Are you in a gang or something?"

He could tell that through the strands of hair that hung over her face she was reading the message on his T-shirt. He popped himself on the chest with an open palm. "You looking at this?"

She flinched, then flipped her hair out of her face with a quick turn of her head and came right back at him with some attitude of her own. "As a matter of fact, yeah. Don't look at me like that! *You're* the one wearing a shirt that says, 'Not a Suspect, I Just Fit the Description.'"

He laughed, but stopped fast. After his recent series of lost fights and crash landings, laughing hurt.

She raised one invisible eyebrow. "And that was funny because...?"

"Long story." He had chosen the shirt out of the Help Yourself closet at St. Ignatius—the nuns had been okay with the message. "I like my shirt better than yours."

"Me too," she admitted. "Do you really live here?"

"Yeah, really. Whoa!" He put both palms down on the cement. The world was spinning left. "Excuse me while I pass out." He dropped his forehead to his knees again.

Feeling her breath on the back of his neck, he turned his head slightly. She was right up in his face again.

"Show me your pupils," she demanded.

He closed his eyes down to a slit. "Why?"

"Open them! I've had first-aid training."

Whoop-dee-doo, he thought. But he opened his eyes.

Her eyes scanned back and forth. He had never looked at a girl's eyes this close-up before. Hers were a freaky pale blue with long white eyelashes, which were freaky too—but pretty. And she smelled nice. He hoped she wasn't breathing in, because his own smell was a whole different story.

"Your pupils are the same size," she decided. "No concussion."

Then why did he feel so dizzy? He propped his elbows on his knees and rested his chin in his hands.

"Ohmygosh!" She pointed at his arm. "You're bleeding."

He looked down and thought he'd pass out for real. The back of his right arm was ground burger. He hadn't even felt it—maybe he *was* in shock. "It's no big deal," he said. "Don't sweat it."

"No. Seriously. You're majorly bleeding!"

"You think this is bad? This is a nada. I saw a guy get shot once."

The girl's eyes opened wide. "Where?"

"Next to the Dumpster behind my building."

Her eyes crossed. "I mean, in what part of his anatomy?"

"Heart. He was shot through the heart. Point-blank."

She slapped her hands over her own heart. "Did he die?"

"What part of 'through the heart' did you not get?"

Her pupils large, she stared into his eyes for a long moment. "What did it look like?" she breathed.

"Blood everywhere." It still made him sick to his stomach. "The shooter must've run through it. A trail of bloody footprints disappeared around the corner."

"I thought you said you *saw* the shooting."

"Sorry, guess I just missed it!" Why was she getting all technical? "The dead guy's name was Frankie. He lived in 3F."

"How terrible!"

"Being dead, or living in 3F?"

"Being dead, of course." She acted all sad about poor dead Frankie, but for her it was like one of Mr. Marvin's newspaper headlines. For him Frankie lying there in his own blood was real—he still had nightmares about it.

Why were they still talking? His arm was bleeding, his head was throbbing, she was weird. It was time to split.

"What's your name?" The girl leaned back on her arms, stretching her legs out again. When the toe of one sneaker touched his calf, she pulled back fast and wrapped her arms around her shins. "Unless it really *is* 'the Mighty Ant.'" Holding up both hands, she wiggled her index and middle fingers, making air quotes. "I saw your little attempt at graffiti."

"You spend a lot of time in drainpipes?" he asked, trying to cover his surprise.

"Apparently not as much as you do." She scratched an ankle. "Actually that was a lifetime first for me."

"Why are you checking out drainpipes all of a sudden?"

She looked away. "It's not the best time to hang around my so-called new *home*. So, what *is* your name?"

"Socko," he said. "Socko Starr."

"Are you joking?"

"Sure. I go around making up crazy fake names for myself all the time—of course I'm not joking!"

She blinked her white lashes. "Your parents named you Socko?"

"Parent. My mom named me Socrates."

Her pale eyebrows pinched together. "You mean like the ancient Greek philosopher?"

"Pretty much." He didn't want to act impressed, but she was the first kid he'd ever met who knew about ancient Greek philosophers.

"'To find yourself, think for yourself!'" she proclaimed.

"Say what?"

"That's a quote from Socrates."

"Oh." He'd never thought of Socrates as someone who had quotes. He'd never thought of him as anything but dead.

She held out a hand like they hadn't been talking for a good ten minutes. "Livvy Holmes."

He didn't want to touch her hand. His was sweaty. "*Your* parents named you Livvy?"

"Olivia. But no one but Mother uses that name. Call me Livvy." Her hand was still sticking out.

"Livvy?" He swiped his palm on his shorts really quick, then shook. "Where I come from the name Livvy would sound just about as snotty as O-livia," he said.

"I thought you said you're from here."

"I *live* here, but I'm not *from* here."

"Where *are* you from?"

"The city."

"Which part?"

"The part where guys get shot through the heart."

"You mean…it was, like, seriously dangerous?"

"You know, drugs, gangs, drive-by shootings. It's pretty scenic."

Did he just imagine it, or did she look excited? "Where are *you* from?" he asked.

"The Heights." She raised her eyebrows, like "the Heights" should mean something to him. When he didn't respond, she shrugged. "It's not, you know, *scenic* like where you're from, but I thought it was pretty perfect. Actually, it's the only place I've ever lived. We had a tennis court in the yard, and Isabella Kennedy next door."

"Who's Isabella Kennedy?"

"Izzy." She tapped the pocket with the cell phone in it. "My best friend since before we were born. Our mothers did Lamaze together."

He had no idea how you "did Lamaze," but he thought it must be nice having your best friend in your pocket.

"Izzy and I talked it over and we agreed that moving is not going to change our relationship."

"Yeah…and how's that working out for you?" he asked. "I haven't talked to my best friend since I moved."

A blue cell phone appeared in his face. "Call him."

He almost reached for it, then remembered. "Can't. His phone's disconnected."

She gave him a sympathetic frown. "Did his parents revoke his phone privileges?"

Socko snorted. "Yeah…something like that." The wall of the pool felt warm against his nearly bare scalp. He stared up at a cloud and wished he hadn't snorted. "Why'd you move here if your old neighborhood was so perfect?"

Livvy roped her arms around her knees again. "Moon Ridge is my dad's project. You know, Holmes Homes?"

"Sure." How could he not know? It was on all the signs.

"My father built lots of the subdivisions around here. But he was always the contractor. This one is all his. I get that he wants to live and breathe the place 24/7, but they didn't even warn me! One day a couple of weeks ago my parents were like, 'Surprise! We're moving!'" She sighed. "I guess you like it. It's safe and you have your own personal skate park."

"I hate it here." Socko checked his arm. The scrape was doing something less than gush—but definitely more than ooze. Blood speckled the floor of the pool. He pressed his elbow into his damp T-shirt and stood. "Nice talking, but I'm outta here." Socko tucked his skateboard under his uninjured arm; he figured he'd better walk it. He still felt kind of dizzy.

He made it as far as the corner of the building before she came trotting after him. "I'll go with you. You don't look too steady."

Neither of them said anything for a while. Every now and then Socko shot a glance at her. She was a good head shorter than he was, but still tall for a girl.

"So, do you live with just your mom?" she asked.

"And my great-grandfather. I only met him a few days ago. We took him in trade for the house."

She stopped. "Excuse me?"

"We take care of him until he kicks and the house is ours."

"That's cold!"

"Don't look at me! It was his idea, not ours."

"What about your dad?"

"Never met the guy," Socko said. "Listen, you don't have to walk me. I'm fine."

She let him get ahead of her, but he could tell she was still there. He could hear her footsteps.

"What grade are you going into?" she called.

"Seventh."

"Seventh? Really?"

He turned to her and walked backwards a few steps. "I repeated second." Great, now she thought he was stupid. "You?"

"Eighth."

He made a right on Tranquility Way, thinking he'd lose her. She made the turn too, just a few steps behind him.

"I'm not following you," she called to him. "Your house is across the street from mine."

"How do you know that? There are, like, a gazillion houses here."

"My father *built* the gazillion houses, remember? I know exactly how many have sold."

Socko looked back. She held up one finger, and then pointed it at him.

Oh man. So there really was nobody wandering around this neighborhood but him. Him and an albino-blonde girl who talked too much. He pointed at the basketball hoop. "You have a brother?"

"No. Girls can play basketball. Dad and I play sometimes—but not that often. He's always busy."

He almost offered to shoot hoops with her—that fall was affecting him worse than he thought. "Gotta go." He jogged up his driveway.

He looked back when he reached his front door and saw the dark car turn onto Tranquility Way. Livvy wiggled her fingers at it as it passed.

The girl had no street sense. None at all. She'd probably never needed any in "the Heights," but she wouldn't last half an hour in his old neighborhood—and this one wasn't as safe as she thought, even if her daddy did own it.

"It's not my job to wise her up," he mumbled. But before opening his front door, he leaned his back against it and watched her jog up her driveway. He didn't even notice when he dripped blood on Delia's brand-new beige carpet.

***

"Who's the dame?" rasped the General. He was parked, as always, at the front window, an unopened book in his lap.

"Livvy Holmes."

"Aw, Sacko." The lone eye glared at Socko's bloody elbow. "Don't tell me you can't even take a girl!"

"Skateboard accident!" He blew past the old man and into the kitchen. As he held his elbow under the running tap, he heard the click of wheels.

When he turned, the General sat in his wheelchair in the kitchen doorway. "Cute girl."

"I guess." Socko pressed a paper towel against the wound.

"You guess? How old are you, Sacko?"

"Thirteen."

"Thirteen, *sir*. I was thirteen when I had my first serious encounter with Mary O'Malley—she caught me cribbing answers off her in math class."

"She fell for you because you were cheating?"

"Fell for me? She turned me in! I got detention for two weeks. That Mary O'Malley was a real spitfire, and it wasn't just her flaming red hair!"

Socko touched his bristly scalp with wet fingers. He had always wondered about his red hair.

The General cocked his head. "You have her hair, all right. Not just the color either. Her hair was thick like yours. Thick and curly." The old man's thin lips twisted in a crooked smile. "Glad you let me cut it. Your hairdo was beginning to look exactly like hers. Word of advice, Sacko. When you decide to get interested in girls of the opposite sex—"

Socko glared at the old man. It wasn't like he hadn't noticed girls. Although he'd never talked to her, he had watched Maya Barrios all last year.

"Anyhoo, *when* you get interested in girls, look for a fiery one, one who can dish it out. Fifty-four years is a long time to spend with a limp noodle."

20
I JUST FIT THE DESCRIPTION

Delia flung her bags down on the kitchen table and grasped Socko's chin with one hand. "Look at you!"

He tried to pull away. "Come on, Mom! It's only a haircut."

She turned his face back and forth, examining the whitewalls the General had shaved above his ears and the brush cut on top. "A Tarantula haircut!" She let go in disgust.

"For Pete's sake!" the General sputtered. "Me and the boys defended the world against Hitler and his Nazi thugs wearing that haircut. Now, if you're done checking out the kid's scalp, I'm famished!"

Delia tossed a couple of burgers in the microwave, then caught sight of Socko's bloody arm. "And what's this?" She twisted his arm so the wound faced her. "How'd you get this?"

"Ow, Mom, go easy! I blew a trick on my skateboard."

"How did I go wrong?" Delia stared up at the ceiling like she expected God to answer her question.

The microwave beeped. Delia sighed, then slid the plate out and plopped it in the General's lap. "Dinner is served."

The General glared at the burger in front of him. "You've got to stop knocking yourself out with all this cooking!" He tossed the damp top half of the bun across the room at the garbage can and missed.

"And you've got to quit knocking yourself out being polite!" Delia snapped back.

The General spun the wheelchair away from her, nearly dumping the plate off his lap, and rolled into the living room.

It suddenly struck Socko—they hadn't set the table in this new house even once. Now there was a ketchup-slimed bun on the floor. Was this the "family" Delia had been so happy to get?

Socko was picking up the bun when Delia said, "I saw Damien today."

He squeezed the damp bun in his hand, then dropped it in the trash. "Yeah?"

"He came into the Phat with Meat and a couple of the other guys."

The electric zap of fear ran down his spine. "He came in with Tarantulas? Did you talk to him?"

"I talked. He said three words."

"Three words?"

"Yeah. Three exactly. I asked, 'How come I haven't seen you for that reading help we talked about?' And he said, 'I been busy.'"

"You asked him about *reading* help?"

"The boy can't read! So then I asked, 'How come you haven't gotten in touch with Socko?' Meat answered that one: 'He been busy.' Meat bought burgers for Damien and the other two. They sat in the corner booth. They were slouching out of there when I said, 'Hey, throw out your trash!' All of them kept right on dragging their sorry butts to the door, except Damien. He rushed back and heaped everything on the tray, then he dumped all of it in the trash. He's still got some good kid in him, I guess."

"I *know* he does, but we left him behind! He's just doing what he's got to do."

"You sure about that? It's kinda hard to tell." She put her knuckles on her hips. "When I saw him with those guys I thought, thank God I got my kid out in time. Then I come home to this!" She leaned toward him and cuffed the back of his head. "What are you doing, joining long-distance?"

"It's summer!" Socko wiped ketchup off his hand and onto his shorts. "And we live in a friggin' desert!" He turned to face her. "Are

115

you really gonna let Rapp have him? Junebug too?"

"You think it's up to me to save them? Sorry, Socko, but I gotta think about us, in the here and now."

"Yeah? Well, us in the here and now sucks!"

"Zip it!" the General snapped. "We've got company."

"What do you mean, company?" Delia hustled into the living room, Socko right behind her.

The old man was staring out the window, an alternating blue, white, and red light coloring his waxy face.

Delia grabbed Socko's injured arm. "What did you *really* do, Socko?"

"Nothing!"

A car door slammed.

The General whistled through his teeth. "Got some size on him."

Striding the path to the front door was a cop even bigger than Officer Charles, the neighborhood resource officer who had regular "conversations" with the guys at the Kludge. Socko caught a glimpse of a man in a suit and tie pacing the driveway across the street. Had the girl turned him in for skating in the pool?

"Anything you want to confess, boy?" the General rasped, pointing out the clear plastic bag loaded with cans of spray paint swinging from the cop's fist.

"No! I didn't do anything!" If skating someplace that wasn't a skate park was a crime, it shouldn't be. And he didn't know a thing about the spray cans in the bag.

"Glad to hear it," his great-grandfather called as Socko vanished into the kitchen. The old man rolled to the door with surprising speed and whipped it open, startling the chunky officer who stood, fist raised, ready to knock. "Yes?" the General demanded.

"Good afternoon, sir."

"Maybe it is. Maybe it isn't. That kind of depends on why you're here."

Socko peered around the edge of the door frame. But he pulled back fast.

Although the wheelchair was blocking the door, the cop on the front step was scanning the room.

The General cleared his throat. "I don't suppose you're selling tickets to the policeman's ball."

"No, sir. I'd like to have a few words with Socrates Starr if he's at home."

"Concerning?"

When Socko snuck another look, his mother was standing behind the General's chair, the two of them forming a double wall between him and the law.

"There's been some vandalism at the other end of the project, over near the pool. Graffiti. Some busted windows."

Socko pressed his forehead against the kitchen wall. Over by the pool? He was just there. He hadn't seen a thing.

"Who says my boy did it?" asked Delia.

The General cleared his throat again. "My money's on the stiff in the suit across the street."

"I'd like to speak to Socrates," the officer repeated. "Is he at home?"

Back door! Go! The voice in his head was Damien's. But Socko didn't listen. He wasn't guilty of anything.

He stepped out from behind the kitchen wall. "I'm here." He wished his voice sounded stronger. "I'm here, but I didn't do it."

"Socko, we can handle this!" Delia clasped her hands, pleading with him to disappear.

"I didn't do it," Socko repeated. He took a step forward.

His mother's penciled eyebrows rose in dismay.

"Seems like the boy can handle this himself," the General said. The wheelchair swept back, and Socko was facing the cop.

His name tag said Officer Dalton Fricke. A walkie-talkie crackled on his belt, all official—yet he looked really young, and his hair was cut just like Socko's. With a change of clothes he'd fit in fine with Rapp and his boys. But Socko could tell Officer Dalton Fricke was not about to do a fist bump with him.

Socko felt his mother's hands on his shoulders as the officer's eyes flicked down to his shirt. He remembered the words printed on it and almost blurted out how he'd gotten it from the Help Yourself closet—but he knew, when dealing with Officer Friendly, you don't volunteer anything.

Through the open door Socko watched the man across the street pace back and forth. His necktie was gray. His shoes were shiny. He had the same white-blond hair and invisible eyebrows as Livvy. He had to be the Holmes in Holmes Homes.

The spray cans jostled each other as the officer thrust the bag at him. "Know anything about these?"

"Never seen 'em before."

"You sure?" Officer Fricke held the bag in front of Socko's face, as though a closer look might jog Socko's memory. "The developer said the tagger did a couple thousand dollars worth of damage."

The bag was in his face, so Socko looked. It was like there was a Help Yourself closet of paints, and the tagger had emptied it. There was paint for metal, paint for plastic—even one can labeled "Clear." Who ever heard of bombing a wall with clear paint?

"Listen," Socko blurted out. "There's been this car cruising the hood. Late model? Black paint job? Tinted windows? I've seen it around here three times now. Just this afternoon, in fact."

Officer Fricke set the plastic bag on the floor, where it rested against the polished toe of his black boot. He extracted a pen from his breast pocket and clicked the point out. "You catch the make on that car?"

"No, but the girl from across the street waved at it when it went by, like, an hour ago."

The cop clicked the pen again and returned it to his pocket. "That car belongs to a real estate agent who was showing a client a couple of houses on Quarter Moon. She's the one who found the vandalism."

Quarter Moon was one over from the street that led to the pool. Socko hadn't seen the vandalism because he hadn't walked past it.

Officer Fricke toed the bag of cans on the floor. "I'll bet there are some nice fingerprints on these cans."

Socko rubbed his damp palms on his pant legs. "They won't be mine."

"Are you his mother?" the officer asked Delia.

The hands on Socko's shoulders squeezed hard. "Yes. And proud of it."

"I need to fingerprint your son, ma'am. We can do it right here." He touched a device hanging on his belt.

"No!" Socko was pulled back so hard he had to do a quick skip to avoid falling as Delia stepped in front of him. "No," she repeated firmly. "I moved my son here so he wouldn't *ever* get fingerprinted. Come on, officer! He's only thirteen!"

"These prints are just so we can check for a match. If there's no match, we dump the prints." Officer Fricke's leather boots creaked as he leaned toward her. "Listen, I don't want to take the boy down to headquarters."

Socko turned his mother around and held onto her soft upper arms. "It's okay, Mom," he whispered. "I didn't do it."

She clamped her lips between her teeth and nodded once. Eyes closed, she rested her forehead against his chest.

"Mom?" This was embarrassing.

She squared her shoulders and turned to the officer. "The test can't mess up? I mean, if he didn't do it, that machine won't say he did?"

"No, ma'am. If those are not his fingerprints on the cans, they won't match."

"Okay then, do it." She wandered across the room and fell into the recliner.

Socko watched his thumb leave a wide electronic print as Officer Fricke rolled it across a tiny screen. With a click, the print disappeared. The policeman grabbed Socko's index finger. He was rolling it across the screen when the General wheeled over to Delia and sat beside her, placing one bony hand on top of her plump one on the arm of the chair. In a second, Socko saw her turn her hand over and grip his.

After taking all ten prints, the officer clipped the device back on his belt and turned to Delia. "Phone number?" He jotted her work number on his pad. "I'll be in touch."

The door closed behind him.

"You should've called him 'sir,'" the General told Socko sternly. "Men in positions of minor authority like it."

Delia walked to the window and threw up her hands. "Take a look!"

Officer Fricke was talking to the man in the driveway.

The General glowered as he rolled to the window. "Don't go jumping to conclusions. The man made a complaint, the officer is updating him. This is America, Delia Marie. With liberty and justice for all."

"What America do you live in? You got the word of a kid against the word of that big-time developer—one who lies like a rug about all the Phase 2 amenities he's going to give us, I might add. Who do you think that officer's gonna believe?"

The General turned the chair toward Socko. "If you didn't do it, you don't have a thing to worry about. Your fingerprints will exonerate you."

Even though he didn't do it, Socko felt his confidence drain away. Holmes of Holmes Homes was probably best friends with the chief of police.

21

YOUR GIRLFRIEND'S HERE

Socko was filling two bowls with Lucky Charms and worrying about the visit from Officer Fricke when he heard a knock on the front door. The cereal box slipped out of his hand, spraying brightly colored moons and stars across the kitchen floor. He stood frozen, cereal bits on the tops of his bare feet.

The wheelchair ticked across the tile floor. Socko heard the door open.

"What do you want?" asked the General, with his usual warmth and friendliness.

"Is...um...Socrates Starr home?" The girl's voice was higher pitched than Socko remembered.

"Well, he's not out parading at this time of the morning!"

Socko let out a relieved sigh. He was mad at her—but if the girl was at the door, the cop probably wasn't.

"You must be his great-grandfather," she said.

"That's the rumor."

"I'm Livvy Holmes, from across the street?"

Now she's acting all polite, Socko thought. *Bet she's sticking out her hand for a neighborly shake.*

"General Starr," the old man rumbled.

"May I come in?"

Socko dropped to his knees. Crawling fast, he tried to herd the Lucky Charms into a pile.

"Socko?" the General bawled. "Your girlfriend's here."

His face on fire, Socko kept his eyes down when the girl came into the kitchen.

"Hi, Socko."

"Thanks for ratting me out." He didn't look up at her, but he could see her brand-new sneakers—a different pair from yesterday. They'd cost a hundred bucks, easy. "You always bust guys for wearing the wrong T-shirt?"

Her bony knees hit the floor. "That's not what happened!"

When he looked over, she was crawling along the baseboard in front of the sink, scooping up the last few pieces of cereal. She stared at the orange star and yellow moon in her hand. "I didn't mean to get you in trouble. I was telling my dad about you when he got the call from the real estate agent. He sort of put two and two together."

"And got six. I notice you didn't straighten him out."

She sat back on her heels. "I tried, Socko. I really tried, but he just wouldn't listen."

The General stuck his head in the kitchen. "What's on the break-fast menu? Ah, I see. Sugary Styrofoam. You care for a bowl, young lady?"

"Thanks!" Livvy looked strangely grateful for the opportunity to eat sugary Styrofoam.

Socko was dumping the last few bits of spilled cereal into the trash when he heard a cupboard door open. He turned. Livvy was reaching for a bowl, and beneath the edge of her shirt he could see the pale skin of her back. He swallowed hard. He was used to seeing lots of Junebug—she wore short tops too—but seeing this much of Livvy Holmes was different. "No cereal at home?"

Just as she'd done the day before, she hid behind her bangs. "I don't want to eat cereal at home."

There was probably nothing but health food at her house. What a brat.

She carried two bowls to the living room and handed one to the General, who grunted and began shoveling in the cereal. She retreated to the staircase and sat on the third step, scrunched up against the wall. Socko noticed how she stirred her cereal under to get it totally

122

soggy before she started to eat. That was gross.

He ate on the sofa, his back to her. Bowls in their laps, they chewed without talking.

Then Socko felt his neck prickle. The girl had to be staring at him. He took a quick look—but it was a false alarm. She was studying the old man, tapping her lips with the back of her spoon. "Excuse me, sir," she said quietly, "but are you in a wheelchair due to a war injury?"

The General turned his chair a couple of clicks in her direction. "I'm in this chair due to the fact I am older than dirt. God and me were kids together. Plus, I was stupid."

"Stupid how?"

"Started smoking when I was eighteen. Quit at sixty-eight. That was what you might call closing the barn door after the horse got out!" He hacked, then spat into the dingy handkerchief he always carried in his pocket.

"My father smokes," she said quietly.

"Yeah? Well, tell him he's a fool."

"I do. All the time."

"Huh!" snorted the General, looking at Socko. "Spunky."

"A spunky snitch," Socko mumbled.

Livvy turned toward him fast, her blonde hair flaring. She delivered the hurt look girls were so good at.

Everyone went back to chewing in silence.

The General's spoon clattered into his empty bowl. "Another sumptuous repast!" He held out the bowl.

As resident slave, it was Socko's job to hop up and take it. He stayed put.

It was Livvy who jumped up, tossed her hair over her shoulders, and held out her hand.

"Thank you," the General wheezed.

Thank you? Socko ditched his own bowl on the couch and strode out the front door. He had never gotten thank-you number one from the General. Let the spunky snitch hang out with the old guy; they deserved each other.

He grabbed his skateboard and launched. He didn't have anywhere to go, so he buzzed Full Moon Circle, going around and around, thinking about Damien and about the cop who might be the next person to knock on his door.

After his fifth lap he was hot. He figured he'd stayed out long enough. The girl must have gone home by now.

He hung a right on Tranquility Way, but he hadn't gone far before he heard the thump of a basketball. "Oh, crap."

She faced away from him, her feet wide apart. The backs of her skinny legs were incredibly white. She bounced the basketball slowly and deliberately, her eyes on the hoop. This was his chance to slide into his house unseen, but he wanted to watch her take a shot. She tossed it up, two-handed, and...

Not even close. The ball hit the corner of the backboard and ricocheted sideways. It didn't have much momentum, though. It hit the ground, did one soft bounce, then rolled into the street. Instead of going after it, Livvy folded her legs and sat down in the middle of the driveway.

Socko stopped the rolling ball with his foot. "You want this?"

"Not really."

He picked up the ball and walked it up the driveway to her. "Here."

"It's getting worse," she said.

"What? Your aim?"

She looked up at him. "No, the fighting. My parents fight all the time now."

Livvy's idea of a fight couldn't come close to the battles between Damien's mom and her boyfriends. "So, go somewhere else. Close a door. You have a bedroom, right?"

"It wouldn't help! The walls are cardboard."

"Your dad builds houses with cardboard walls? Nice."

She didn't seem to notice his sarcasm. Instead she hugged herself. "This morning's fight was the worst. That's part of why I showed up so early at your house."

He stared at the hole in the toe of his left sneaker; it was definitely time to make an exit. He glanced over at his house, then sat down cross-legged on the pavement across from her. "Yow!" He quickly shifted his position so that just the seat of his shorts and the soles of his shoes touched the driveway. "Your legs must be asbestos."

She almost smiled.

"So. What was the fight about?"

"Money. Mom acts like we're broke."

"Wish my family was broke the way your family's broke. You own all these houses, right?"

"True." She took a deep shaky breath and sat up a little straighter.

"Okay…so…problem solved." He got to his feet.

She popped to her feet too. "You want to take a look at the vandalism? It's somewhere near the clubhouse."

"It's on Quarter Moon. The cop told me," he added when she looked at him funny.

She dusted off the butt of her shorts. "We'd better tell the General first."

Wasn't it his job to say that? "You getting tight with the old guy?"

"I like him. He's nice."

Nice? The word must have a different meaning in "the Heights."

22
THE DEFENSE

Your dad thinks *this* is worth two thousand dollars?" A couple of small glass panes in the front door were smashed. The rest of the damage was in the form of spray paint spewed across the garage doors.

"Does it matter what it's worth?" Livvy watched him closely. "Don't you think it's just *wrong* to do this to somebody's property?"

"Sure. Whatever." He turned away and started walking.

"You think vandalism is okay?" She got in front of him and blocked his path. "Socko!"

"What!"

"Just tell me why you did it."

"Did it?" He looked over his shoulder at the blast of four-letter words on the garage door. "What makes you think *I* did it?"

"Yesterday the real estate agent saw someone running away as she pulled up, a kid in a black T-shirt."

"Then it couldn't have been me, could it?" He started walking again. "I was with you when she cruised by."

Livvy hurried to catch up with him. "You were, weren't you?"

"Exactly what did you try to talk your dad out of?"

"Prosecuting you! I told him that with your childhood…and, you know, where you come from…your family and all… I told him he should let you off."

"But I didn't do anything! And what do you know about my childhood? You've never even met my mom. She would kill me personally if I messed up like that." Angry, he was walking fast, but Livvy just lengthened her stride.

"I was standing up for you, all right? I was trying to *help*!" He dropped the board on the ground to skate away, but she grabbed his arm. "Sorry! I made a mistake! I jumped to the wrong conclusion." She let go and turned away. "Oh, forget it."

He only realized they were in front of the skeleton house when she walked through the door frame and sat down on the steps.

Socko stood with one foot on the skateboard, pushing it back and forth. This was his chance to split. But sitting with her elbows on her knees and her chin in her hands, she looked as defeated as Mr. Marvin in his chair in the lobby of the Kludge.

"So you made a mistake, big deal. I'll get you back for it later." He left the board at the curb and joined her on the stairs. It was her turn to smart-mouth back, but she didn't. She didn't say anything. What was he supposed to do now?

"See those beams?" he asked, pointing up. "I walked across one of them the other day."

She blinked slowly and then tipped her head back. "Get out!"

"Yeah. I did it barefoot. Those are my socks over there." As soon as he pointed them out, he wished he hadn't. They were shriveled and dirty. But Livvy didn't waste any time checking out his socks. Instead, she bounded up the steps. When she got to the landing, she sidled over to the edge and stared at the floor below. "It's a long way down, isn't it?"

"Nine, ten feet, easy," he said, following her up the stairs.

She placed the sole of her right sneaker on the beam, then the left.

"I didn't say *you* had to try this." Wishing he was holding a two-by-four for balance, Socko eased out onto a beam a few beams away from the one she'd chosen.

"You know, this is sort of like walking a balance beam." She took another step and looked over at him. "Like in gymnastics?"

"I guess." The only "gymnastic" equipment at Grover Cleveland was half a dozen dingy gray mats so old the padding inside had turned to concrete.

Livvy balanced carefully on one foot and raised her other leg. "Ta-da!"

"Would you be careful?" Even though she'd given him the whole first-aid lecture the day before, she was a little bit like Damien in the stupid-risk department.

"No worries. I took five years of gymnastics."

Socko scuffed out to the middle of the span and lowered himself cautiously, his heart pounding, until his butt was safely parked on the beam. Livvy stepped toward him from beam to beam, walking lightly on the balls of her feet, then sat on the beam next to his, facing him.

Why hadn't she just sat down where she was? She was sitting so close now that if he swung his legs, he'd kick her.

Up close, she wasn't like Damien at all. She was a girl, and her girl-ness was beginning to get to him. "I better go now…gotta check on the General." He pressed his palms against the beam, about to get back on his feet, but decided that if he tried to stand he'd probably get down the same way he had the last time. He already knew it would be painful, why add embarrassment?

Luckily he thought of another way. Before the city tore it down, he'd spent a gazillion hours at the park near the Kludge, messing around on the rusty jungle gym, hanging by his hands and knees, kicking his feet over his head in a flip dismount. The beams were a little close together for that move. Besides, that would be like showing off. He decided to keep it simple.

Reaching to her left, he grabbed the beam she was sitting on and let his body drop so that he hung for a moment by his arms, then let go.

"Not bad." said Livvy as the beam she was sitting on twanged. Socko had barely straightened up from his own landing when the soles of her sneakers hit the floor. "Yes!" She threw her arms up over head. "I really stuck my landing."

It was definitely time for him to split. Just then the phone in her pocket began playing something classical. He was turning away when he felt a tug on his belt loop.

"Wait!" One finger in his belt loop, she hit the Talk button on her phone and pressed the cell to her ear with her free hand. "Oh, hi... Of course, Mother." She rolled her eyes skyward. "But Mother, I didn't storm off! I just went away... Now? Nothing."

Socko whispered, "Ask her if she heard from the cop."

Livvy's finger slid out of his belt loop. "I know...but do you guys have to fight about everything?"

Socko circled Livvy, trying to get her attention. "Ask!" he hissed.

She covered her eyes with her hand. "It's scary when you two fight."

"About the cop?" he whispered.

She put a finger to her lips. "By the way. Did you hear back from that policeman?"

He waited to hear the news. It felt like red ants were walking on his arms.

"Okay," Livvy said. "Good to know."

Socko opened his eyes wide at her.

"Sure. Chinese is fine... I don't know, just get me some dim sum... I love you too." Livvy thumbed the End button and slid the cell into her pocket. It rang again instantly, this time with a little jingle of bells. She whipped the phone out of her pocket and turned away from Socko. "Where've you been, Izzard-Lizard? I've been trying to reach you since forever!"

He stood stunned. "Hey!" He stepped in front of her. "About the cop?"

"You've been cleared." She turned away again.

He turned with her. "So—I'm off the hook?"

"That's what 'cleared' means." She looked annoyed, but after watching him for a second, her look softened. "Izzy? Two minutes. Don't go anywhere." She hung up and pocketed the cell. "Of course you're off the hook. You didn't commit the crime."

He sat down on the curb hard.

"Socko?" She sat next to him. "What's wrong?"

He leaned forward, holding his head in his hands. "You ever know anyone who's been sent to juvie?"

"Juvie?"

"Juvenile hall? Kid jail?"

"No. I guess not."

"I have. Plenty." He stared at the patch of road between his sneakers. "Some of them didn't even do the stuff they got sent up for."

She put a hand on his back, then quickly folded her hands and squeezed them between her knees. "Are you sure they didn't?"

"Yeah, I'm sure! Your dad wanted to nail someone for the damages, so why not me? I fit the description."

"Not 'someone,' Socko. He wanted to nail the perpetrator." She slipped the phone back out, punched a button. "Izzy?"

Disgusted, he stood up and walked away. When she followed him, he picked up his skateboard, but listening to her talk to her friend, he wished he'd skated on ahead. He felt like he was eavesdropping on a personal conversation as she described what had happened with her parents. But they didn't get far before she came to a sudden stop. "Is that Daria's voice? Is she at your house?" The eager glow Livvy had been giving off since Izzy called dimmed. "Sure. No problem. We'll talk later."

Livvy closed her cell and slipped it into her pocket.

Their houses were just ahead. He expected her to follow him inside, invited or not.

Instead, she turned up her own driveway.

"So...bye." He walked backwards until she disappeared into her house.

***

Socko and the General played Rummy 500 at the kitchen table, a Nature Channel show about meerkats on in the background.

"Another player wouldn't hurt," the General grumped. "What about that girl across the street? Maybe she'd pay attention to the game."

"I'm paying attention." Socko turned away from the five meerkats who were standing tall on their skinny back legs.

"Maybe we can talk Delia Marie into joining us," said the General as the multicolor car pulled into the driveway.

130

Delia plunked a bag of apples down in the middle of their game. "Take a look at these babies! Three dollars and twenty-nine cents for twenty-six apples, I counted them! That's less than thirteen cents each!"

The General lifted the bag off the rummy discard pile. "Bet you didn't buy 'em at Donatelli's."

"Don't even talk to me about Donatelli! He's been robbing me all these years. I found this discount grocery store right near Home Depot—it's like a Home Depot of food! I got two-for-one family-size boxes of Cocoa Puffs and ten packages of Ramen noodles for a buck ninety-nine."

"Welcome to America, Delia Marie." The General picked up a card and inserted it in the fan of cards in his hand. "But next time, buy bananas. These pearly whites?" He tapped one of his unnaturally white teeth. "Glued to my gums. One good bite and you have an apple with teeth."

"Thanks for the mental image!" Delia carried the groceries into the kitchen.

A car pulled into the driveway across the street. In a moment a thin woman in a long black skirt and a red blouse climbed out, a plastic sack over her arm. *Must be Mother,* Socko thought. Balanced on high heels, she stood as straight and skinny as a meerkat. The bag with slashy Chinese characters printed in red on the side looked like it outweighed her.

"Do either of you know what dim sum is?" he asked, watching the woman walk up to the house.

23
ONE HUGE RAT

Socko and Livvy lay on their stomachs at the edge of the empty pool. The early morning sun cast a sharp shadow across the floor of the blue concrete hole.

"That is one *huge* rat!" Livvy breathed.

Socko took his eyes off the animal and stared at her—she had to be kidding. It was definitely an opossum. Even living in the city all his life, he knew that.

The opossum rambled to the deep end of the pool, tried to scrabble up the wall, then slid back down. "It'll never get out that way," said Livvy. The opossum lay quiet for a few seconds. "You think there's something wrong with it?"

"Maybe it's overheated or something." The animal tottered to its feet, then stumbled out of the shadow. In the sunlight its fur had a greasy shine.

"Did you see rats that big when you lived in the city?"

She *wasn't* kidding; she really thought it was a rat. Socko decided to string her along. "Oh yeah, we had 'em that size and bigger. Not in our apartment, but around the Dumpsters and stuff." He didn't want her to think they'd had rats personally. But even though Delia had kept their place clean, rats came in now and then from other apartments. Sometimes he'd wake up to the snap of a springing trap, followed by the scream of a rat that was only half-dead—another thing he'd never tell Livvy about.

"I've seen rats at the pet store." Livvy rested her chin on her folded arms. "But they weren't this big, and they were cuter."

He wished Damien were here. Damien knew how to take a story right up to the edge. "This is a different species. *Ratus giganticus.*"

Livvy looked suspicious. He kept a straight face. *Ratus giganticus* walked into a side wall, then shook itself.

She knelt up. "I guess you'll have to teach me to skate somewhere else."

"We can't just walk away and leave him in there."

Her nose wrinkled. "I don't know, Socko. It might be rabid."

The opossum yawned, showing off sharp yellow teeth.

"But if we don't help it get out, it'll starve or die of thirst."

"You're right." Livvy dug for the cell in her pocket. "Let's call someone."

"Who? The rat suicide helpline?" Socko jumped into the pool, the smack of his sneaker soles reverberating off the pool walls. The opossum whirled around to face him. Socko held out his hands. "It's okay, man, it's okay." The opossum puffed up until every hair stood on end. Socko was within three feet when its mouth gaped and it let out a hiss.

Socko fell back a step.

"Give it up, Socko. It's not worth getting bitten!"

Socko didn't want to get bitten, but he didn't want to give up either. "Wait. Genius idea." He ran at the short wall and vaulted out of the pool. "I'll throw something over it."

They found a dusty blue tarp near one of the heaps of dead trees.

"How are you going to do this?" she asked.

"You know, toss it over him and wrap him up." He and Damien had never been much into planning. They got an idea and they did it.

"What if it runs out from under the tarp and bites you?"

"I won't get bit!" Socko jumped back into the pool and held the tarp out in front of him. Advancing inch by inch, he tried not to step on the plastic or rattle it. Unexpected sounds seemed to incense the opossum.

Although it was hissing and flashing its yellow teeth, he noticed that the animal was backing steadily toward the wall at the deep end. Socko began to feel sorry for it. "Hey, I'm not trying to mess with you. I just wanna get you outta here."

Livvy danced along the edge of the pool, following the action. "Don't let it squinch itself up against the wall! You won't be able to get the tarp over it. Socko, it's about to squinch!"

"Go over there and make a loud noise. Scare him my way."

Livvy dashed to the edge at the deep end. "Happy birthday to you!" Her thin, high-pitched voice cut through the air. Socko wished he could cover his ears. And he wasn't the only one. "Happy birthday to you!" Her singing enraged *Ratus giganticus* so much, it charged.

No time to think, Socko flung the tarp over the opossum and fell on it. Hoping he hadn't landed on it too hard, he knelt, bunched the blue plastic around the animal, and picked it up.

"Good work!" Livvy reached out. "Pass him to me." Her blonde hair riffled in the wind, brushing his arm as he handed up the heavy bundle of crumpled tarp. Walking to the shallow end to climb out, he could feel the place where her hair had touched him.

By the time he reached her, the way-to-go look in her eyes was gone. She stared up at him through her bangs. "He isn't moving, Socko. At all."

It's playing possum, Socko thought. *This is so cool!* "I forgot. The bigger species of rats have weak hearts."

"You mean you killed him?"

"Guess we'd better check."

While he scouted for a good place to lay down the opossum, Livvy followed him anxiously. "If he's alive, he's got to be suffocating inside this tarp!"

Socko wanted the opossum to wake up someplace where he'd feel at home. But when it came to natural habitats, there weren't many choices around here. He settled for a spot near one of the heaps of bulldozed trees. Wildlife liked brush piles, and this was a brush pile on steroids.

Livvy set down the bundle and stepped back. "You do it."

When Socko unwrapped the animal, it lay on its side, paws curled against its chest. Saliva foamed in its open mouth.

Livvy dropped to her knees. "It looks really dead."

"It can't be!" Socko's knees hit the ground too. "It isn't bleeding or anything." He'd seen plenty of dead animals on nature shows dangling from the jaws of a big cat or a bear; he'd seen Frankie dead in the alley behind the Kludge. There was always blood.

"You fell on it pretty hard."

He shoved his hands into his pockets. His first encounter with a wild animal and he'd killed it.

"Oh, gag!" Livvy slapped a hand over her nose and mouth. "Can dead things rot that fast?"

But for Socko the sudden putrid smell was good news—make that great news. He knew that to put off predators, opossums could emit a rotten smell.

"I know you didn't mean to kill it, Socko, and it's only a giant rat, but ten minutes ago it was alive," Livvy said softly. "Sad. You think we should bury it?"

Socko saw a paw twitch. "Hey, watch this." He held his open hands over the dead rat. "Rise!" he commanded.

The word had barely left his lips when the possum yawned and scrabbled to its feet. After giving its stiff fur a shake, it turned its back on the pile of dead trees and ambled slowly away into the scraped landscape.

"Socko! What—what just happened?" Livvy sounded suspicious.

He shrugged. "A miracle."

He could tell she knew he had tricked her somehow, but she hadn't figured it out yet.

"I don't want to learn to skate anymore," she said.

"Fine." It had gotten too hot for skating in the pool anyway, and he hadn't wanted to teach her to skate in the first place. They went back to his house, where Livvy told the General all about the "giant rat."

The old man listened intently. "Sounds more like a possum to me."

Socko reached into the refrigerator to grab the milk. "Yeah, it was."

"Wait! It was an opossum, and you knew it all along?" Livvy asked.

"Well, yeah."

"Socko! That was a mean trick! Thanks a lot for making me look stupid."

"You *were* stupid. Who doesn't know the difference between a rat and a possum?"

Livvy turned and flew out the front door, slamming it hard behind her.

Through the window, Socko and the General watched her surge across the street. "Definitely not a limp noodle," said his great-grandfather.

Socko didn't get it. If he'd tricked Damien, his friend would've said, "Good one!" and then gotten him back for it later. And who cared about looking stupid? He looked stupid all the time.

24
INVINCIBLE!

When he woke up the next morning, Socko rolled off his cot and walked over to the window. It looked pretty quiet across the street.

Maybe no one was stirring at Livvy's house, but the day had started a while ago at his. Delia was standing in the driveway dressed for work. Paper hat pinned to her hair, she was staring at the dirt in the yard, which had yet to show a hint of green.

Socko pulled on a T-shirt and shorts, shoved his feet into his sneakers, and snuck down the stairs.

"Boo!" rasped a creaky voice.

Socko clutched his chest. "Don't *do* that!"

The General was already at the window, seated in his wheelchair. He was wearing his GI pajamas (today's baggy boxers were splotched with American flags). "Delia Marie's outside lecturing the grass seed," the old man said. "Seeds need regular watering, not crazy talk. Tell her to buy herself a hose."

But Socko planned to talk to her about Damien, not lawns. He pushed open the front door.

"And you just have to work a little harder!" his mother said, shaking a finger at the yard.

He closed the door behind him. "Mom? You *do* know you're talking to dirt, right?"

Delia clenched her fists. "We traded everything so we could have a lawn. We had friends. I could walk to my job." She held out an arm.

"Get over here. I need a little sugar."

Hoping no one across the street was watching, Socko trotted over to her. His mother's arm hugged his waist. His arm draped her shoulders. "Hey, Mom, are you shrinking or something?"

"It sure feels that way." The arm around his waist tightened. "Socko? I gotta tell you something."

"Yeah?" The worry-sick feeling sat like a weight in his stomach.

"I walked by the old place yesterday," she said. "I haven't seen Junebug for a couple of days and I thought maybe Damien would talk to me if he was by himself. Lucky thing Mr. Marvin was in the lobby to let me in."

"Guess he didn't get evicted yet." Socko wanted to slow the story down, afraid to hear the "something" Delia had to tell him.

She didn't seem to be in a hurry either. "Can you believe it? He said there are new people in 4A."

Socko felt strange, like someone else was wearing his clothes. And where could Damien go now when he needed to hide?

"The elevator was broke, of course. I had to climb the stairs—I sure don't miss *that*."

"Did you see Junebug?"

"No. Her aunt opened the door with the chain on—you know how she does. She said Junebug and Rapp had had a big fight, and now they were out somewhere making up. But she did have some good news. Junebug finished her nurse's aide program, number two in her class!"

"Did she get a job?"

"Not yet. Her aunt said she's filled out loads of applications, but so far nothing."

"Then what was the point?" He stepped out from under his mother's arm so he could see her face. "What about Damien?"

She rested her broad back against the car door and sighed. "I knocked and he came out—his mom and her boyfriend were home, yelling like usual. Boy, was that kid jumpy. He kept checking the hall, checking the stairwell door—all the time checking. I told him you want to talk to him. He said talking wouldn't help."

"Take me back home just once, Mom. I gotta see him!"

"I am not taking you back, and don't even think of trying to get there on your own. A clean break is the only way."

"He's still my best friend!"

"Listen, he sent you something." Delia opened the car door and reached into the glove compartment. "Here." She turned around and flopped Damien's Superman cap into his hand.

Socko stared at it. "Why's he giving this to me?" Without Damien's head inside it looked flat, like it had been run over. "This hat makes him invincible."

"I don't know, he just said to give it to you. He's wearing a new hat these days."

The cap's original blue had faded to gray. On the inside, printed on the sweatband in ballpoint pen, were the words "Propty of Damien Rivera. YOU TOUCH YOU DIE!"

"Damien never takes this hat off."

His mother lifted the cap out of his hands. "Things change." She reached up and tried to put the cap on his head, but he pulled away.

"If you don't want to wear it, I could use a little invincibility!" She plopped the hat on her own head and pointed at the lawn. "Grow!"

Socko didn't laugh. "Seeds need water, Mom. Buy a hose."

"Okay, I'll buy a hose." She took the hat off again and rubbed her thumb slowly across the embroidered *S*. "We're on our own here, Socko. You, me, and the old man."

"I *hate* it here."

"Maybe this isn't the dream I hoped it would be, but it's still way better than what we had. The Kludge is an ugly old place, a dead end, and I'm glad we're out of there." He didn't answer. "Come on, Socko," she begged. "I'm not getting much backup from the General, but *you* I count on."

He looked away.

Something bumped his arm. "Go on, take this." His mother was holding Damien's hat out to him. "He wants you to have it."

***

139

He was locked in an upstairs bathroom when he finally set the hat on his head. Nothing about it felt or looked right. He could see in the mirror that it sat too high—Damien sure had a small head. He flipped the cap off, adjusted the strap to its largest setting, and put it on. He pulled the bill way down on his forehead. This was the way Damien wore it.

It fit better now, but it was still Damien's hat. Why had his friend sent it to him?

Maybe Damien didn't need it anymore. If he was hanging out with the Tarantulas, he probably thought he was invincible for real. But he had to know that with Rapp things could go bad fast. No, if Damien was wearing a Tarantula hat, he was just going along to get along.

Or maybe sending the hat was a message. But if it was, Socko couldn't figure it out. Did it mean Damien needed help? If only he could talk to him.

He wandered back to his room, leaned on the windowsill, and stared at the house across the street.

As he watched, its front door opened. Livvy trudged across the street, her fists clenched.

The doorbell rang. "Socko?" the General yelled. "Your girlfriend's here!"

Socko didn't answer. In a few seconds he heard the front door open. "He's in the john," said the General. "I think he fell in."

Socko was miming bashing his head into the wall when he heard Livvy sob. He stopped mid-bash. What was *that* all about? He eased himself down three steps, to the point where the staircase turned, and sat down. He couldn't see what was going on, but he could hear the conversation.

"They promised! They absolutely promised!"

"Who promised what?" asked the General.

"My parents! They promised I could always go to Haworth Prep, no matter what."

"Circumstances change," said the General. "I doubt they built Moon Ridge thinking they'd only sell one house. Unless I miss my guess, their business is in trouble."

"That's not it. They think public school will be *good* for me, a broadening experience."

"Nothing wrong with public school." The General wasn't offering any sympathy.

"But I *have* to go back to Haworth. All my friends are there. And it's ten times better than a public school."

"We need a more up-to-date authority. Socko? Pick your butt up off that step and get down here."

Socko jumped. How did the General know he was parked on the stairs?

Livvy was sitting on the floor with her back against the door when Socko came down. "Are you going to tell me how *great* public school is?" she asked.

"It's not great, but it's okay," he said. "I've gone to public school all the way—and look at me!"

She was looking at him—more specifically, at his hat.

"So what do you want to know?" he asked before she could make a comment.

She squeezed the handkerchief that usually rode around in the General's pocket—he must have passed it to her during the tearfest. Socko only hoped the old guy hadn't used it first. "What's public school like?" she asked.

"It's like...school. You do stuff with words and numbers."

She leaned forward. "Will they have algebra? I did pre-algebra last year."

"I guess." All the kids Socko knew at GC were still struggling with post-arithmetic.

"Do you think they'll have a debating team?"

"We didn't have one at my old school." All "debates" at GC ended with two teachers pulling the debaters apart. "Does it matter?"

"I was team captain at Haworth."

"I'll bet you were," said the General, folding his hands over his belly.

"What about school uniforms?"

"You wore a uniform? Is Haworth some kind of Catholic school?"

"No, just very traditional. At Haworth we wear plaid pleated skirts and white blouses with the school emblem embroidered on the pocket." She ran a finger across her chest where the emblem would be, then blotted her eyes with the handkerchief. "Izzy and I were signed up for all the same classes this year."

Socko put a hand on Damien's Superman lid. "That's tough." Since Damien had been held back, they wouldn't have been in any of the same classes. But he and his best friend would've still hung out together.

"Is Haworth one of those girls-only schools?" asked the General.

She nodded. "It'll be kind of strange being in classes with guys."

"Lucky for you Socko's here to give you a little real-life practice. By the time you get to public school you'll know what to expect."

Livvy wadded up the handkerchief again. "That ball cap he's wearing is putrid! Don't tell me it's public-school-boy typical."

"Yup," said the General. "Along with stinky sneakers and sweaty T-shirts."

Livvy sniffed. "I have *so* much to look forward to…"

Socko saw her lips tremble. She stood up quickly and opened the door.

"Glad we could cheer you up!" said the General as the door closed behind her.

They watched Livvy cross the street, but she only made it as far as her own driveway, where she began shooting hoops. She threw the ball hard, like she was mad. It didn't improve her aim any.

Socko ate breakfast with his great-grandfather, then looked out the window again. She was still there.

"You could sneak past her, maybe," said the General.

Socko was getting used to the old man reading his mind. "It wouldn't work."

"Chicken."

***

She whirled around the moment she heard his front door open.

"Just going for a walk," he said.

"I'll come with you." She set the ball down in the driveway. "I'm tired of not hitting the hoop."

They walked in silence until they reached a barely developed part of the subdivision.

Basements had been dug, the displaced dirt heaped in crumbling mounds. Socko had assumed the soil at Moon Ridge was pure sand, but just inches below the surface it turned to brick red clay. Having been excavated first, the sand was at the bottom of the piles. The exterior of each mound was pure clay.

In a rain, these mounds would turn slick as heck. Add a large square of cardboard and they'd be decent sledding hills.

Damien would have seen the possibilities immediately. Livvy didn't even seem to notice the mounds, let alone their potential. "It's getting hot out here," she complained.

He was about to turn for home when he happened to look past a fence at the end of the cul-de-sac. "Hey, I see green!"

She shaded her eyes. "That's Lorelei Meadows. My dad worked on that subdivision a few years ago."

Socko sprinted to the fence, stepped up on the bottom rail, and threw a leg over.

Livvy followed him slowly. "What are you doing?"

"Checking it out. Is it illegal or something?" He dropped to the other side of the fence, landing soundlessly on a thick carpet of grass.

"Illegal, no. Pointless, yes." She boosted herself up onto the fence. "Hey, wait for me!"

25
THE PERP

Socko dropped to one knee and brushed his palm across the dense blades of grass.

"You look like a pilgrim." Livvy perched on top of the fence, legs swinging.

"It's not like this where I come from," he said, sitting back on his heels. The road and houses and sidewalks were nearly identical to the ones in Moon Ridge, but here the blank spaces in between had been colored in with the green of lawns and trees, dotted with the bright pixels of flowers. He was looking at his own neighborhood three or four years down the road—the Moon Ridge Estates his mother had imagined when she stared at the brochure.

He crossed the narrow strip of grass and hit a sidewalk, which he followed past a house with a sundial on its lawn. Livvy hopped down off the fence and ran after him.

The next house had a bed of purple flowers planted in front. Individual flowers were dropping and lifting like piano keys played by an invisible hand.

"It's just bees," Livvy said.

"*Just* bees? Eight out of every ten bites of food you put in your mouth was made possible by bees."

"Thank you, O magnificent bees!" Livvy lifted her palms and bowed from the waist. "I get it that everything is green, but this is so completely ordinary." She lifted her arms and let them fall. "I mean, what's here? Some lawns, a few flowers, trees so little they need sticks to hold them up. We had *real* trees in the Heights...grandfather oaks."

So it wasn't the Amazon rain forest—or even the Heights. It was still way better than what Socko was used to.

From behind a nearby house he heard the whoop and splash of kids in a pool. Judging by their voices, the swimmers were probably older—high schoolers, maybe? Curious, he headed toward the noisy house—and that's when he saw it. Lying in the grass, one wheel resting on a coil of garden hose, was a cherry red and black ripstick.

He pointed it out to Livvy. "I saw a board just like that by one of the houses in Moon Ridge."

"Really? Maybe kids from here are coming over to Moon Ridge to check out the dirt!"

Ignoring her joke, he ventured up to the driveway, then stopped.

"Socko? What is it?"

He stared into the dark cave of the house's open garage, letting his eyes adjust. A new SUV was parked on one side. On the other wall were shelves. He sidled a little closer to the house, stopping near a tall bush halfway up the driveway. "Look at that."

Livvy peered into the garage too. "Look at what? We're in somebody's yard, Socko."

"See those paint cans lined up on that shelf? Take a look at the empty spot closest to the door."

Livvy squinted, then her eyes opened wide. "Ohmygosh!"

Although the interior of the garage was in deep shadow, sunlight hit the end of the last shelf. Even from the sidewalk it was easy to see that the low wooden shelf was stained with dark, rusty rings too small to be made by cans of house paint.

A door at the back of the garage swung open and a tan, sun-blond guy in wet Hawaiian-print trunks came in from the backyard. He was fifteen, sixteen, easy. As he sauntered over to a refrigerator near the garage's large open front door, Socko and Livvy ducked behind the bush.

"Go on, Socko," Livvy whispered. "Confront him!"

"I don't know…"

"Come on. You're tough. You've seen a guy shot through the heart, point-blank. And you're way taller than he is."

"I could probably take him," Socko whispered back, giving himself the benefit of the doubt. "But if someone calls the cops, which one of us do you think'll get slammed against the squad car door?"

"But *Socko,* he did it!" breathed Livvy. "We have evidence."

"Tell your dad to send Officer Friendly over."

They heard the refrigerator close. The boy turned toward the door that led to the pool. Before Socko could stop her, Livvy sprinted the rest of the way up the driveway. "Hey, you!"

The guy swung around. Eyebrows raised, he touched himself in the middle of his chest. "Me?"

Livvy stopped just outside the garage door. "Have you by any chance paid a visit to Moon Ridge Estates recently?"

"Why? Who wants to know?"

"Quite a few people, actually." She spread her feet wide and planted her knuckles on her hips. "Did you spray-paint profanities all over a house in Moon Ridge Estates?" she demanded.

"No. Why would I?"

Peering out from behind the bush, Socko could see how the boy's eyes tailed away from her.

"What if I told you there was a witness?" Livvy bluffed.

There was a long pause, and then Socko heard a pop as the guy pulled the tab on the can in his hand. "Get lost, little girl."

Although he hadn't been spotted, Socko shifted uneasily.

"I said, get lost!" The guy reached out with his free hand and gave Livvy a shove.

Socko touched the *S* on Damien's cap and stepped into view. Hoping his slow walk looked confident, not scared, he strode up to the open garage door.

"Hey." He stopped right next to Livvy. "How's it goin'?" The guy was much smaller up close. Socko was not only taller, he was bulkier.

"Holy crap!" the guy breathed, falling back.

Socko took another step toward him, thinking, *this must be what it feels like to be Meat.*

The guy raised his voice. "Pete? Trevor?"

Two more blonds slouched through the door of the garage and stood there, dripping on the concrete floor. "What's going on, Brad?" asked Pete or Trevor.

"Your friend vandalized a house in Moon Ridge Estates, my father's project," Livvy said. "He isn't too happy about the damage."

Both guys repeated Brad's eye fade. *They were all in on it,* Socko thought.

Brad seemed to expect his two unwelcome visitors to go away quietly now that he had backup—but that wasn't going to happen. Socko ran his hand over the rusty rings that stained the shelf. "Looks like a couple dozen cans of spray paint should be sitting right about here."

One of the blonds turned on Brad. "I told you we shouldn't of—"

"Shut your face, Trev." Brad looked at Socko and Livvy. "You two are trespassing."

Livvy let out a sudden, bloodcurdling scream. "Get your hands off me!" she yelled.

The guys jumped, and then traded confused looks. Socko was just as mystified.

"Leave me alone!" she shrieked.

A second door flew open. "Bradley!" A woman in a crisp white tennis outfit stepped into the garage. "What is going on here?" She saw Socko and Livvy. "Is everyone all right?"

"I'm Olivia Holmes," Livvy volunteered, her voice perfectly calm now. "My father built this house. A couple of days ago your son vandalized a house in my father's current project, Moon Ridge Estates."

The woman whirled and faced her son.

Brad opened his eyes wide. "I don't know what she's talking about, Mom."

The woman pursed her lips. She stared at her son hard before turning back to Socko and Livvy. "Unless you have some proof, it's your word against my son's—and I trust my son."

But not much, thought Socko. He tapped his fingers on the shelf.

"Excuse me, ma'am, but should there be cans of spray paint on this shelf?"

The woman looked at the conspicuously empty stretch of shelf, blanching when she saw the rings of rust. "Bradley!" She turned on her son. "First you get suspended for drinking, then you scratch your father's BMW. Speaking of your father, do I need to call him and ask what should be on that shelf?"

"Hey, it was Pete's idea!"

***

"We so kicked butt! And how did you like my scream? " Livvy held her hand up for a high five.

Socko kept walking, his head down. "What just happened back there? Those guys come right out and admit they did it, and Brad's mom says there'll be consequences. Then she gets on the phone with your dad to make sure there aren't any."

"I bet they'll get grounded, or lose their driving privileges."

"Big deal. Is your father gonna call Officer Fricke and turn them in?"

"I doubt it." Livvy put a sneaker on the bottom rung of the fence. "It takes forever to get the money if you go to court. Brad's mom already said she's going to pay the damages."

"But they messed up his property!" Socko jumped down on the Moon Ridge side of the fence. "When *I* was the suspect your father had a cop at my door in a heartbeat."

"The situation was different. Now we know who did it and Brad's parents are going to pay for the damage."

"Oh, I get it. Brad and Pete and whoever don't fit the description. They have money, so they get off. No wonder jails are full of guys like me!"

She walked beside him, watching the ground. "You're right," she said at last. "They're guilty. They should be punished. I know my dad won't call the police, but...we could."

"Like they'd listen to us..."

"Maybe we can get the General to do it."

"Oh, crap! The General!" He knew he'd catch it for being gone so long, but maybe once he got past the crackle of complaint, he'd convince his great-grandfather to make that call. It was time for a little of that "justice for all" the General claimed all Americans were entitled to.

When they reached Tranquility Way, Livvy veered off toward her own house. "I'll be over in a minute."

The first thing Socko noticed as he jogged toward his own house was the vacancy at the front window. The old guy must be pretty mad.

He slipped inside. The wheelchair stood empty in the middle of the room.

"General?" His voice echoed, but there was no answer. Then, through the arch that opened into the family room, he saw a few inches of the brown Naugahyde recliner. One scrawny arm and claw-like hand hung down its side.

"Sir?" Sometime after they'd left, the old man had climbed back into "bed" and dozed off again. Old guys did that.

Socko crept toward the silent family room and stood in front of the recliner. Not moving at all, the General was the oldest-looking thing Socko had ever seen. He was oddly slumped too, toppled to the right.

Socko tried to detect motion, but there was none. He felt his own heart start beating weird. The arm that hung down seemed barely attached to his great-grandfather's body. In fact, all of him looked as if it had been strung together with worn-out rubber bands.

Socko put a finger on the old man's shoulder. When nothing happened, he put his whole hand down, feeling the bones under the thin skin. "General, sir?" Socko gave the bony shoulder a shake. His great-grandfather slipped lower in the chair.

"Crap! Oh, crap! Oh, crap!" The General was dead. But how could he be? He was alive when they'd left—alive and complaining.

But in all of Socko's experience, nothing had ever looked deader—including Frankie with a bullet through his heart.

If the old man *was* dead, he and Delia had fulfilled their side of

149

the contract. The house was theirs—but Socko hadn't wanted the stupid house in the first place.

Eyes stinging, he stared at the crumpled body in the chair. "How could you leave Mom and me alone in this desert? I was starting to like you!"

He heard the front door open. "What's for lunch?"

Socko stood still, his back to Livvy.

"Socko?"

He turned away from the body in the chair. "The General... croaked." He'd tried to make his voice sound strong, but instead it shook.

"Oh, Socko!" She threw her arms around his neck. A shock wave ripped through him as his face was buried in her hair. Taking a surprised breath, he smelled green apple shampoo.

She let go fast and stepped away from him. Knotting her hands, she stared at the pitiful body in the chair with tears in her eyes. But the sad look quickly changed and she dropped to her knees. "General?"

She brought her face to within inches of the shriveled corpse. "Please stop this, General. You're scaring Socko." When nothing happened, she stage-whispered, "I'm onto you, you old faker." Then she spread her hands. "Rise!"

Socko let out a hoarse scream when the corpse straightened up in the chair.

"Aw, heck," said the General. "I was just having a little fun with the kid."

Socko was stunned silent, caught between gratitude, embarrassment, and a fury he could almost taste. "You were *faking* it?" His voice was quiet but hard, the armored-up voice his mother called "attitudinous."

"It was a joke, Sacko!" The recently dead General rubbed his palms back and forth on the arms of the chair. "I was playing possum."

"That was supposed to be funny?" Socko roared.

The General pouted. "You two lit out of here without even a howdy-do. You were gone so long I got worried. I don't know what you're all worked up about anyway, Sacko. You did it first, pulling that fast one on Livvy."

Livvy put her hands on her hips. "Told you playing possum wasn't funny."

Socko collapsed to the floor, where he sat cross-legged staring at the tile in front of him. He hadn't felt this exhausted since he and Damien made that hour-long crawl up the fire escape chute.

"Sacko?"

He heard the *whoosh-snap* of the recliner being brought back to the upright position, followed by the scuff of slippers. He didn't look up to see where the General was going. He was done with the old man.

The corduroy toes of a pair of mole colored slippers slid into his circle of vision and stopped. A bony hand clamped down on his head. "It's been so long since anyone's liked me I guess I've forgotten how to act. I won't scare you like that again. Next time I look dead, go ahead and order flowers." Socko tried to lift his head under the weight of the old man's hand so he could look up, but the General would not ease up, would not let go. "So, we'll just forgive and forget, okay, Sacko?"

"Quit calling me Sacko!"

He felt the grip on his head relax. "Okay," the General whispered. The weight of the hand lifted. The old man patted Socko's head gently one time before coming down with a firm slap. "And now, like the young lady says, what do we have for lunch?"

Socko stared in disbelief. "What do you *think* we have for lunch?"

Socko pushed himself to his feet and went to the kitchen, glad that for once Livvy didn't follow him.

He still felt funny about the hug. And smelling her shampoo.

26
A GLINT OF METAL

Those three stupid seconds of hugging Livvy had changed things, big-time. Now, when she knocked and the General made his usual your-girlfriend's-here remark, Socko felt his face flush.

The knock had come early this morning.

The General wheeled his chair around. "Your girlfriend's here—"

"Cut it out!" Socko whispered, his face burning. He got to the door first and opened it.

"Hey, Socko." Livvy was standing there, wrapping a strand of blonde hair around one finger. Her face was kind of red too. She hurried past him and walked over to his great-grandfather. "Good morning, General."

He glared first at her, and then at the plate in his lap. "Get a load of this breakfast!"

Livvy took a long look at the cold burger and fries on the plate in front of him. "Guess what *I* had for breakfast?" she asked, sitting down on the floor at the old man's feet.

"What?"

"Matzo ball soup."

The General snorted in surprise, but recovered fast. "At least you get some variety. Nothing but reheated burgers and fries around here, with an occasional bowl of Styrofoam and milk thrown in."

Socko grabbed his Nintendo and fell onto the couch.

"Doesn't anyone cook anymore?" the General grumped.

"My parents sure don't. They say they're too busy."

"It's not like it's hard. Heckfire, during the war I fixed grub for a whole company—that's four platoons, which is, oh, about a hundred and twenty men. If I can do it, anyone can do it."

"Then why don't you?" Socko mumbled, pushing buttons.

Livvy scooted closer to the wheelchair. "Teach me how to cook. I'll cook for both of us."

Socko waited for the old man's excuse—he already knew the answer would be no.

"Nah. I'm too old to take the heat in the kitchen. And I got too much arthritis in my hands." To demonstrate, he made a fist and winced.

Livvy jumped to her feet. "Tell me what to do. I'll do everything." She ran to the kitchen. When she came back, she folded her legs under her and sat back down on the floor with a pencil in one hand, a scrap of paper bag pressed against her knee with the other. She looked up expectantly. "What ingredients do we need?"

"Depends on what we want to make, doesn't it?"

"Apple pie?" Livvy suggested. "Fried chicken?"

The General raised his wiry eyebrows. "Let's start with something simple, like SOS."

"What does SOS stand for?" she asked, her pencil hovering.

The old man snorted. "Let's just call it 'Slop on a Shingle.'"

Livvy wrote down the ingredients the General rattled off: chipped beef, milk, white flour, salt, pepper, and white bread.

It sounded to Socko like the makings of a school lunch.

"Anything else?" Livvy turned the scrap of paper so the General could read it.

Feeling invisible, Socko left the Nintendo on the couch and slid out the front door.

He was spending too much time with Livvy anyway. Besides, he had things he needed to think about, like coming up with a genius idea to get back to the old neighborhood so he could see Damien—having Livvy around all the time was distracting him.

He jumped on his skateboard and was rolling down the road when he heard the ring of sneakers on the pavement behind him.

"Wait!"

He stopped and let her catch up. "Thought you were taking cooking lessons."

"Later. We need ingredients."

He popped the board up and carried it. They turned down the next unexplored street on the circle, Lunar Lane. "Are we going anywhere in particular?" Livvy asked.

"Nope."

"Okay." She walked along beside him.

When Socko realized he might get caught watching her, he began looking intently at anything that wasn't her—which was pretty much the usual. Houses. Pavement. Dirt.

The houses on Lunar Lane looked as vacant as any of the others they'd passed, but these were more complete than most. Socko was scanning a gray house when an unexpected glint of metal caught his eye. Fear zinged from his scalp to the soles of his feet—it was the rear bumper of a maroon Trans Am.

It had taken a while, but Rapp had come after him. Had Delia gone back to "messing with Junebug"?

Livvy touched his shoulder. "Socko? You're hyperventilating." She followed his gaze. "What's a car doing back there?" She took a step toward the house. He grabbed her arm.

"What?"

"Wait a sec. Let me think." He focused his eyes on the ground. Staring at Rapp's car made his brain seize.

"Ohmygosh!" she gasped.

Sure that the next thing he'd see—possibly the last—would be Rapp, Socko raised his eyes slowly.

A baby in a sagging diaper had toddled out from behind the house, mosquito bites all over its pale arms and legs. Hugged to the baby's bare chest was a gray stuffed dog that had probably once been blue. The baby gave them a gummy smile and held out the toy. "Daw-gy."

"Emily?" a hushed voice called from behind the house. "Em, where are you?" A woman in shorts and a stained T-shirt rushed around the corner of the house and swept the baby into her arms. The woman was small and looked very young. Suddenly seeing them, her eyes grew wide. "Oh…hi," she said. "We didn't hurt anything."

"It's okay." Socko didn't know why, but people always said that when things were not okay, and it wasn't hard to tell things here were definitely not okay. Still, Socko was breathing easier. When he looked again, the car behind the house was just an ordinary maroon car, not Rapp's chariot of fear. It wasn't waxed and shiny. It wasn't even a Trans Am. Only the color matched.

Livvy reached for the cell phone in her pocket.

"What are you doing?" Socko asked softly.

"Calling my dad. They broke into that house."

"It's a baby and a mom," he whispered back. "And so what if they broke in? What could they steal, the doorknobs?"

Livvy inhaled sharply. "Socko…look!"

The man who had stepped from behind the house was big and had several days' growth of beard. His jeans were filthy, his hands black with grease.

Livvy took a step toward him. "My dad owns this house. If you leave now you won't get into any trouble."

The woman glanced at the man, then she turned to Socko and Livvy. "We can't leave. Something's wrong with the car." She rubbed her eyes with the back of her wrist.

"Not now, Ceelie," the man said gently. "Listen, we don't want any trouble. I'm fixing the car. We won't be here long." He closed his hands into fists.

Livvy looked at the clenched fists, then over at Socko.

"He's nervous," Socko whispered. "They're in a jam, Livvy." He raised his voice. "Can we help?"

"We'll be fine," said the man. "We'll be out of here as soon as I get the car running."

The woman sat down on the ground, the baby clutched to her chest, and let out a sob.

***

155

Socko stopped the small group at the end of his own driveway, watching the frown on the face at the window deepen. "Hold on a sec."

Livvy threaded her arm through Ceelie's. "We'll wait out here."

"Yeah, let me go in first," Socko said. "I need to explain things to my great-grandfather."

The door was barely open when the old man started. "Looks like somebody dumped a litter of kittens." His one good eye pinned the family huddled at the end of the driveway.

"They're in a jam," Socko said. "Luke lost his job and they've been camping in one of the vacant houses."

"Luke? Is that big guy some old friend of yours?"

"No. I just met him, but—"

The General hacked loudly and spat into the wastebasket he kept parked beside his chair. "Last I heard, houses are private property. Oh, but I'm sure there was a welcome mat out at the one they've been 'camping' in."

"Come on, General! They don't even have water."

The old man turned his chair away from the window and stared into the kitchen. "I'm too old for all this mess!" he shouted at the refrigerator. "All I want is to die quiet and on my own terms—not in some drool palace surrounded by geezers who are all off their nuts. Is that too much to ask?"

"Don't you think the baby looks hot?"

"Tarnation!" The chair turned, *click, click, click.* The General took a look and then glared at the baby's parents. "Any fool knows you cover a baby's head in the sun if you don't want its brains to fry."

Socko's nails bit into his palms. "Are you going to let that baby's brains fry?"

The General pressed his lips together.

Socko turned away from the family standing in the hot sun and faced his great-grandfather. "It's up to you, sir. Can they come inside?"

"All right, all right!" the General sputtered. "But these are my terms. They take showers. We feed 'em supper. They call their relatives, and then they vamoose! Am-skray! No pajama party, no listening to their sad story. We put their relatives on the case, and they move on."

156

"I'll call Mom and get her to bring extra burgers."

"*You* dial. *I'll* talk."

Socko punched in the number and handed the phone to his great-grandfather. He wanted to invite the family in out of the heat but he had to hear what the old man would say to his mother; he didn't quite trust him.

Phone to his ear, the General pointed a gnarled finger at the scrap of paper Livvy had dropped on the floor and clicked his fingers. Socko handed it to him. "Put Delia Marie Starr on... No. I can't hold until the fries are up." He poked at the inside of his cheek with his tongue. "Delia Marie. We have company for supper. I'm cooking."

"*You're* cooking?" mouthed Socko.

The General covered the phone. "We're finally getting up to numbers I can handle," he snapped. "Besides, Livvy'll pester the daylights out of me until we cook something together. SOS is so crappy she'll never ask again." He uncovered the mouthpiece. "Delia Marie? Write this down." As he read the list of ingredients, he glared at the woman and baby at the end of the driveway. "Better pick up a package of those paper diapers too... What size? I don't know. The kid's about as big as a good-sized turkey."

When Socko and Livvy ushered the family inside, Luke walked right over to the wheelchair. He held out a hand, then seemed to notice how greasy it was and hid the hand in his pocket. "Luke Olson. Thank you, sir. These are tough times and we appreciate your help."

"Tough times, hah! I lived through the Great Depression, son. My mother made soup out of twice-cooked bones. I know what hard times are and this little hiccup is nothing."

"Feels like a pretty big hiccup to me." Luke ducked his head. "Anyhow, thanks for the help."

"Yeah, thanks," Ceelie whispered.

Socko signaled Livvy into the next room. "The General said they could take showers...but we don't have enough towels." Not only did they not have enough, but the towels they had were thin and bald, with most of the fuzz worn off.

"Be right back." Livvy returned in a few minutes with a pile of

157

royal blue bath towels so thick she had to keep them from spilling out of her arms by holding the stack steady with her chin. When she passed them to him, Socko couldn't believe how cushy they were or how good they smelled. Had they ever been used?

He showed Luke and Ceelie to two of the three and a half bathrooms and grandly gave each of them a couple of towels.

When Delia got home, Socko intercepted her in the driveway. "Tell me what's going on," she said. Her smile grew as he explained. "Is the old man having a niceness attack?"

"If he is, it's temporary," Socko said. "He's kicking them out right after supper."

***

When Luke saw the diapers in the top of one of the bags Socko carried in, he looked stunned—then embarrassingly grateful.

"Give the vittles here," the General ordered, commandeering the two bags of groceries. He balanced them in his lap. "Come on, Livvy. We've got cooking to do."

"I'll be your sous-chef!" said Livvy.

The General grimaced. "I worked with a cook named Sue in the army, a guy. Army cooks all had strange handles."

"What was yours?" she asked.

He clamped his mouth shut and rolled into the kitchen.

She hurried after him. "Come on... Tell me!"

The sound of splashing and a voice singing about the eensy weensy spider filtered down from an upstairs bathroom. Delia smiled and grabbed the package of diapers. She headed up the stairs, leaving Socko and Luke in the living room with nothing to look at but each other.

Luke shoved his thumbs into the back pockets of his jeans. "We don't want to put you all out any longer than we have to. But we can't go anywhere 'til I get the car running, and I can't do it without a little help."

"I'll help," Socko offered, "but I don't know anything about cars." Fixing cars was one of the things he'd missed out on by not having a father—he didn't know much about sports either.

Luke grinned. "You don't have to *know* anything. You just have to have strong hands."

***

Socko liked standing next to Luke, their heads under the hood. And it turned out his hands were plenty strong.

Twenty minutes later Luke said, "That should do it." He had Socko sit in the driver's seat. "Okay," he called, head still under the hood. "Crank 'er up!" Socko gripped the key. They cheered when the engine turned over.

Luke pushed the hood shut with both hands.

Before driving to Socko's, they gathered up the blankets and everything else that was on the floor of the house and piled it in the already-overflowing backseat. Luke relocked the house. "Go on," he said, climbing into the passenger seat. "You drive. It's an automatic." He showed Socko how to put it in gear and leaned back in the passenger seat.

Socko's pulse hammered. He drove as slowly as the General, the wheel slick with his own nervous sweat, but he didn't drive over any curbs or mow down any street signs. When he pulled into his driveway, Luke cuffed his shoulder. "That was pretty smooth!"

By the time they got into the house, Ceelie was putting the last few pieces of silverware on the table.

"Grub's ready," the General announced. "Sue?" he called, and Livvy traipsed out of the kitchen holding a steaming pot. Her face was pink and sweaty, her normally board-straight hair wavy from the steam.

At the General's order to "park it," they all sat, Ceelie with Emily in her lap. For the first time since the move, the china that had come with them from the Kludge was set out, with forks and knives on either side. Ceelie bowed her head and grabbed Luke's hand, which everyone but the General took as a signal that they should do the same.

Socko found himself holding Luke's hand on one side, Livvy's on the other. Her hand felt warm. He stared at the platter of stiff slices of toasted white bread.

"Our heavenly Father, thank you for bringing us to this safe haven, and for this abundant meal…"

Socko checked out the steaming pot of lumpy paste. SOS was definitely school-lunch-worthy.

"And thank you for the kindness of these good Samaritans."

The General coughed.

"Through Christ our Lord, amen."

Luke was lifting a fork to his mouth when the General asked, "Do you all have family?"

Luke set down his loaded fork. Ceelie swallowed the bite in her mouth and blotted her lips with a napkin. "I have a sister in Michigan," she said quietly. "But she has three kids in a little bitty house. Her husband's out of work too."

"Still, family are the folks who have to take you in." The General looked pointedly at Delia.

Ceelie's eyes were shiny again. "Oh, they'd take us in, but I couldn't do that to them."

"How about you, Luke?" the General asked. "Got anyone on your side who isn't down on their luck?"

"No, sir." Luke picked up his fork again, the SOS on it now definitely cold. "But we'll manage."

"How?" the General demanded.

Socko wished the old man would leave it alone. If Luke knew the answer to that, the Olsons wouldn't be eating school paste at a stranger's table.

When dinner was over Ceelie insisted on doing the dishes, which took a while. Neither she nor Delia trusted the dishwasher. Neither one of them had ever had one. Ceelie washed, and Delia dried. Livvy held Emily in her lap. The baby clutched a spoon and was banging it against the table. The General and Luke were talking, not about where the family would go, but about Luke's work as a landscaper. The General asked question after question as if he was really interested.

As he listened to them talk, Socko forgot the General was about to kick the Olsons out. He wondered if this was what family felt like.

27
ONE HAND WASHES THE OTHER

Livvy jumped, then slid her cell phone out of her pocket. "Hi, Mother."

Pinned down by the baby in her lap, Livvy was facing away from the front windows, but Socko could see a car in the driveway across the street. Livvy's mother stood next to it, a cell phone pressed to her ear.

"Can I stay a little longer?" Livvy smiled at Emily, who was waving the spoon around. "I already ate."

Socko watched the man who had accused him of vandalizing Moon Ridge get out of the car. He was holding a big sack of carryout, this time from a restaurant called Thai-One-On.

"Livvy," said the General. "Ask your parents to come over. It's time we got acquainted."

"Can you guys come over here a minute?" Livvy's eyes closed as she listened to their conversation. Although he couldn't hear a word they were saying, Socko could tell the couple in the driveway wasn't exactly thrilled about the invitation.

"Great!" Livvy's eyes opened wide. "See you in a sec!" She handed Emily to Delia and ran to the door.

"Wipe your chin, Luke," rasped the General. "And look intelligent. You're about to have a job interview."

Luke took a swipe at his chin with his paper napkin and stuffed the napkin in the pocket of his jeans.

Livvy leaned out the door and pulled her mother and father inside. "Everybody, these are my parents, Tim and Marsha Holmes!"

Socko noticed the way his own mother smoothed the front of her blouse as she looked at Marsha Holmes. Livvy's parents obviously spent a lot of money on clothes, haircuts, and manicures. They looked like they belonged in a place like Moon Ridge. But they also looked tired. The tie around Mr. Holmes neck hung crooked. His wife had circles under her eyes that makeup didn't hide.

Tired or not, their smiles flashed on like emoticons. Everyone shook hands. Delia gave Mrs. Holmes a hug. "So glad to finally meet you!"

"It's a pleasure to meet you too," said Mrs. Holmes, taking a step back. "Livvy says such nice things about all of you. We'll have to have you over for dinner sometime." She eye-signaled her husband with a quick glance at the door.

"Absolutely," said Mr. Holmes. "You'll have to excuse us for now, though." He held up the bag of carryout. "Dinner isn't getting any warmer." With his free hand on his wife's back, Mr. Holmes turned toward the door.

A battered wheelchair cut off their retreat. "Now that we've got the nicey-nice out of the way, let's cut to the chase. Mr. Holmes, from the look of things I'd say you're in a pickle."

Socko saw the shock on Livvy's face.

"I beg your pardon?" said Mr. Holmes.

"Nothing dishonorable about it, son. The way I hear it the whole country's in a pickle. And that includes Luke here."

Luke dipped his head in agreement and stared at the floor.

"The economy being what it is, Luke and his wife and baby are living in a car at the moment, but normally Luke is a landscaper. The subdivision he was working on went belly-up."

"Which subdivision?" Mr. Holmes asked Luke.

"Buena Vista."

Mr. Holmes nodded grimly. "Dave Mason's project—I didn't know it had gone under."

"Oh, yeah," said Luke. "A couple months ago."

Mr. Holmes dragged a hand down his face.

"Mr. Holmes, I don't see you selling a lot of houses," the General pressed. "And you won't if you don't get a little greenery going. I'm thinking that maybe the two of you could help each other out. Put Luke and his family up in one of these houses you have so many of, and in trade he'll plant up a few of the yards, as well as that bare dirt around the entry to the project."

Socko stared at the General as though he had just pulled a rabbit out of his hat. But would Livvy's dad go for the idea?

"Tim?" Mrs. Holmes said quietly. "This is ridiculous! We are not *that* desperate."

Livvy looked back and forth between her parents. "How desperate are we?"

"Cash flow is a little tight right now, honey," her father said, "but we're fine."

"Then why can't we help Luke and Ceelie?"

"It's kind of complicated, Liv." Mr. Holmes turned to his wife.

"Mother, please?" Livvy begged.

"We are *not* a charity, Olivia," Mrs. Holmes whispered.

Socko saw Luke stiffen.

"We don't want charity, ma'am," Luke said. "I do an honest day's work for an honest day's pay. You can call Dave Mason. He'll give me a reference."

Livvy stood between her parents, looking back and forth. "Mother? Daddy? We'll help the Olsons, won't we?"

Mr. Holmes put a hand on his wife's shoulder. "What do you say?" She sighed. "All right."

"Thank you, thank you!" Livvy gave her mother a hug.

Having given in, Mrs. Holmes looked even more tired, but the emoticon smile switched back on.

"Now, if you'll excuse us," said Mr. Holmes, steering his wife toward the door. "It's been a long day. We'll firm up the details in the morning, Mr. Olson."

"Thanks," Luke said, watching Mrs. Holmes's stiff back as she walked out.

164

"One hand washes the other," the General called after them. "This'll turn out good for everyone."

Mrs. Holmes was opening the door when Delia said, "Just a second, Marsha." Delia had been walking back and forth to the laundry room all evening, delivering stacks of clean clothes. She walked into the laundry room one last time and came out with Livvy's mountain of towels. "Thanks for the loan."

Mrs. Holmes raised her eyebrows at her daughter before turning to Delia. "Keep them, please."

"Are you kidding?" Delia tried to force the towels into the woman's arms. "Take 'em! Towels cost money."

Mrs. Holmes held up a hand. "No, really. I insist. They're not the right color for any of our new bathrooms." She slipped her arm through her husband's and headed for the door. "Olivia, I expect to see you at home in fifteen minutes. Good night, everyone."

"Night," added Mr. Holmes.

"Come over anytime," Delia called after them, hugging the stack of towels.

Livvy didn't do anything with her fifteen minutes. She just held the baby and rocked nervously back and forth.

"I'll walk you," said Socko when the time was up.

"No kissing on the first date," the General rumbled as they walked out the door.

Livvy didn't even blush—so Socko didn't bother to either.

"Sorry I got you in trouble about the towels," Socko said. "But I don't get why your mom was so bent about taking them back."

"Mother's acting weird lately. Plus she's a germ freak."

"You can't catch homelessness." He thought it was kind of funny, but Livvy didn't laugh.

As they walked through the open door of the three-car garage, Socko spotted a large map leaned against the wall. Having spent days making a map, he had come to appreciate their ins and outs, and this one was as big as the classroom map that had been his bedroom wall at the Kludge. "Nice map."

"Map?"

"Yeah, over there." It was only when he walked over to it, Livvy at his heels, that Socko realized he was looking at Moon Ridge Estates.

He was about to check it out and see how it compared to his own map when Livvy whispered, "That should be hanging on the wall of their office." She stared at Socko, a look of panic on her face. "They're going out of business!"

"No way. They'd tell you if it was that bad."

"Really? I didn't know we were moving until my mother began putting things in boxes! They don't tell me anything."

Not being told anything was hard for Socko to imagine. Delia shared *all* her worries with him—her hours were going to be cut, she didn't have the rent money— sometimes way more than he wanted to know.

Livvy's eyes darted around the unfinished garage. "What if we can't keep *this* house?"

"Why wouldn't you? Your dad owns Moon Ridge."

"It's not that simple…" She put her hand on the doorknob, then rested her forehead against the door. "Oh, Socko. I don't want to live in a car."

"You got two nice ones to choose from."

She slipped into the kitchen without looking back.

"Just trying to cheer you up," he told the closed door. "Sorry."

28
LOOKS LIKE A FUNERAL

The next morning Socko grabbed Damien's hat off the doorknob. He turned it around in his hand until the *S* faced him. He hadn't thought about Damien all that much lately. "Been busy," he said under his breath, and put the hat on. He crept out of his bedroom, then hesitated in front of the closed door next to his, pretending for a second it was Damien sleeping in there.

"It's okay, Em," said a woman's voice from inside the room. "Go back to sleep."

His mother and great-grandfather were drinking coffee at the kitchen table. "Still sleeping?" Delia whispered, pointing up.

Socko nodded.

"And tonight they'll be someplace else," said the General, but Socko noticed that he was keeping his voice down too.

Delia heaved herself to her feet and put her cup in the sink. "Walk me out," she said to Socko. At the car she pressed a crumpled twenty-dollar bill into his hand. "Give this to Ceelie for groceries. Don't tell the General."

Socko was hiding the twenty in his pocket when the sun peered over the edge of the earth and an orange light raked across their dirt yard. "Hey, Mom! Check out the lawn!"

"Goodness!" Delia had been watering the dirt for days, using the "gentle showers" setting on the sprinkler head so she wouldn't dislodge the seeds. Now, seemingly overnight, a million tiny blades had sprung up and were standing straight and green. "It isn't a lawn yet," she said, hugging herself. "But it's a start. It'll be the best lawn in Moon Ridge Estates."

"It'll be the *only* lawn in Moon Ridge Estates."

His mother punched his arm. "Smart-mouth. With Luke here there'll be more. But ours will still be the best."

"Because it's ours?"

"Right." She stared at the cloudless sky and frowned. "The TV says it's supposed to rain today. Doesn't look like it, though. Our lawn could use a good, deep soak. If it doesn't rain this morning, go out and water it good, okay?" She tapped the *S* on Damien's hat and climbed into the car.

"What was that for?" Socko asked as she rolled down the window.

"Rain. And the Olsons. Junebug too."

"What's wrong with Junebug?"

"Same old same old. Forget I mentioned it."

Just then, Livvy and her mother came out of their house. "Good morning, Marsha!" Delia called. "Thanks again for the towels."

Mrs. Holmes waved and got into the car. Livvy hurried across the street. "Look!" She showed Delia and Socko a silver key. "It's to the house next to yours."

"More neighbors," said Delia with a contented sigh.

***

"My parents and I talked last night and it's okay about the map in our garage." Livvy put the key on the kitchen table and helped herself to a bowl of cereal. "They're moving to a different office. A smaller one," she admitted, stirring the oaty clusters into the milk. "So I guess it's not totally okay. But at least now I know there's a good reason why I'm not going back to Haworth. It was a relief to find out that they weren't just messing with my life."

"Money?"

"Temporary cash flow. We all have to make a few sacrifices, but Dad says everything's going to be okay."

"Can I take a look at the map before they move it?" he asked.

"Sure."

She finished her cereal, washed the bowl and spoon, and set them in the drainer.

Crossing the street, Socko checked the sky. In the time since his mother had driven away, the TV's prediction of rain had become more believable. A ceiling of clouds hung low over Moon Ridge Estates. It seemed to flatten the already flat landscape.

Livvy rolled up the big garage door and turned on the bank of lights.

All of Moon Ridge Estates appeared in crisp black and white. Although the proportions were different, it looked a lot like his map. He found Full Moon Circle and traced it until his finger reached Tranquility Way, where it hung a left. "We live here." It took another minute for him to find what he was looking for. "Hey, here it is!" he whooped.

"Here what is?" She pulled her hair back with one hand and took a closer look at the spot he was pointing to. "Oh, that..."

The Wildlife Area abutted the golf course and was almost as big. The whole area was textured with little symbols. "Trees?" he muttered, matching the symbol to the key. The only trees he'd seen there were lying dead on the ground. "Did they move the Wildlife Area?"

"No." She let her hair slide out of her hand. "The partners decided an eighteen-hole golf course would be better for sales than a nine. Dad had to go back to the county commission and get a variance."

"Holy crap! He bulldozed it?"

"He's a developer. It's part of his job."

"Did you see what it looked like when it was a forest?"

"I never saw Moon Ridge at all before we moved here. But I'm sorry! I know how much you like nature."

Socko shrugged off the hand she put on his arm and strode out into the rain that had just begun to fall.

***

169

While rain pelted Moon Ridge, the General taught them to play a card game called Crown and Anchor. They bet saltines. Socko didn't feel like talking, and Livvy didn't seem to either. "You two are about as much fun as a toothache," the General grumped. "I almost wish the Olsons were still around getting underfoot instead of next door."

Although Livvy always seemed to want to prove she was the best at everything, she was less than her usual competitive self. But since Socko couldn't be bothered with trying and the General was on a losing streak, she managed to build a tower of saltines six inches high.

It was early afternoon when Livvy's pocket began jingling classical music. She slid out her cell. "Yes, Mother?" She listened a minute. "Be right there." She pushed away from the table and stood. "Gotta go. The partners are coming for dinner tonight."

"Tell them there's nothing left to bulldoze," Socko called after her.

"Nothing but Holmes Homes," the General observed as Livvy dashed out the door into the falling rain.

"What are you talking about?"

"I'm talking about the partners putting her folks out of business." The old man began divvying up her saltines. "The only money Moon Ridge has made so far came out of my pocket."

"Her dad said it was just a temporary cash flow problem."

The General frowned at the last saltine in his hand, then dropped it on Socko's pile. "Shutting down the whole shebang would fix that."

Socko kept on playing, but he barely noticed as all the saltines migrated to his great-grandfather's side of the table.

Manuel's old car crawled into the driveway at five. Delia's face appeared and then blurred as the one working windshield wiper swatted the rain away. Socko expected her to use the button on her keychain to open the garage door since it was raining; instead the headlights went out and the lone windshield wiper stopped in mid-swish. The car door opened.

A long red spear emerged first. Popped open, it became a tiny umbrella—it must have come with the car. Delia rolled out. Although it was raining so hard the drops bounced off the umbrella, she just stood there.

"The grub isn't even good when it's dry," the General complained as rain fell into the open top of the bag that hung on her arm. "Is Delia Marie having a stroke?"

Socko ran out in the rain. "Mom?" He blinked the rain out of his eyes.

She didn't even look at him. She just stared into the rain. He crushed himself up against her under the umbrella to keep the rain out of his eyes and looked too.

He had never given it much thought, but their yard ran downhill to the road. In this heavy rain the edge of the driveway had become a swiftly moving river. When it reached the street, the river turned, spilling along the curb until it poured through the metal grate that covered the storm drain.

The lawn they had spread and stomped and watered and exhorted to grow had become a flotilla racing down the driveway, a million tiny green sails. Moon Ridge's best and only lawn was disappearing beneath the road.

Socko stepped into the rushing torrent. Sprouts swirled around his ankles. Some clung to his socks, but most whirled by, dancing their way to the drain.

He felt a warm hand on his arm. "Come on, Socko. We'd better go inside before the burgers get any more waterlogged and we have to listen to himself."

"But...our lawn..."

"I know, I know." She linked her arm through his. Already soaked, they walked slowly up the path.

"In case you missed it, the lawn just washed away," Delia announced when they stood dripping inside the front door.

"It was bound to happen," said the old man. "At least you gave it a try."

Delia wiggled her feet out of her sopping sneakers. "And I'll give it another one too. There's plenty more seed at Home Depot. We *are* going to have a lawn!"

The General gathered the cards as Delia thumped into the kitchen. "You'll have a lawn if the whole shooting match doesn't go up in

171

smoke," he wheezed. He cocked his head toward the driveway across the street. "Behold. The partners."

Three unfamiliar black cars sat parked at Livvy's, the rain glistening on their perfect paint jobs. The General rapped the edge of the deck of cards against the table. "Looks like a funeral to me."

29
CLICK

When Livvy didn't show up to bug him first thing the next morning, Socko walked over and knocked on her door. He wasn't going to make a habit of it or anything, but he was worried about what the owners of the three black cars had had to say.

She slid out the door, closing it behind her. The dirty pink shorts she wore were the ones she'd had on yesterday.

"How'd the meeting go?" He gave her a thumbs-up and raised his eyebrows.

She answered with an emphatic thumbs-down, her eyes shiny.

Socko looked away, embarrassed. He spotted a flattened cardboard carton leaning against the wall of the garage—which reminded him of something. "Are you throwing that box away?"

"I guess."

"Can I have it?"

"Sure…but why?"

"I'll show you. Follow me."

He dragged the piece of cardboard as they walked, having second and third thoughts about what was probably a stupid idea. "So what went down at dinner?"

"We ate." Livvy shoved her hands into the pockets of her shorts. "After dessert Mother sent me upstairs. I went, but only partway. I sat in that blind spot where the staircase turns and listened to what they were saying. Oh, Socko! The partners are getting ready to pull out!"

The General had been right. "That's tough," Socko said.

"Tough?" She gave him a wide-eyed stare. "It's a disaster!"

It was bad, sure, but disaster? "It'll be okay. Your parents'll find other jobs."

"They don't have jobs! They have a *company*. No more company, and they'll have to lay off all their employees."

"What employees?"

"My dad's finishing out a couple of contracts on other projects. He has his people there, but that work will dry up soon, and then they'll all be out of a job. I don't know what we'll do. My dad owes so much money."

Socko listened to the scratch of the cardboard as he dragged it down the road. This was way bigger than not having the rent—and he thought he could cheer her up? Fat chance.

They had reached the part of the development cratered with future basements. Socko stopped beside the largest mound of excavated earth. He stood the cardboard on edge, then let go. "We're here," he announced as it landed flat on the ground.

Livvy didn't seem to notice the dirt mountains. Instead her eyes went to the nearby fence they'd climbed a few days earlier. "We're not going after Brad and his friends, are we?"

He shook his head.

"And please tell me we're not going over to Lorelei Meadows to admire the grass."

"Nope." Suddenly either of those options sounded less dumb than what he had in mind. He stared at the flattened cardboard box he'd felt so lucky to find. Forty-gallon hot water heater. Energy Star. The printed words glared up at him.

"So…why are we here?" She was looking at the flattened box too, a puzzled look on her face. Damien popped into his head. Damien was the friend who would have gotten the connection instantly. Damien was used to making do, pretending every piece of trash was something else. With Livvy staring at the cardboard, it turned from a genius idea back to what it really was. Garbage.

"Hey!" She dropped to a squat and ran a hand across its surface. "I bet if we dragged this to the top of that pile of dirt we could ride it down."

Surprise and then relief flooded his chest. "And why do you think I brought it here?"

Livvy picked up the cardboard and balanced it on her head. Holding it in place with both hands, she ran halfway up the hill, then started to slide. "Aaaaah!" Never letting go of the cardboard, she dropped to her knees and careened back down the clay slope.

The edge of the cardboard slammed into Socko's stomach, knocking him down. He sat with his legs out straight, serious dampness creeping through the butt of his shorts.

Livvy unfolded her legs so they stuck out straight too. From knee to ankle each shin was striped with mud.

Socko figured she'd give up after checking out her muddy self. Girls weren't into getting slimed. Instead, she jumped to her feet. "Come *on*," she said.

"Was that a smile? Did I detect a smile?"

She stuck her tongue out at him.

With each failed attempt to scale the clay mountain, the sliming got worse. Socko rolled. Livvy belly-skidded. She pushed herself to her knees and looked at the red clay stains on her formerly white blouse—then tried again.

"Queen of the Hill!" she crowed when they finally reached the summit. "And King!" she added.

They rested the cardboard Livvy had carried up the hill on both of their heads. Each of them held onto an outside edge with one hand. They weren't in a hurry to try out the cardboard sled. It had taken them so long to scale the mud mountain, and they'd be at the bottom again in one quick slide.

Socko looked down at the massive shadow of the hill with the two of them, tiny mountaineers, on the top. The shadows of their legs and arms were spindly. The cardboard, caught edge-on by the sun, was reduced to a single line.

"Click," said Livvy softly.

Socko's short hair made a gritty sound against the cardboard as he turned his head. "Click?"

"You know, like taking a picture? Izzy and I made it up. We say it—said it—when some moment was worth remembering."

"And this is a click?"

She pointed to their shadows. "We look like hieroglyphics." She did an Egyptian thing with her arms, bending them at sharp angles, the cardboard resting on her head.

He Egyptianed his free arm, watching the shadow do the same. "Click," he whispered, then felt kind of stupid. "Let's try this baby out." He set the cardboard down on the flat top of the mound. "You sit up front."

Livvy climbed on and gripped the leading edge of the cardboard.

Socko sat down behind her, one leg on either side. "Now, I guess we...sort of...inch forward." He dug in with his heels, trying to propel the cardboard forward.

She stretched her long legs out past the edges of the cardboard and dug in too. When they lurched over the edge, she let out a little scream. "That was anticlimactic," she said when the cardboard sled hung there like a bug on flypaper.

The words were barely out of her mouth when the cardboard began to slide.

Socko tapped Damien's Superman *S* just as the slow creep turned to an avalanche of speed. When they hit level ground at the bottom of the hill, he slammed into Livvy's back, ripping the cardboard edge from her hands. She skidded off the sled on her knees, then stood, checked out her legs, and shrugged. "What's a little more mud?" She looked up the hill. "Too bad it was over so fast."

Their slide had smoothed out the tiny watercourses cut by rain, squeegeeing the clay flat and leaving a dark, shiny path. "It would be even faster if we went down again," said Socko.

"Come on!" Livvy grabbed his hands and pulled him to his feet.

It *was* faster. Way. And this time when they hit the level ground they skidded farther. "Again?" he asked.

They rode the cardboard sled until it was so soggy it fell apart. "We'll snag another big box before the next rain," he said as they walked away.

"Hope it rains before the partners put my dad out of business. Who knows where I'll be after that."

"It's not definite. They haven't pulled the plug yet."

"Yet," she repeated.

Livvy looked as worried as she had when they'd set out from her house—and a lot muddier. So much for cheering her up.

They hosed off in Socko's yard. The water in his sneakers bubbled between his toes with each step as they squelched into the house.

The General made them put towels on the kitchen chairs before they could sit. "How'd that meeting go last night, young lady?"

Behind Livvy's back Socko zipped a finger across his own throat to let his great-grandfather know how it had gone—and to shut him up, but it was a little late for that.

"Terrible. The partners might pull out."

The General drummed his fingers on the kitchen table. "I was afraid of that."

"I want to help my parents, but they think I'm too young to even know about it!"

"Strange times we're living in. Strange times. Used to be kids were *expected* to help. Once, back when I was a kid during the Depression my mother gave me four cents to buy bread at Lewis's General Store. Ma knew it cost five but she only had four. It was my job to get that bread."

Livvy listened intently, her heels hooked over the edge of the chair, her arms around her shins. "What did you do?"

"I walked slow with my hand in my pocket. I kept picking up and counting those pennies: 1...2...3...4. It was four every time."

Socko slipped off his soggy sneakers and tipped his chair back against the kitchen counter. A couple of weeks before the move he had made a walk like that—only he was heading to Donatelli's with Damien to get Louise a pack of cigarettes and they'd had no money at all.

"I was almost to the door when I had a bright idea," the General said. "I stopped and tore a hole in my pocket so I could make like I'd *lost* one of my pennies."

Damien had had a bright idea too—and a dead cockroach.

"I grabbed a loaf of bread," his great-grandfather went on, "and then I put the four cents on the counter in a pile. Mr. Lewis counted them into his palm and then held out his hand. I felt around in my pocket and acted surprised."

Socko had acted surprised too—surprised to discover that there was a dead roach on top of the pile of chicken wings under the heat lamp.

The General mimed turning his pocket inside out. "I showed Mr. Lewis the hole in my pocket, but he wasn't fooled. Instead he handed me a broom and let me work off the last penny."

When Socko had showed Mr. Donatelli the roach, he *had* been fooled—or at least distracted long enough for Damien to reach behind the counter and snag a pack of cigarettes. Socko wished he could have offered Mr. Donatelli some work in trade for the cigarettes, but the shop owner didn't trust kids.

"I'd be happy to do any kind of work to help my family earn money," said Livvy. "But things are different now."

The General shook his head. "If you can't help them earn money, maybe you can help them save."

Livvy put her head down on her knees. "I got all over them about not sending me back to private school. I told them if they *really* loved me they would never make me go to public! But I didn't know we were in real trouble until last night."

The General leaned toward her. "So lie. Tell them you changed your mind. Tell them you decided it would be fun to go to public school with your boyfriend, Socko."

Livvy blushed. "There are some lies *nobody* would believe."

"You're right," the General agreed. "Sorry I suggested it."

She went to the living room window. "No cars," she reported. "I'll lie to Mother as soon as she gets home."

"You want to do something right now?" the General called. "Luke's planting posies down by the guardhouse. Bet he wouldn't mind some help."

"What do you say Socko? Want to help Luke?" she asked.

She sounded pretty happy about digging holes in the hot sun. He was too. Doing something—anything that might help—beat worrying.

***

The General eyed Socko and Livvy as they came in the front door, glaring at their dirty hands. "I didn't think the two of you could look any worse, but you managed it."

"We straightened up the sign so it doesn't look like it's falling over anymore," said Socko.

"Bet that looks a little more dignified."

"And we planted about a zillion marigolds. And, let's see, we put in tithonia, gomphrena, and verbena." As Livvy ticked the exotic flower names off on her fingers, her father's car pulled into the driveway across the street. "What was that creeping plant with little yellow flowers?" she asked Socko.

"Livvy," the General said, cutting off the recitation. "Ask your father to come over for a minute if he'd like a little good news."

Livvy dashed out the door. When she came back, her father was walking slowly behind her. Even though the guy had caused him a lot of trouble, Socko felt sorry for him. His whole body drooped, as if the dinner with the partners had put a huge weight on his shoulders.

"You know the guard booth Luke and the kids just prettied up?" the General asked. "How'd you like an old geezer to put in it? Someone to open and close the gate?"

Livvy's dad looked disappointed. A geezer in the guard booth didn't seem to be his idea of good news. "You can sit in the booth," he told the General, "but I can't pay you."

"Not me!" the General snapped. "This geezer's name is Eddie Corrigan. We were in the war together. After us boys came home, he hung

179

around my store for better than fifty years, supposedly working. The only way to fire him was to sell out. Vermont's getting too cold for him—and he misses my smiling face."

Socko saw one corner of Mr. Holmes's mouth turn up—which was twice the smile the General wore.

"They sold their big old house a few months ago, moved into a little apartment. His wife Lil is sick and tired of having him underfoot, so she likes the idea of a bigger house and a guard booth to stick him in. He likes the idea of being in law enforcement. I told him you might even throw in a uniform."

"I can arrange that."

"And a gun."

"A gun?" Mr. Holmes puffed up his cheeks and blew out.

The General contemplated the ceiling for a second. "I think he'd settle for a big flashlight."

30
THE BAD PENNY

S ocko overheard a phone exchange between the General and his old army buddy. "It's all squared away. You get the booth," the General wheezed into the phone. "And did I tell you about our eighteen-hole golf course and clubhouse loaded with activities?"

"What golf course?" Socko asked when his great-grandfather hung up. "What activities?"

"So I told a few stretchers." The General stabbed a finger at the house across the street. "I don't want to see that fella over there lose his business; he's got family."

"Right. And it isn't because you want your friend to move here. Admit it, you miss him!"

"Miss him!" The General slapped his skinny thighs with his palms. "For better than sixty years Eddie Corrigan was an irritation, a rock in my shoe! Like a bad penny, he just kept turning up. The best I can say is I was used to him."

"I have a friend I was used to—"

"I know," the old man said, cutting him off. "Delia Marie and I have been talking about this Damien Rivera kid."

"You have?" Socko saw a glimmer of hope.

"If what Delia Marie says is true, he's happy where he is." The General lifted his bony shoulders and let them drop. "Sometimes friends move on—personally I've never been that lucky—"

"He's not happy! He's just doing what he has to do to stay alive!"

"Maybe so, maybe not. Either way, I think you deserve an answer to that question."

The glimmer was back. "And how would I get an answer?"

"Ask Damien."

"Ask him how?"

"Therein lies the conundrum. Delia Marie has made up her mind. She won't take you back to the old neighborhood. I lack wheels." He gave the arm of his wheelchair a quick slap. "At least not the kind we need. Maybe when Eddie gets here, we can steal his car."

Was he serious? With the General, Socko could never tell, but it sure sounded as if his great-grandfather had given him permission to find a way to get back to the old neighborhood to talk to Damien.

***

Socko couldn't get the conversation with the General off his mind. He thought about it every morning, standing in the hot sun with Luke and Livvy planting flower beds. He thought about it in the evening as he was playing cards with the General. He thought about it at night as he stared into the darkness, his great-grandfather snoring and coughing downstairs.

He was still thinking about it one morning when he knocked on Luke's door, ready for the day's gardening assignment. The Holmes Homes truck that was always parked in the driveway was gone, but Socko figured Ceelie could point him to the part of the project where Luke was working; they'd been starting earlier and earlier to beat the worst of the heat.

Ceelie opened the door, Emily on her hip. "Oh, hi, Socko. Luke's in the city today, running errands for Mr. Holmes."

Errands in the city... The words chimed in Socko's head.

It was like he could hear the powerful angel voices that used to come out the open doors of the AME church down the street from the Kludge. He rushed back home.

"I think I have a way to get back to the old neighborhood!" he said, barging through the front door.

"Hold your horses, kid." The General crossed his arms over his skinny chest. "Explain."

While Socko explained, the General chewed on the insides of his cheeks and frowned.

Socko waited for a sign of approval, but the frown didn't go away. It was looking like it had been a big mistake telling the old guy. The General must have been joking with him that day, not authorizing a sneak trip to see Damien. What if his great-grandfather put his foot down now, insisted they run his idea by Delia?

The General cleared his throat. "There's an old military saying that goes like this: 'Sometimes it is better to beg for forgiveness than to ask for permission.'"

"What does *that* mean?"

"It means that I know nothing about your little plan, and Delia Marie won't hear it from me." The fingers he put on Socko's arm felt as dry and cool as notebook paper. "But Socko, if you should happen to carry out this plan you never told me about, I expect you to exercise the utmost caution, do nothing stupid, and get your patoot back here as soon as you have your answer. No heroics. It would simply be a recon mission. Compree?"

"Compree."

When he saw Luke that afternoon, Socko asked if he could ride along on his next trip into town. "I have to check on my best friend."

"That okay with your folks?"

"The General authorized it." Socko hoped Luke wouldn't go back to the General to make sure, or worse yet, ask Delia. And that wasn't his only problem. Somehow Socko was going to have to convince Luke to let Damien ride back with them to Moon Ridge.

Hopefully when the time came, Damien would have one of his genius ideas.

For days, Socko and Livvy helped Luke plant the gardens around the clubhouse, Socko waiting, not very patiently, to hitch a ride back to the old neighborhood. Although the need for the ride to happen right now itched him all the time, he didn't talk to anyone about it, not even the General. He was afraid his great-grandfather might reconsider.

But his great-grandfather had other things on his mind—namely, not acting excited that his own thorn-in-the-side best friend, Eddie Corrigan, was about to move to the neighborhood.

***

Luke straightened up from the landscape boulder they'd just rolled into place beside one of the clubhouse paths. "Might be going into the city this afternoon," he said. "If I am, I'll pick you up."

"All right!" Lucky for Socko, Livvy was off at the dentist and the General was probably too distracted to care. This was the day the Corrigans were to arrive.

Socko needed a shower, but he couldn't risk being naked and wet when Luke came by, so he stood at the kitchen sink and let the cold water pour over his head. He vaguely heard the blast of a horn through the sound of running water.

"Unnecessary ruckus!" the General exclaimed. "Socko?"

Socko rushed out of the kitchen, furiously rubbing his head dry with a kitchen towel, but the Holmes Homes truck was nowhere to be seen. Instead, a baby blue Cadillac Coupe sat in the driveway.

"The bad penny turns up!" the General huffed. "It's Eddie Corrigan and his lovely wife Lil. You may as well show them in."

Socko's first view of Eddie Corrigan through the bug-specked windshield included a straw hat with a plaid band and a pair of milky blue eyes that peered back at him from under the hat's brim. The window powered down. "You must be Socko!"

"Pleased to meet you, Mr. Corrigan." Socko opened the door for him.

"What the hey? Call me Uncle Eddie. And this is the wife, Lil."

The woman seated beside Uncle Eddie was large, like Delia. She wore a dress with giant daisies printed on it. "Hello, honey," she said.

The old man climbed out of the car but his back stayed as bent as a question mark. One hand on top of his hat, he squinted up at Socko. "Hoo-ee! How's the air up there? I remember when I used to be tall."

The General rapped his knuckles on the window.

Uncle Eddie lifted his hat to salute his scowling friend. "Sure have missed that friendly face!" He tucked his thumbs into his white plastic belt. "So how has Cookie been treating you, son?"

"Cookie?"

Uncle Eddie's laugh was a sharp honk. "He didn't tell you? That's what we called him in the army."

***

While the Corrigans settled in the living room, the General ordered Socko to rustle up some grub.

"Yes, Cookie—I mean, yes sir." Socko beat a hasty retreat and heated half a dozen burgers while Uncle Eddie and "Cookie" caught up over lunch (Uncle Eddie did most of the talking). His wife read aloud from the Moon Ridge Estates brochure. "Lush lawns. Modern landscaping. Golf course." After each item she stared pointedly at the General.

"You don't even play golf, baby doll," Uncle Eddie soothed. "And my booth sure looked spiff-a-roo. The moving van should be here by six. You'll feel better with your stuff around you. Our daughter Jeanie and her husband packed us up," he explained. "We diddle-dawdled our way south so we'd get here about the same time as the truck."

They were just finishing their burgers when a second horn blasted in the driveway. Socko looked out the window and saw Luke seated at the wheel of the Holmes Homes pickup.

"Nice meeting you," Socko called as he headed toward the door, "but I gotta go!"

"Halt!" A surprisingly strong hand gripped his wrist.

"But I have to—this is my ride!"

The General's grip tightened. "You will exercise extreme caution at all times, private. You will do nothing to give me reason to regret this mission I know nothing about."

"Yes, sir." Socko dashed out the door and climbed into the truck. When he looked back at the house, his great-grandfather's face was at the window. The old man nodded once. Socko nodded back.

185

31
LIL' D

I t wasn't rush hour, so the trip to the city was fast—the distance had seemed so much longer when he was lying awake in bed trying to figure out how to get back to the old neighborhood.

"I'll drop you off," said Luke as they exited the interstate. "But I only have a couple errands, so it'll have to be a quick visit. How do I get there?"

"Um…I think you turn here," said Socko. They cut through a neighborhood in which all the signs were in Spanish. "Try a…right at that bodega." In the next neighborhood the buildings looked vacant.

This was a possibility Socko hadn't considered. What if he couldn't find his way back home?

Then suddenly the gray concrete pile that was Grover Cleveland Middle School was in front of him. "Here! Turn here!" Socko strained forward in his seat, tugging against the belt.

He saw a Tarantula tag on a Dumpster and Mrs. A. walking Puppy Precious past Two Guys Pawn Shop. Even though she was Meat's mother, he wanted to jump out and kiss her. He was home!

Then he remembered his mission.

As they rolled past the familiar storefronts he repeated a silent chant: *make it easy, make it easy.*

They reached the corner of his street. "Stop here." Socko scanned the block— Damien was just coming out of Donatelli's. Alone! Although it looked like things were going to be easy after all, Socko's palms went all sweaty. "See ya, Luke. Thanks for the ride."

"Half an hour. Be on this corner."

"Sure." Socko slammed the door behind him. He cupped his hands around his mouth. "Yo, Damien!"

His friend turned toward him fast, then looked back over his shoulder at Donatelli's plate glass window. He hesitated just a second before running down the long block toward Socko.

Socko ran too, wondering what they were supposed to do when they reached each other. Hug? High five?

Damien stopped a few feet away from him. "Hey," he said. "Nice lid."

"Superpowered. You want it back?"

"Nah. I kind of replaced it." That's when Socko noticed that the bill of Damien's new cap pointed to the side.

"What happened? They make you join?"

Damien shrugged.

"Don't worry about it. Soon as Luke—Luke's the guy with the truck—soon as he comes back I'll get you outta here."

"Like an abduction?" The crooked grin was pure Damien, but it dimmed fast as he looked over his shoulder. "Not a great idea. A lot has changed since you blew outta here. I gotta stick around."

"Why?"

"My mom and the latest boyfriend."

"What about 'em?"

Damien took another quick glance toward Donatelli's. "It's kind of complicated." He touched his new cap—the same way he'd always touched the *S* on his old one. "Let's just say that in my present situation it doesn't hurt to have some brothers around."

"Brothers?"

At the sound of a sharp whistle, Damien turned fast. Rapp, Meat, and some other guys were standing in front of the door to the convenience store.

Damien looked at Socko. "Gotta go—" He did a stutter step backwards. "And you should get outta here." He took off.

Socko watched the soles of Damien's sneakers as he flew past the Jumbo Dollar, the Rockin' Wok, the newsstand, and the vacant store that used to sell scratch-and-dent appliances.

Damien had nearly reached Donatelli's when Socko started running too. Was he crazy following his friend right into a nest of Tarantulas? Definitely. But he kept on running.

By the time Socko got to them, Damien was already slouched against the wall between Rapp and Meat, his slumped back resting easy against the brick wall, like he'd been there all along. Only his chest pumping in and out proved he'd just run hard.

Meat's head pivoted slowly. "Well. Look who's here." Rapp made a point of not noticing him. The others took their cue from the gang leader. Still, Socko could feel it. They were on alert.

Rapp continued to lean against the wall, but one hand slid into the baggy pocket where he kept his knife. Socko's legs began to shake, remembering the last time he'd crossed Rapp.

He had to concentrate on his friend. This was his one chance to figure out what was going on. "Damien?"

No response.

The Damien Socko knew moved like a scribble, fast and all over the place. But now, surrounded by the gang, Damien even blinked slow. And it wasn't just his face that was playing dead. He was barely moving, like he was in a trance.

But Socko had seen the smile. Damien hadn't faked that. "Can I talk to you a minute?" he asked.

Rapp and Meat shifted against the wall, framing Damien even tighter. Rapp's hand emerged from his pocket. He flipped the knife in the air. It landed on his palm with a soft slap.

Socko was shaking, but he kept at it. "It won't take long, just a couple minutes. It's nothing to do with you guys."

"What you say to one brother you say to all," Rapp said. Two guys Socko didn't know pushed away from the wall. Redeploying, they took up positions behind Socko on the sidewalk.

"It's cool, Rapp." Socko held out his empty hands. "I just wanna talk to Damien."

"Give it up, man." Meat's voice sounded almost kind.

Socko knew that it was time to go. Past time. "Let him walk to the corner with me. You guys can watch," he babbled, "I just want to talk to my friend for two minutes. Just two minutes."

Rapp swung his elbow and nudged Damien. "How 'bout it? You wanna take a walk with your little friend?"

Damien barely shrugged. "Guess I'm fine right here."

"That's it then. Conversation over." Rapp smiled at Socko. "You heard Lil' D."

A bead of cold sweat ran down Socko's spine, but he didn't move.

"Something wrong with your hearing?" This time Meat didn't sound so friendly.

Socko felt the two guys behind him step closer. He kept his eyes on the convenience store's plate glass window, hoping to use it as a mirror to show him what was going on behind him. What caught his eye instead was Mr. Donatelli lurking between two racks of chips, watching the scene on the sidewalk. Despite the audience, Socko knew he was on his own. Whatever happened next, the store owner would swear he hadn't seen a thing.

Socko concentrated on the images reflected on the glass. In the background was the empty street, three parking meters. He saw himself and the two guys, who now stood so close behind him he could hear their open-mouth breathing.

Something was about to snap; Socko could feel it.

His reflected view of the street blurred, and the side of a truck hid the street. Although the words read backwards on the glass, he still recognized them: Holmes Homes.

"Hey!" Luke's voice was strong.

When Socko whipped around, Luke was standing in the open driver's door of the truck, his muscular arms resting on the roof of the cab. "You ready?" He looked past Socko. "Hey...Damien?"

Damien put a hand on his chest. "You talkin' to me?"

"Yeah. How about if you ride along with us?"

Socko watched Luke's face for Damien's answer.

Luke nodded once. "Okay. Suit yourself. Let's go, Socko."

Socko stumbled past the two guys nearest the street and fell into the passenger seat. Although the confrontation was over, he could barely walk. Safe inside the truck, he looked back at Damien as they pulled away from the curb. Just like last time, he was leaving his friend behind.

"You all right?" asked Luke.

"Fine." Socko took a deep breath and fastened his seatbelt. "That was a quick half hour."

"I got a few blocks away, then something told me I'd better swing back. Sometimes these neighborhood punks can be just as dangerous as a real gang."

"Thanks." Rescued again. Rescued every time.

His mind went to Moon Ridge, where he acted all tough in front of Livvy. What a joke. He might "fit the description," but he was gutless. Livvy would have stood up to the Tarantulas better than he had.

Collapsed against the truck door, Socko listened to the tires grumble over the cracked tar.

Maybe Damien was getting by the only way he could. But Socko clung to the fact that the goofy grin his friend had given him when Rapp and the others were out of the picture was real. Damien lived.

The first of Mr. Holmes's errands involved picking up an envelope from a glass office building. Socko sat in the double-parked truck while Luke dashed inside. If he had been dropped on this street, Socko wouldn't have known where he was. Could this be the same city? All the men going in and out of the building wore suits and ties; the women were dressed like Livvy's mom.

What had almost gone down in front of Donatelli's could never happen here.

Suddenly Socko understood. The old neighborhood wasn't the whole world. It was just a box—a really small one. But Damien didn't know that.

He'd never been outside the box.

***

The old man was sitting ramrod straight in his wheelchair when Socko came through the door. "What in the Sam Hill took you so long?" the

190

General demanded. "Did you get in the way of any more punches?"

"No, sir."

The single eye looked Socko up and down. "Your front looks okay. Any damage on the back?"

"No, sir." Knowing the General would demand proof, Socko turned in place.

"I've been on high alert ever since you left, which made listening to Eddie Corrigan's babble even more annoying than usual. I kept wondering what I would tell Delia Marie if you went and got yourself killed."

"Thanks for the confidence."

The General drummed his fingers on the arms of the wheelchair. "Report on the mission."

"Mission not accomplished." Socko put his foot on the bottom step of the staircase.

"Halt."

Socko let his head drop back and stared at the ceiling. All he wanted to do right now was go to his room and close the door. He did *not* want to play soldiers.

"Would you just tell me what happened, son?"

Socko turned and sank down on the step. Keeping it simple, he told the General the basic story, thinking as he explained it of a dozen better, braver things he could have done. The General listened in stony silence.

"And that's about it, sir. Can I go to my room now?"

"Idiot!" the old man snapped.

"I am *not* an idiot!" Socko snapped back. "I...I couldn't think of what to do. I wimped, okay? I couldn't think at all...those guys—"

"*You're* not the durn-fool idiot, Socko. I am! I should never have let you go back there. Anything could have happened. And your mission most definitely *is* accomplished. You are never ever to go back there again. Compree?"

"Compree." Socko knew that saying he understood was the only way to get the General to say, "Dismissed!"

But understanding and obeying were two different things.

32
FAREWELL PHAT

Why didn't you take me with you?" Livvy asked. They were riding in the back of the truck along with dozens of flowering annuals in plastic pots.

"It was kind of spur-of-the-moment. And anyway, you were at the dentist." He hadn't planned to tell Livvy about his visit to the old neighborhood, but who else could he talk to about it?

Now that he'd told her what had happened, she sat in silence. Socko figured she was still mad at him, but then she stretched out a leg and touched his foot with hers. "I know it didn't work out, but what you did yesterday was really brave. You're a stand-up guy, Socko."

Despite all her rich-girl weirdness he was starting to like her, at least as a friend—and maybe as a girl of the opposite sex. And even though it was just sneaker to sneaker, not skin to skin, her foot was touching his. So maybe she liked him too.

But if she did like him, it was only because she didn't know the real him. He pulled his foot away. "I'm not who you think," he said.

"You're not Socko Starr?" she joked.

"I'm not brave. Sure, I'm big, but I'm harmless. A leaf-eater." He told her about the scene with Rapp on the roof—the primo example of how brave he wasn't. "Junebug saved Damien, not me. I was too scared."

She paused. "Were you scared yesterday?"

He stared past her. "What do *you* think?"

"But you did it anyway. Being scared was smart. Doing what you did even though you were scared? *That* was brave."

"Like it did any good." But he felt a little better. Not about Damien, but about himself. Maybe he wasn't the biggest wuss that ever lived.

Maybe just the second or third.

***

Riding in the back of the truck after a day of hard labor, surrounded by a sloshing sea of empty plastic pots, Socko stared at his hands. In the last few days he had planted so many bushes, trees, and annuals that his fingertips were cracked. Both he and Livvy had pink, peeling sunburns.

Watching the parade of vacant houses go by, Livvy looked as worried as he felt. "Hear this, Universe!" she announced. "I don't want anything for my birthday or Christmas. I just want people to buy houses here at Moon Ridge."

"They will," he said, but he didn't believe it. Why should things start going right all of a sudden? Moon Ridge would go bust and Livvy would disappear just like Damien.

Socko needed a shower, but when he got home he felt too tired to haul himself up the stairs. Instead, he fell onto the sofa and stared at the ceiling.

His view of the ceiling was eclipsed. A wrinkled face hovered over him. "What're you doing, Socko, worrying about Damien again?" The old man didn't wait for an answer. "Worrying never solved a thing. You either fix the problem or you forget about it. You tried to fix it yesterday, but it couldn't be fixed. It's time to forget it and move on." He turned the wheelchair toward the kitchen.

"What if I can't forget it?"

The wheelchair turned slowly back his way. "You have to. It's time to cut your losses, private. Damien is collateral damage."

Socko pushed himself up on his elbows. "What's collateral damage?"

193

"The unintended damage caused by an action. You moved out of the neighborhood and Damien joined the gang. End of story, so forget about it." The General wheeled his chair into the kitchen.

"Not gonna happen," Socko mumbled. He was an elephant when it came to not forgetting.

***

Socko was still splat-flat on the couch when Delia came waltzing in from work an hour late. "Big news!" Her face was flushed.

Socko turned his eyes her way, too tired to do more. He hadn't even noticed she was late. Between worrying about Damien and the collapse of Moon Ridge, he was way overscheduled in the worry department.

"Didn't anyone hear me? I said *big news*," Delia repeated, enunciating carefully.

"So spill it, Delia Marie," demanded the General.

Delia folded her arms on top of her stomach. "Guess!"

"I'm not dead yet?" the General ventured.

"Bigger! I overheard a guy in the Home Depot say the day manager at the fast-food place next door got caught helping himself to money out of the cash drawer."

The General raised his bushy brows. "A clerk with sticky fingers, that's your big news?"

"They fired him—which he deserved—and just like that, no more day manager! I walked myself across the parking lot and told them I was there about the job."

Socko sat up fast. "Why?"

"Why? Don't be a doof! Because I need a new job."

Socko had never thought about her leaving the Phat. Didn't she always call it *her* place? "Did you get the job?"

But Delia was spinning the story out, making it last. "The manager looked me over and right away, the usual came up."

"Which is?" the General quizzed.

Delia spread her arms. "Let's just call it my full figure. I dropped the word 'discrimination,' and the temporary day manager got the regional manager, a little bitty thing named Nikki. My manager, Paul, would have said, 'So, sue me,' but Nikki folded fast. They're not very tough out here."

The General was wearing one of his rare smiles. "But *you* sure are!"

"I take after you, old man."

"You got that right, big girl." They both grinned.

"So," she said, "long story short, I start next week."

"But...you can't!" said Socko. "What about Damien and Junebug?"

"Damien..." She waved a hand. "There's no talking to him anymore. And Junebug? Before I leave, she's dumping Rapp. I'll make sure of that if it's the last thing I do. Without that loser she'll be okay."

"Get real, Mom. If she dumps Rapp she'll need her own witness protection program! You will too. He'll know you made her do it."

"If he does, so what? I'll be long gone. Junebug's a big girl, Socko. She can do this thing. She'll be fine."

"No she won't. She'll be dead."

Socko stormed up to his room and fell onto his cot. He was mad—and something else. Relieved? With the connection broken, he couldn't be responsible for Damien. He could concentrate on the life he had here.

But what kind of guy tosses away a friend like a burger wrapper?

If only yesterday had gone down different! What would have happened if Rapp and his boys hadn't come out of Donatelli's? Would Damien have climbed into the truck? Would he be here now? Socko couldn't let go until he found out. Luke would never take him to the old neighborhood again, but what if he drove himself back to the Kludge? He knew the fundamentals of driving. He could feel his heart beating hard in his chest, but he had to find a way to do it. He had to be the stand-up guy Livvy thought he was.

He had barely begun to plan how and when to sneak off in the car when he heard a faint knock on his door.

"Socko, can I come in?" Delia didn't wait for an answer. She walked in and stood over his cot. "I have something for you."

The blue envelope she put in his hand was from the electric company. It was addressed to Louise Rivera. Socko turned the envelope over. On the back was a mess of Scotch tape and the words: FOR SOCKO STARR ONLY. He looked up at his mother.

"No," she said. "I didn't read it. But if Damien asks you to do something stupid, you say no. I didn't have to give this to you, but I trust you, Socko." She made a big point of closing the door behind her when she left.

He wished she hadn't said she trusted him, because this had to be the word he'd been waiting for from Damien, saying to come get him. He tore open the envelope.

The Riveras had a past-due balance of four hundred and thirty-seven dollars—by now their lights had been cut off for sure—but that couldn't be his friend's message. He turned the bill over. Damien's note was scrawled on the back.

> *Socko—thanks for coming back but this is the way it is now. I owe Rapp and the guys. Mom's boyfriend sent her to the ER a couple times and I couldn't do nothing. Rapp and Meat made it so he won't bother her no more. The gang's not bad like we thought. I got brothers now and plenty 2 eat. Don't show up or try to call. If you were still here it would be different. But I gotta think about now.*
>
> *Lil' D*
>
> *PS: Tell your mom to quit messing with Rapp's GF. The message on the car means bizness.*

Socko stumbled to the window. Rapp's message was tagged on the front passenger door, black and heavy. The blast of paint had been so strong it had run under the stencil and dripped down the car door. The tarantula was oozing black blood.

"Mom?" He took the stairs two at a time. He had to make Delia promise to forget about breaking up Rapp and Junebug.

But his mother refused to take the threat seriously. "Once I change jobs, how's Rapp gonna find me?" Like the General, she told Socko to forget about it.

Later, lying in the dark, his elephant brain worked overtime wondering what Rapp had done to Louise's boyfriend, afraid it would happen to Delia when she got between Rapp and Junebug—because that was just what she meant to do.

33
LAST ORDERS

Delia pinned her paper hat to her hair. "How do I look?"

Socko shrugged. Her orange and brown smock and slacks were as clean—and as ugly—as they were at the start of any workday.

"Did you notice? New lipstick for my last day!"

Considering all that might happen today, he couldn't believe she was hung up on lipstick. He'd showed her the spider on her car door. She'd covered it with a blast of spray paint of her own and gone right on saying she'd make sure Junebug dumped Rapp.

"Mom, about—"

"Last orders?" she called to the General as he rolled out of the bathroom. "How about a Crispy Fried Salad?" she teased.

"I wouldn't serve that barf to a dog! But I'll take a few of those pies. They go good with the dishwater-weak coffee you serve around here."

"And what can I get for you, young man?" she asked Socko.

"Whatever." It was like he was the only one who knew a planet-destroying meteor was headed for earth. "I'm going with you," he said, following her to the car.

She sighed as she lowered herself into the driver's seat. "It's just a day at work, Socko."

"Mom. About Junebug and Rapp, leave it alone! I'm beggin'!"

"I've worked too hard for that girl and she's worked too hard for herself. She wants to dump him, but she needs a little help and that's where

I come in." She jammed the key in the ignition. "I'll take care of it before I come home."

"You actually think Rapp will just let her dump him?" She had never watched Rapp dangle somebody off the roof of the Kludge. "Seriously, I gotta go with you!"

His mother looked past him and smiled. "Good morning, Luke."

"Morning, Delia." Luke strolled over and rested his palms on the edge of the open window. "It's your last day, right? They throwing you a party or anything?"

"Yeah, all the burgers I can eat."

"Sounds good to me." Luke walked to the company truck parked in his driveway next door.

"Hey!" Livvy sprinted across the street from her house. "I'll ride with you guys to the clubhouse." She walked up to Manuel's old car. "Be careful today, Ms. Starr." She turned away fast and climbed into the back of the truck, squeezing in behind the tarp-covered bushes Luke and Socko would be planting around the pool.

Delia raised her penciled eyebrows. "You been talking to Livvy about today?"

"Yeah." Socko jerked on the handle of the car's back door—he'd forgotten it had been permanently locked by a sideswiping collision. "At least *she* listens."

His mother put the car in reverse and backed out.

"Hey, wait!" He jogged along beside her.

"You worry too much. It'll be fine," she called. The car sped away.

Luke stuck his head out the truck window. "Ya coming, Socko?"

Socko stared after his mother until she made the turn and the car disappeared behind a house.

"Come on, man! It's only gonna get hotter."

Socko knew he should be sitting in Manuel's old bomber beside his mother. Instead, he climbed into the back of the truck with Livvy. They sat facing each other, sharing the narrow space between the tailgate and the blue tarp.

"Worried about your mom?" Livvy asked.

"Yeah."

"Me too," she said.

They rode in silence for a minute. "Did I tell you my parents are throwing a big open house for real estate agents next week? They're even filling the pool. So, no more private skate park."

"It's too hot for skating anyway." Socko appreciated the fact that she was trying to distract him, but it wasn't working. Something was going to go down today in the old neighborhood, something bad.

And when it did, he'd be planting bushes around a swimming pool.

***

Livvy gave Socko a last concerned look before disappearing into the club-house. Today she was helping her mother set up the new headquarters of Holmes Homes. Livvy's parents had decided to locate their smaller office within the subdivision, and the office had to be ready for the open house.

"Sure would be better to plant these when the weather is cool," said Luke, tossing back the tarp. "But according to Mrs. H. the area around the clubhouse has got to look good by next Sunday." They hauled bushes out of the truck and set them down at the edge of the pool. Soaked with sweat, Socko wrestled the last bush out, then stopped to raise the tailgate. He turned and rested his back against the truck—by now his mom was pulling into the parking lot at the Phat.

Staring at the empty pool, he tried to imagine past this day. He was in the water swimming…his mom was on her new job…today had gone off without a hitch.

They just had to get from now to then.

"This is gonna be a neat trick," said Luke as they dug closely spaced holes around the pool. It had been Socko's idea to plant a hedge just past the concrete deck that edged the pool. With the hedge in place, a swim-mer would see greenery, not the vast wasteland of scraped earth and piled tree trunks.

They planted the first row of bushes in silence.

Luke lifted his ball cap and wiped his forehead with the shoulder of his T-shirt. "Earth to Socko. You okay?"

Socko realized he was just standing there. "Yeah, I'm fine I guess."

"Take a break. In this heat, you gotta pace yourself." Luke snagged a bottle of water out of the cooler in the truck, then jumped into the shallow end of the empty pool and walked down the incline. He squatted in the shade of the wall at the deep end. Socko followed him and sat down, his back against the wall.

Luke took a swig out of the bottle and passed it to him.

As the icy water jolted down his throat, Socko tried to think of a way to bring up the situation with his mom. He needed to talk about it or bust. If Luke said to forget it, he'd relax a little. Maybe he *did* worry too much.

Taking the water bottle back, Luke gave him a sidelong glance. "Now, tell me what's bugging you."

Socko heaved a sigh of relief and told Luke about Rapp and Junebug and what might go down because it was his mother's last day at the Phat. "She thinks she's gonna bust up Rapp and Junebug and everything will be okay!"

Although he barely commented, Luke was definitely listening. When Socko finished, Luke looked worried too. It didn't fix things, but Socko appreciated the company.

After the break, even though the temperature was climbing, Luke picked up the pace. At noon they wolfed the lunch Ceelie had packed, then went right back to work.

"What time does your mom get off?" Luke asked, tamping the last bush into the ground with the sole of his boot.

"Three."

"Guess that cuts out the possibility of showers."

Socko did a double take. "Are we going back to the neighborhood?"

"Yup. Soon as we rehydrate." They'd chugged down all the water in the cooler, but Luke led Socko over to the hose that snaked from the wall of the clubhouse and twisted the tap. Water bubbled out the metal end of the hose as Luke passed it to him. Although it was warm and hose-flavored, it was the best water Socko had ever tasted. He was actually going to do something, and Luke was going to help.

"Chances are, everything'll be fine." Luke took the hose, the water splatting on the ground at his feet. "But we'll be there if your mom needs backup."

"You gonna get in trouble for using the truck?"

Luke swallowed half a dozen big gulps. "Nope. Mrs. H. has some stuff that needs to be dropped off in town." He handed the hose to Socko and headed for the clubhouse. Luke held the door for Livvy, who was coming out.

As she walked toward him, Socko noticed the blue shirt Livvy was wearing. It made her eyes look bluer. "Hi, Socko," she said.

"Hi."

She held her hair back and drank out of the running hose in Socko's hand. "You guys done for the day?"

"Pretty much." Socko twisted the tap shut.

"Good. I'll catch a ride."

"Uh…we're not going home," he said.

She stared into his eyes until he looked away. "You're going back to the old neighborhood again, aren't you?"

He nodded once.

"I have to come with you!"

"I don't think Luke'll go for bringing the boss's daughter along."

"Then we won't ask him." She scrambled up onto the truck bed.

"Come on, Livvy. I don't want to get him in trouble for helping me out."

"He can't get in trouble for something he doesn't know about!" She covered herself with a tarp.

Sometimes it's better to ask for forgiveness than to ask for permission, Socko thought.

The tarp had barely stopped moving when Luke came out of the clubhouse, looking over the address on the envelope in his hand. He tossed a bunch of garden tools into the back of the truck. Socko hoped Luke would figure out she was under there, but even though a shovel handle hit the tarp, Livvy kept still.

Socko knew he should tell. Luke was doing him a huge favor.

But he still hadn't said anything when they passed Uncle Eddie's guard booth, and by then it was too late.

34
JUNEBUG

Fear prickled Socko's scalp. The Tarantulas were in the parking lot of the Phat. Rapp's Trans Am was parked next to Delia's old junker. Damien sat cross-legged on the hood of Delia's car—nobody sat on Rapp's classic. The others stood around, smoking. Rapp paced.

"I don't think they noticed us," said Luke, parking the truck so it was hidden by an oversized van. "And if we're lucky they won't recognize us walking in. What the—" Something in the rearview mirror had caught his eye.

When Socko turned around, Livvy was stepping over the tailgate onto the bumper. Her hair looked damp, her face hot. She walked up to Socko's open window. "Sorry, Luke. It was my idea."

Luke looked at Socko. "You knew about it?"

"Yeah, I knew."

Luke shook his head. "We'll talk about this later."

"I just had to have one last Phat burger," Livvy joked.

Socko grabbed her arm as she turned toward the Phat. "You can't see them, but the gang is right over there, across the parking lot."

"Ohmygosh!"

"If I had time I'd take you back, but I don't," Luke whispered. "So this is what you're going to do, Livvy. You're going to get in this truck and duck down behind the jump seat while Socko and I go inside. Keep the windows rolled and lock the doors."

"I'll die of heat stroke!"

Luke ignored her. "Socko, walking to the door we can use this van parked next to us for cover, then that Suburban'll hide us some." He reached back and lifted a big straw hat off the pile of tools that jammed the space behind the driver's seat. He dropped it on Socko's head right over Damien's Superman lid. "They only saw me once, but they know you, so keep that hat pulled down. They may recognize us, they may not. Either way we're gonna walk in like all we want is a burger and fries."

"Let me walk with you on the side that faces the parking lot," Livvy urged. Her voice was excited, like this was some kind of adventure. "Please? They've never seen me before."

Socko didn't like the idea.

He could tell by the way Luke dragged his hand down his face that he didn't either, but it was a logical suggestion—and leaving Livvy in the truck wasn't exactly a great plan.

"All right," Luke said, "but we act casual and we don't look at 'em. You got that, Livvy?"

"Got it." She took Socko's arm as he climbed out. "Pretend I'm your girlfriend," she whispered. "They don't expect you to have one, right?"

"That's for sure," he whispered back.

Casual, thought Socko, but being casual was hard under the circumstances—especially with Livvy hanging onto his arm.

He meant to go through the door without looking back—but at the last second he looked over his shoulder. A shock went through him. Despite the farm-boy hat and the fake girlfriend, Damien was watching him.

Livvy tugged him through the door and the smell of fryer grease engulfed him.

Luke strode up to the counter.

The paper hat sat on Delia's head at a crazy angle. "Socko, Luke—Livvy!" As soon as Socko's mother said her name, Livvy let go of his arm. "What're you doing here?"

"We had a hankering for a Phat Burger," said Luke.

"I want the three of you out of here right now." Delia cocked her

204

head toward the front windows. "We have a situation going on, and I got more than I can handle already."

Luke leaned across the counter. "You clock out in twenty minutes. I walk you to your car. End of situation."

"Not quite." Delia pointed out Junebug huddled in the far corner of the back booth. "I got that girl in a mess of trouble and I have to get her out of here," she whispered. "May I take your order?" she asked Luke more loudly. They were beginning to attract attention.

Socko hurried to the booth, Livvy right behind him. He had concentrated on convincing his mom to leave Junebug and Rapp alone, not on what would happen if she didn't.

Collateral damage, he thought, scooting into the seat opposite his old babysitter. *But not if I can help it,* he added silently as Livvy slid in beside him. Junebug had saved him so many times, it had to be his turn to save her.

It should've been impossible, but Junebug had gotten thinner since he saw her last. The nurse's watch hung loose on her arm. In front of her on the table was a super-sized milkshake. Socko tapped the back of her hand with his finger. "Hi, Junebug."

"Yeah, hi."

"This is Livvy."

Junebug's eyes settled on Livvy. "You his girlfriend?"

Livvy hesitated. "Maybe."

Socko turned toward her fast.

"I said *maybe.*"

"Lucky you," said Junebug. "He's a good kid."

Livvy drew a sudden sharp breath. "What happened to your arms?"

Junebug checked out the bruises that braceleted her skinny wrists. "I tried to fight back and got dragged. Old news. That was last week." Junebug swiped at an eye with her knuckles, then grimaced, seeing the smudges of blue eye shadow on them. "Oh great, now I'm melting."

Livvy stared at Junebug as if she were some exotic butterfly. "You're still very beautiful."

"Ugly would be better right about now, but thanks." She gave Livvy a weak smile.

"What went down with Rapp?" Socko asked.

"I had him meet me here. Your mom's idea. Delia said this was neutral territory." Socko saw Livvy's eyes dart to Junebug's hands as she nervously tapped on the tabletop. "Rapp bought me a shake. I broke up with him. He stormed out. But I knew that was too easy. He was back in ten minutes—with his posse."

Junebug's straw made a nervous squeak against the cup's plastic lid as she slid it up and down. "Are they still out front?"

"Uh-huh," said Socko.

"So, what're you doing just sitting here?" Livvy asked.

"Basically?" Junebug lifted her bony shoulders and let them drop. "Waiting to die." A shadow fell across the table. She cringed and slid toward the wall.

Socko looked up. "It's okay. This is my friend Luke."

"Hey, Junebug." Luke dropped to a squat. "I'm gonna get you out of here," he said softly. The muscles in his neck looked tense. Socko could tell Luke didn't like any of this.

Junebug bit her lip as she looked Luke over. "Thanks for the offer. You seem strong and all, but if you think I'm walking out those doors you better think again."

"There's a window in the ladies' room," Socko said.

Livvy gave him a funny look.

"I cleaned the restrooms a few times for money," he told her, then turned back to Junebug. "If you go out that way they won't see you."

"You think you could climb out?" Luke asked.

Junebug looked at the restroom door, then back at Luke. "Guess I could fly if I had to. But that window's real high."

"I'll boost you up," said Socko.

"No." Livvy took a deep breath. "I will. It's the *ladies'* room, Socko."

Junebug raised an eyebrow at Livvy. "You sure?"

Livvy nodded.

"Now hold on." Luke puffed up his cheeks and blew out. Socko knew he was wondering how out of control things were going to get with the boss's daughter.

Socko didn't like the idea either, but there were several people in the booths facing the restroom doors, so it couldn't be him. And they had to sneak Junebug out, period. "All right," Socko said. "Livvy goes in with Junebug."

"Okay, okay," Luke whispered. "We'll pull around back. Don't climb out until you see us, you got that, girls?"

Junebug picked up her giant purse. Hugging it, she teetered toward the ladies' room door on her high-heeled sandals like she was so scared, she had forgotten how to walk.

"Be careful," Socko whispered as Livvy slipped out of the booth. Her hair flared as she turned to look back at him, then she quickly disappeared through the restroom door after Junebug.

Delia sent Socko and Luke out to the truck with two big bags of carryout. With his hat pulled down, Socko walked so Luke stayed between him and the gang. This time he watched the ground, but for a moment it felt like the easy mind link he and his old friend always had was back. Damien knew that one more person had gone in the door than had come out. Would he report that fact to Rapp?

Out of sight behind the van, they climbed into the truck. Luke backed out. His straw hat jammed down, Socko stared straight ahead as they left the parking lot.

Luke drove several blocks before doubling back to make the turn on the street that went behind the Phat. "With any luck we'll be there and gone in two minutes," said Luke.

Socko gripped the seat. "What about my mom?"

"She'll come off shift and walk out the door. Rapp'll see she's alone and go in after Junebug. By the time he figures it out, your mom will be long gone."

Ahead on the left was the orange and brown box that was Phat Burger. Before the front parking lot was hidden by the building, Socko had a quick view of the gang. While all other eyes were watching the front of the restaurant, his friend's were on the truck. To score major points with Rapp, all Damien had to do was tell him that a suspicious pickup had just pulled in behind the Phat.

Luke eased in next to the Dumpster and parked, but he kept the engine idling. He checked out the space behind the seats. "Only room for one," he said. "Junebug'll have to hide under the tarp like Livvy did."

A frosted window on the back of the building lifted and a skinny arm slid out. The big black purse dangling from the hand whumped to the ground, spilling as it rolled onto its side. Next out was a foot with an ankle-buster sandal hanging off the toes.

Socko got out of the truck and ran toward the building. "Jump!" he whispered hoarsely. He kept glancing to his right, sure that at any second Rapp and his boys would surge around the corner. "Come on!"

When Junebug rolled out of the window, Socko caught her and stumbled back a couple of steps.

"Get her to the truck," Livvy called softly from above.

He looked up for a fraction of a second. Livvy's blonde hair hung down, sweeping the dingy cinder block wall, then he turned and staggered toward the truck. Behind him Livvy's sneakers smacked the ground.

Luke was standing in the truck bed. "Hand her up," he told Socko.

"My purse! My purse!" Junebug whispered frantically as they covered her with the tarp. "I got my books in it, my certificate—all my stuff!"

"I'll get it." Livvy sprinted back over to the fat pig of a purse. While she swept what had spilled back in, Luke dove into the driver's seat. The purse in her arms, Livvy scrambled into the truck's jump seat. "Come on, Socko, get in!" She reached over the seat in front of her and slapped it. "Now!"

Instead, Socko closed the passenger door behind her. What if Luke was wrong about the gang letting his mother leave? He stuck his head through the open window. "Get 'em outta here, Luke. I'll ride with Mom."

"No!" Although her lips were almost blue with fear, Livvy tried to push the seat forward so she could get out. "If you stay, I stay too!"

"*That* ain't gonna happen." Luke crossed his arms on his chest and blew out. "We'll *all* sit here 'til your mom pulls out in…" He checked his watch. "Three minutes."

"No, Luke. I'm sure Damien spotted us," Socko whispered.

"If he had, they'd be all over us by now. Or else he's still your friend." Luke leaned across the seat and pushed the door open. "Get in. As soon as Delia comes out, we roll."

They sat, the engine still idling. Socko took off the straw hat and rolled up the brim in his hands. "How're we going to know when she comes out?"

Luke pointed out the narrow strip of street visible beyond the edge of the building. Delia's car would cross that street as she drove away.

"Assuming they let her get to her car," Socko mumbled. Windows down, they listened for anything that might let them know Delia had walked out the front door of the building.

But all the sounds Socko had missed in the silence of Moon Ridge got in the way. The AC unit behind the Phat roared, and somewhere a street or two over some guys were arguing, a truck beeped as it backed up.

"So, this is where you're from." Despite all the noise, Livvy was whispering.

When he turned around, she was staring at the tarantula painted on the Dumpster. "Yeah," he whispered back. "This is where I'm from."

"Ten seconds." Luke stared at his watch. "Now!"

Although the danger meter at the back of Socko's neck was going crazy, nothing happened. Then a wall of sound surged over the building, a tidal wave of four-letter words and electronic bass that he could feel like a second heart throbbing in his chest.

Rapp had unleashed the power of the Trans Am's mighty stereo. Rapp knew it was three o'clock too. Was he signifying that his patience had run out, or was he covering up something that was happening to Socko's mom? Socko grabbed the handle and threw the door open.

A hand gripped his upper arm. "Wait!" Luke ordered.

The wait was no more than a minute, but during those sixty seconds Socko felt as if he would fly apart not knowing what was happening on the other side of the building.

"There she is," said Luke.

Socko saw a turquoise car door flash by, then an orange one. Delia was at the wheel, staring straight ahead.

"Go!" said Livvy. "Go!" As Luke pulled across the street that ran up the side of the Phat, Socko felt the blast of the radio full force; the parked Trans Am seemed to pulsate. The Tarantulas were gone—they must have swarmed the Phat as soon as Delia left. Only Damien, the lookout, had stayed with the car.

Socko touched the *S* on the Superman lid. Maybe Damien saw him, maybe not. If he did, Socko hoped Damien would know he was saying thanks.

For once in his life Damien had kept his mouth shut.

***

"Nice little jaunt?" asked Uncle Eddie, raising the barrier arm.

"All in a day's work," said Luke as he pulled through the gate.

Socko glanced back at the wooden bar and the old man in the guard booth. Both would be a joke to Rapp if he wanted in, but first he'd have to figure out that Junebug was here, and to storm Moon Ridge he'd have to know Moon Ridge existed. If Damien hadn't ratted him out when he was right there just feet away from the gang, why would he spill now?

Livvy knelt on the jump seat and slid the window behind it open. "Junebug? You can come out now."

The plastic tarp stirred. Pushing it aside, Junebug sat up slowly. She watched the blank faces of brand-new houses stream by. Despite the heat, she kept the tarp wrapped around her like a blanket.

Socko wished he was riding in back with her. He'd tell her that this place was weird at first but that you get used to it. He'd explain that Moon Ridge was like one of those islands where birds evolved, losing the ability to fly because there were no major predators.

"Shoot," said Luke as they pulled into Socko's driveway. "Looks like I'm heading back to the city." He snagged Mrs. Holmes's envelope, which stuck up from between the seats.

"Sorry about that," said Socko.

"You're safe from him here," Livvy assured Junebug through the open window.

But Socko was worried about a different "him" as he climbed out of the truck. He trotted up the driveway, leaving Livvy to bring Junebug inside.

"Delia Marie!" the General rasped as Socko opened the door. "This is completely unacceptable! We've already done our share. More than our share. We can't save everybody!"

"What did you want us to do? Let her gangsta boyfriend kill her?" Socko's mother yelled back, tossing her paper hat in the garbage.

"Who do I look like, Mother Teresa? There must be someplace else she can go."

"If there was, do you think we would've brung her here?"

Socko watched Livvy help Junebug down out of the truck. "General, sir?"

"Don't interrupt, young man. Your mother and I are having a difference of opinion!"

"Take a look."

"At what?" But the old man rolled his chair over to the window. "Gonna break her fool neck," he muttered, watching Junebug stand, swaying slightly in her too-tall heels.

"She's kind of in shock," Socko said. "Up 'til a few minutes ago she thought she was going to die today."

"Hang out with the wrong people and…" The words fizzled. "Skinny little thing, isn't she? Wears way too much makeup."

"But she's a good girl," Delia insisted. "She was just in over her head."

The General sighed. "All I wanted out of our little arrangement was peace and quiet. No fuss. And what do I get? Homeless families, girls with crazy boyfriends…all kinds of mess. You knew there was going to be a problem—I heard you two whispering about it. Why didn't you talk to me? We're a family."

Socko and Delia stared at each other over the old man's head. When, amidst all the complaints and threats to "call my lawyer," had they become a family?

But they had.

Delia put her hand on the General's shoulder as the front door slowly opened and Livvy helped Junebug inside.

"Mother Teresa?" Delia said softly to the General. "I got someone I'd like you to meet."

35

MY SUMMER ON THE MOON

H is name is Rapp Robinson and he drives a maroon Trans Am," Socko said, putting Uncle Eddie on alert. "I don't think he's going to come, but if he does, don't try to do anything. Just call the cops."

"I saw that girl sit up in the truck after you all pulled through. Wondered why she was riding back there. I get off in half an hour, but if you want I can sleep in the booth." Uncle Eddie picked up the flashlight he always kept handy and swung it like a weapon.

Socko took a good look at the old guy and his flashlight and told him to go home after his shift. If Rapp showed up in the middle of the night, Uncle Eddie would get himself killed—or else he'd sleep right through it.

All that evening Socko prowled quietly from window to door, checking the road. Sometimes he stopped and rolled his shoulders, but his muscles stayed tight.

The General and Delia watched a couple of game shows. Junebug's eyes were pointed toward the set, but after a little while she curled up on the sofa, her sparkly shoes on the floor.

Socko's mother and great-grandfather quietly debated where to put the girl for the night. They had a room for Junebug, but no bed. "Leave her here on the couch," the General said. "I'll be close by in the recliner if anything happens."

Socko wondered, had the General or Uncle Eddie ever noticed they were old? What would either one of them do if something actually *did* happen?

***

The next day Livvy's mom offered them a fold out couch, which Luke and Socko horsed up the stairs. Without even opening it, Junebug stretched out and went to sleep again.

It was late afternoon by the time she wandered down the stairs. Socko and Livvy were playing cards with the General. Delia was reading an old magazine, enjoying the luxury of two days off between jobs.

"Hi." Junebug stood in the door, her thin arms wrapped around herself.

"Cuppa coffee?" the General asked, laying down his cards.

Junebug nodded.

Socko was surprised when his great-grandfather made the coffee himself. He wasn't Mother Teresa yet, but he sure was headed that way.

As the General handed her the cup, Junebug's eyes seemed to focus for the first time. They were fixed on the hand holding the cup. "How do you do you even zip your fly with those long nails?"

"How is that any business of yours?" he shot back. "Actually I do almost everything with great difficulty," he admitted. "But I got too much arthritis in my hands to cut 'em myself, so I'm kind of stuck."

"You should've told me!" said Delia. "I got scissors." Socko and his mother had never thought the General might need help with cutting his nails or anything else. They'd taken his orneriness as an order to leave him alone.

"Scissors! I can do better than that." Junebug disappeared into the living room where her fat purse sat on the end of the couch. She returned with a small plastic case and a piece of paper. "I'm a certified nurse's aide." She presented the General with the paper and unzipped the case with a flourish.

"I'm sure you are," he said, offering her his hand.

After Junebug had cut, buffed, and filed his nails, the old man

214

admired them for a moment. Then he zeroed in on her with his good eye. "You want a real challenge?"

"Feet?" she asked.

"You know it, sister!"

"Sure thing, but first I better let my aunt know I'm okay. Delia, can I borrow your emergency phone? My cell's gone. I took everything out of my bag, but it wasn't in there."

Socko remembered the contents of Junebug's purse scattered on the asphalt behind the Phat. Livvy must have missed the phone in her hurry to pick everything up and get out of there.

***

"It's been two days," said Livvy. She and Socko were in the back of the truck, heading toward the day's planting site.

"I know," said Socko. But something was still bothering him. Despite being a Tarantula, Damien hadn't ratted him out when he left with Junebug. Damien was still more loyal to him than he was to Rapp—and all Socko could do in return was go back to planting with Livvy and Luke?

He tried to come up with something as he dug holes. He'd told Damien he'd have his back, but so far Damien had covered for him every time.

It was late afternoon, and the sun was beating down by the time Socko walked over to the guard booth. "See anything?" he asked Uncle Eddie.

"Nope. No desperadoes, hoodlums, horse thieves, racketeers, mobsters, or malefactors. Not even a stray dog." The old man sounded disappointed. "You think we're in the clear?"

"I guess."

Uncle Eddie gazed at the empty road that ran in front of the subdivision. "I'm thinking about bumping the threat level down from orange to green."

"What does green mean?"

"Low probability of a terrorist attack."

"I don't know...you might wait another day or two."

"Okey dokey."

"See ya, Uncle Eddie."

***

Socko walked along, watching his feet and thinking thoughts that went about as far as a hamster running in its wheel.

"Hey! Pool's full!" When he looked up, Livvy was striding toward him wearing a polka-dot two-piece swimsuit.

He avoided looking at her white stomach with its frowny belly button, concentrating instead on her weird tan. Like his, her pale skin turned bright pink in the sun. Her burn started and stopped so abruptly it was like she was still wearing her shirt and shorts. He pointed to the flexible foam logs resting on her shoulders. "What're those?"

"Pool noodles." She tossed him the purple one. "Want to stop at your house and change into your swimsuit?"

Socko didn't have one. "Why waste time? I can swim in my shorts."

Livvy dipped a toe into water that was pink with the sunset. "Nice!" The pool noodle she tossed in landed with a splash.

Socko threw his in too and shucked his T-shirt. Livvy stared at his pale chest a moment, then looked away. "Let's jump on three!" she said as he draped his shirt on one of the bushes he and Luke had planted.

Embarrassed by his own exposed skin, he launched before she'd even said "one." The water was cool but not cold. His feet touched bottom. He opened his eyes in response to the explosion of Livvy hitting the water. Slowed by the water, she drifted down, her eyes open too. Her hair, tinted orange, swirled around her face like flames, and silvery bubbles escaped from the corners of her mouth. Together, they popped to the surface.

"Ohmygosh! This is so great!" Livvy slicked back her wet hair with both hands, then paddled lazily toward the yellow pool noodle. She hung her arms over it.

He fanned his own arms in big circles and tried to act cool. Was she his girlfriend?

"There's that thing at the school tomorrow, the open house?" she said. "You think your mom could take us?"

"She starts her new job tomorrow."

She frowned. "My parents can't take us either. They're meeting with the guy who wants to buy those houses on Orbit Lane." The deal was being offered by another builder, one who was buying distressed properties at bargain prices, then finishing the houses and selling them at a profit. Livvy had told Socko that her parents didn't like the idea, but that the sale of six houses would make the partners happy. "Maybe Junebug can drive us."

"Or we could give it a pass." School would start soon enough.

He rolled onto his back and hung still in the water, listening to the hum of the pool pump, smelling the chlorine. For a second he imagined he was on the roof with Damien, but it felt faint and faraway. He was in a swimming pool with a girl. He was wondering what it would be like to kiss a girl in a pool when a wave surged over his face. He stood up, choking, chlorine burning his nose. "Why'd ya do that?"

"To get your attention?"

He vaguely remembered some *blugga-blubba* sounds coming through the water. "Did you have to get my attention by drowning me?"

"Sorry." She stood up too. A water droplet dangled from each earlobe. "What do you think our new school will be like?"

"I dunno." His old school had been as dead and decayed as the president it was named after. According to Livvy the new school was almost as new as the houses in Moon Ridge Estates. How was he supposed to know what *that* would be like?

"Come on, Socko, predict."

"I predict...rubber pizza in the cafeteria."

She twisted her wet hair with one hand and pressed it against the back of her head. The water held it in place. "What do you think will happen the first day?"

"We'll write what we did on our summer vacation." His first day last school year, Socko had written about exploring the North Pole. He'd read a book about it over the summer while sweating in their apartment. The assignment was dumb anyway. No one at GC did anything on their summer vacation.

"Last summer I went to Switzerland," Livvy said. She scooped up water in both hands and watched it slip away between her fingers.

"And this summer you're saving Moon Ridge Estates."

"And Junebug." She dove under the darkening water and then came back up. "And Luke and his family. You can write about that too—unless we're in the same English class. Then I call it."

She'd forgotten he'd be in seventh, she'd be in eighth, and even if they were in the same grade, she'd be in the smart class. He'd be in the one where kids killed time sharpening pencils.

But even if by some fluke they were in the same class, he'd still write about it. He already had a title picked out: My Summer on the Moon.

"It's all good," Delia had said that morning. "Rapp is history and tomorrow I start a new job!"

But even if they never saw Rapp again and her new job was great, it *wasn't* all good—it was just different. A lot had happened since he and Damien had busted the Hurtler celebrating the start of summer vacation.

Like meeting Livvy.

He thought again about kissing a girl in a pool, but Livvy was climbing out.

36
A CALL FROM JUNE GRIMES

Delia tugged at the blouse of her new uniform. "Is it too tight?"

The General wheeled his chair closer and squinted his good eye at her.

Don't say it, Socko begged silently. The uniform looked like it had been painted on.

"Avoid sneezing!" the old man advised.

"Oh, dear!" Delia clasped her hands.

"I think she looks hot!" said Junebug, who was pulling Delia's hair back into a bun.

"Hot?" the General snorted, the lone eye staring. "The color looks good on you, Delia Marie." Orange and brown had been replaced by a pale blue. He gave her arm a pat. "Anyway, it's not the uniform, it's the girl *in* the uniform. Give 'em heck, honey!"

She winked at him. "You know I will."

Socko walked Delia to the car and held the door. She climbed in, setting her purse on the seat beside her carefully. An employee handbook stuck out of the top. "That reminds me," she said. "The new place won't let staff bring food home. It sure is going to be different working for a chain! So, no more greasy burgers—unless I pay for them. And you can forget that!"

"One of us better learn how to cook," said Socko.

"One of us already knows how to cook." Delia waved at the General, who was watching from the window.

Great, thought Socko. SOS on a regular basis.

Delia tapped her cheek. "Come on, give me a little sugar."

When he leaned in and kissed her cheek, she touched the *S* on his hat. "Big day for both of us, huh? New job for me. New school for you. Have a great time at the open house."

"I'm going?" He'd written the whole thing off.

"Junebug's driving. Livvy's parents are lending her a car. Livvy worked it out."

"Hope it's the convertible," he said, although all he really wanted to do was slide through the last two weeks of summer, school free.

***

Livvy let herself in without knocking. She was wearing a yellow knit dress and yellow sandals. "I know. Too yellow, but Mother insisted." She stopped and stared at Socko. "Tell me you're going to change."

He glanced down at his cutoffs, sneakers without socks, the T-shirt that said, "I Brake for Cheese!" He'd tried to dress up for the open house, but his one pair of good pants was suddenly too short. Going as himself wasn't his first choice, but it turned out to be his only option.

"Pretend you don't know me." Socko adjusted Damien's lid, pushing it down lower.

"Not the hat! Please, please, please! Anything but the Superman hat!"

"Not negotiable." Wearing the hat was as close as he could get to having his best friend with him—plus today he needed all the invincibility he could get. "I'll walk ten steps behind you."

She was about to launch another attack on his outfit when the cell phone on the kitchen counter rang.

"Saved by the bell," mumbled the General.

Socko vaulted into the kitchen, sure that something had gone wrong on his mom's new job, but when he picked up the phone, it said June Grimes was calling. Someone had found Junebug's lost phone. "Hello?" he said.

The breathless voice on the other end of the line was a kid's. "He's on his way!"

"Damien? Is that you?"

"No! This is the ghost of the cock-a-roach we zapped in the microwave! *Yeah,* it's me. Who else would risk getting obliviated to warn you? Listen fast. I only got seconds while Meat runs a bag of puppy chow up to his mom. Rapp went to Junebug's aunt and said he wanted to apologize to Junebug and she bought it. Her aunt didn't know the address but she told him Moon Ridge Estates. He lit out of here, like, fifteen, twenty minutes ago. I'm sorry, I'm sorry—gotta bail!"

"Damien!" Socko heard the click. Fifteen, twenty minutes ago? He had to mobilize, but Damien had always been the one with ideas. The phone in his hand rang again. He popped the button without checking the caller ID. "Damien!"

"Holy mother of Mike!" Eddie Corrigan's voice sputtered in his ear. "That guy you warned me about just drove up."

"Whatever you do, don't raise the gate!"

"Raise the gate? He broke it right off with his car when I wouldn't let him in! Couldn't stop him, but I put a honey of a dent in his trunk with my flashlight."

The phone nearly slid out of Socko's sweaty hand. He caught it and pressed it to his ear. "Which way did he go?"

"The long way. Turned left instead of right."

"Did you call 911? Uncle Eddie? Did you—" The phone went dead. Socko stared at it stupidly. Delia's cheapo pay-as-you-go phone had just run out of minutes.

When he looked up, the General and Livvy were in the kitchen doorway. "What the devil is going on?" asked his great-grandfather.

"Junebug's old boyfriend." Socko kept his voice down. Although Junebug was upstairs, he wanted to make sure she didn't hear what was going down. "He just drove his car through the gate—broke it clean off."

221

"Rapp's coming here?" Livvy gasped.

"Call 911," the General ordered.

"Can't," Socko whispered. "The phone's dead."

They both turned to Livvy, who was permanently attached to her cell. She held out the sides of her skinny knit dress. "No pockets. I'll run across the street and call from home."

Socko practically stepped on her bare heels as they raced out his door and across the street to her front door.

She tried to turn the knob. "I must've locked it!"

"Key?" he asked.

She rested her forehead against the door and closed her eyes. "No pockets."

"Go back to my house, get inside. I'll run to Luke's."

"I'm going with you!"

"No!" They were arguing about who would do what when a maroon Trans Am blew past the entrance to Tranquility Way. Socko heard the skid, then a squeal as Rapp threw it into reverse.

In a heartbeat the car sat idling in the street in front of Livvy's house. Rapp hung an arm out the window and gave the door a slap, fingers spread so the spider tattoo near his thumb was prominent. "Yo, Socko."

He stepped in front of Livvy. "Hey, Rapp."

"This your new place?"

"No!" Livvy stepped out from behind him. "*I* live here."

"So, where do *you* live, Socko?"

"On the other side of the project." Socko could see the General's white face at the window across the street, his wrinkled palms pressed to the glass.

"Where?" Rapp demanded. "Junebug called, said she's ready to go. I ain't got all day."

Socko pointed down the street. "Okay...so...you turn around, get back on the circle, then make a right at Eclipse, then—"

"Climb in."

"The address is 327 Eclipse. It's real easy."

"Get in."

"Sure, okay." By now Uncle Eddie had called 911; help would be here any second. But just in case, Socko turned to Livvy. "Tell Uncle Eddie I'll help him out later."

"No!" She grabbed his hand and started to run, dragging him along. Rounding the back corner of the house, she gave one last hard tug and pulled him out of sight. "You are not getting in that car!"

The engine roared, growing suddenly louder—and the Trans Am whipped around the corner of the house.

Livvy screamed, but the car's ferocious lunge stopped. Rapp's tires churned the dirt as they fought to get traction. Still holding Livvy's hand, Socko jerked her in a new direction. "Cross the street!" They ducked behind a house on the other side of Tranquility and kept running. Rapp must have driven over a curb as he followed them and knocked his muffler loose. Like a dog that had just had its muzzle taken off, the snarl of the engine exploded, but the sound seemed to be going away from them.

Livvy fell back against the wall of an empty house and closed her eyes. Struggling for breath, Socko watched her heartbeat tick in one eyelid. Her eyes opened. "Socko, why are you breathing like that?"

"I'm okay." It wasn't a full-blown asthma attack, but he could feel his chest getting tight.

The engine sound was growing louder, and Livvy peered around the corner of the house. "Ohmygosh! He's coming this way!"

Socko looked too. Dragging beneath the car, the muffler clattered and sparked. "Maybe he won't spot us." But the car was slowing.

"Like the yellow dress," Rapp called from the street.

Livvy pulled back. "I told Mother this outfit was a terrible idea!"

"Where's Junebug, Socko? Come on, I just wanna talk to her."

Rapp sounded reasonable but Socko's heart pounded. He knew how quick Rapp's temper could flare up.

"I'm your worst nightmare, kid. Your worst. The longer you make me chase you, the deader you'll be."

"Can you run?" Livvy whispered.

"Yeah," he wheezed.

"If we stay off the roads it'll be hard for him to follow in the car. We'll lose him."

"*I'll* lose him." He held onto her shoulders. "Soon as he…chases me…go to my house…get inside…"

"No! I'm going with you."

"When Rapp says 'dead' he means…like…no longer breathing."

"You're barely breathing right now. You *need* me!"

The Trans Am revved.

"I mean it…get lost!" Before he let go of her shoulders he pulled her toward him fast. He kissed her right on the mouth, then took off.

"What was that about?" Livvy yelled, taking off after him.

"I don't know…quit following me!"

She wouldn't quit following him and Rapp wouldn't quit following them. If only she wasn't wearing that yellow dress. It fluttered like a flag as she ran, leading Rapp on.

They ran through dirt yards, cutting across the spokes of the wheel of streets. But despite the dragging muffler, Rapp didn't hesitate to go off-road. His spinning tires threw up volcanic plumes of dust.

Socko felt as if someone had kicked a hole in his chest. Still, he leapt curbs, pounded across streets. He coughed…and kept going.

"The tubes!" he gasped, jumping another curb. To lose Rapp they ran a zigzag pattern between houses. If they could duck into the drainage pipes on Harvest Moon he could stop, catch his breath, figure out what to do.

The tubes were just ahead when the Trans Am lurched into sight. Rapp's arm hung out the car window. "Run little bunnies! Run, run!"

Shoulders hunched, they barreled through one of the tubes. The small but mighty ant flashed by, and they were out the other side.

"Follow me!" Livvy doubled back, losing Rapp, then veered off and dashed into the see-through house and up the stairs. She danced out onto one of the beams and sat. "Come on, Socko!"

Socko coughed as he ran up the stairs, coughed harder as he stumbled out onto the beam. He sat down hard beside her. "Why…are we here?" he choked. He couldn't see the strategic advantage in hiding in a house without walls, but she was smart, she had to have a reason.

"You can't breathe!"

"I'm breathing!" He gripped the beam with both hands, afraid he might pass out. "I used to…have asthma, but I'll be okay. I…I…just have to calm down." They listened for a minute, but couldn't hear the sound of Rapp's muffler dragging. "Maybe he won't find us," Socko said.

"Maybe not." She glanced at him, then looked away. "Did you ever kiss a girl before?"

"No. That was a first. You?"

"A first."

"Good." Was that the right thing to say? He was in uncharted territory. The hairs on the back of his neck stood up. "You hear that?" Before she could answer, the car came into sight.

"Sorry, Socko, sorry," Livvy whispered. "Coming up here was a stupid idea."

"He still might not see us."

"You think he can miss us with me wearing this dress?"

The Trans Am pulled slowly into the driveway. "Well, what do we have here?" The fingers on the hand hanging out the open window tapped the door lightly.

As Rapp shut it down, the engine made a choking sound.

In the sudden silence Rapp climbed out of the driver's seat and took a slow walk around his "classic" car. A flashlight dent in the trunk harbored a pool of shadow. He kicked the dragging muffler. "Look what you made me do." With his right hand he imitated the shape of a gun, closed one eye, and took aim at each of them. "Bam. Bam."

Livvy barely moved her lips. "Does he have a gun?"

"I dunno."

They both let out an involuntary yelp when Rapp reached through the open car window. He retrieved a pack of cigarettes from his front seat and slid one out. "Why so jumpy? I ain't begun to put the hurt on you yet." The cigarette bobbled in his mouth as he spoke. "Last chance, kiddies." He tossed the cigarette pack through the open window of the Trans Am. "Take me to Junebug and you two are free to go on breathing. I'm bein' generous."

"How'd you even figure out Junebug was here?" Socko called. He already knew it was Junebug's churchy aunt, but the only hope he had was to kill time. By now someone had to have called 911.

"Your buddy told me." Rapp paused to light his cigarette. "Lil' D was happy to draw me a map. More than happy to."

Socko remembered Damien running a finger along the map on the back of the brochure. Could Rapp be telling the truth? Socko closed his eyes a moment, and thought back to Damien's call warning him that Rapp was coming.

"The kid sure is loyal," said Rapp, obviously enjoying the fact that the word "loyal" cut two ways. "I value that in a foot soldier." He glared up at them out of the tops of his eyes. "And in a girlfriend."

Socko looked sideways at Livvy.

"Hey!" Rapp pronged his fingers at them. "Eyes here. This is how it's gonna go—I'm done playin'. You two come down and take me to Junebug."

"*I'll* come down," Socko said. "She stays up here."

"No!" Livvy grabbed Socko's hand. "I don't think he has a gun," she whispered.

Rapp lifted a foot and crushed the cigarette butt against the sole of his boot. "That's it. Playtime's over." He strode toward the house and ran up the stairs, but his boots didn't ring like they did on the metal steps to the roof. The space around Rapp was bigger here—and that made him smaller.

Socko felt the wood give under the gang leader's weight as he placed a foot on the beam. Rapp's gangsta pants usually kept one of his hands busy acting as a belt, but he was going to need to hold his arms out for balance to walk the beam. His boxers ballooned above his drooping waistband. A bead of sweat dripped off his nose as he placed his other boot on the beam. His spread arms bobbled, like he was a kid playing airplane.

Livvy let out a nervous laugh.

Rapp found his balance. "You think that's funny?" He slipped the knife out of his pocket.

Livvy drew a sharp breath.

With one small click, Rapp was big again. The bare blade in his hand caught the light as he took another awkward step. In the distance they heard the faint *waa-waaa* of a police siren. Rapp froze.

Socko squeezed Livvy's hand as the sound grew louder. Someone had made the call.

But the siren never got any closer. Instead it grew fainter and fainter until it faded to nothing.

"Bet some old lady called 911 'cause her kitty's up a tree." Rapp danced a step closer. "This ain't so hard."

"Do like you did last time," Livvy whispered. She reached over and latched onto the next beam with both hands. He did the same. As they slid off the beam they'd been sitting on, Socko heard the twang of the two-by-four's rebound, followed by a thud and a loud groan.

Livvy stuck her landing, but Socko hit the floor off balance and pitched forward. His hands were sliding across the rough wood when something shiny landed in front of him with a *thwack*. The knife that had fallen out of Rapp's hand quivered between his splayed fingers, the blade driven into the floor. Socko looked up.

Rapp lay on the beam above him, his arms and legs wrapped around it.

Gripping the handle of the knife, Socko jerked it free. He pushed the button and retracted the blade.

"Come on, Socko!" Livvy urged. "Come on! Come on!" And they ran.

The knife in his hand felt wrong. He didn't want it, but he didn't want to leave it where Rapp could find it either. Without breaking stride, he dropped the switchblade into one of the plastic pipes sticking out of the ground and followed Livvy as she took cover behind a house.

37
MOON LANDING

They stood, trying to catch their breath so they could run again. "How long can we keep this up?" Livvy gasped.

And that's when it hit him.

He and Livvy were the prey, Rapp was the predator. But in the wild the predator, no matter how superior, lost the prey more often than he caught it—especially if the prey knew the territory.

He grabbed her wrist. "This way!"

She held back. "This way! That way! We can't outrun him. We need a plan!"

"I've got one. Run, now!"

"Now?" They could hear the muffler scraping along the street as the car slowly prowled. "He'll see us!"

"I'm counting on it," Socko said. "We're not running away anymore. We're leading him."

"Leading him where?"

But the car had reached the distance that tripped an imaginary wire. "Go!" Socko yelled, and they took off again.

They zigzagged toward Socko's goal, Rapp sometimes no more than a few car lengths away.

The dragging muffler threw sparks as it bounced along Blue Moon Drive. Socko and Livvy dodged from one house to the next, Livvy's dress the bright flag that waved Rapp on. "Hear that?" Livvy panted. "Another siren!"

"Almost there!" They were running behind a row of houses as the Trans Am paralleled them on the street. Temporarily out of sight, Socko slowed and held out his hand for Livvy to stop. "The clubhouse is just ahead. When I tell you to, we'll run for it."

"We can't get in," said Livvy. "There's no one there."

Rapp leaned on his horn.

"I know!" Socko yelled over the horn blast. "I want you to break left, go around back. Stop at the deep end of the pool."

"Aren't you coming with me?"

"No, but it'll be okay. Trust me."

She stared at him for a long moment. "Don't be a hero."

"Me, a hero? Not a chance. Now, go!"

The horn was still blaring as they pelted toward the brick building. Livvy kept running, but Socko stopped. He was relieved when the yellow dress disappeared around the corner. Behind him the horn blast stopped. He turned and faced the car that idled half a block away.

Rapp floored it.

Socko's legs ached to run but, feet spread, he faced the onrushing car. He stood his ground until its double headlights became the multiple eyes of a hunting spider—and then counted to three. When the Trans Am jumped the curb, Socko bolted for the opposite end of the clubhouse.

The car swerved and kept bearing down on him—if Socko slowed, he'd be under its wheels or splayed across the hood. It hadn't looked like this in his mental plan! He had pictured a lot more space between him and the car's grill. Slapping a hand against the brick wall, his momentum whipped him around the corner and he gained a few feet.

Livvy stood at the deep end of the pool. As if the yellow dress wasn't target enough, she was waving her arms. She'd figured out the plan.

If things had gone as Socko had imagined, he would have had time to get out of the way—but there wasn't time or space. The hedge was just ahead. Desperate, Socko jumped the hedge, took a couple of stumbling steps, and smacked down flat on the water in the shallow end. As he went under, a shock wave billowed past him.

He staggered to his feet. The Trans Am had sailed over him, clearing the shallow end completely and plunging into deep water.

The car's open windows belched bubbles. Water closed over its roof. The engine sputtered and died.

Socko couldn't believe it. His plan had worked!

A police siren wailed in the distance. It was still far away, but getting closer. "Told you I had your back, Damien," Socko said quietly. He heard a splash behind him and turned. Livvy had run along the side of the pool and jumped in at the shallow end.

She stared at the sunken car. "Why doesn't he climb out?"

The bubbles coming up were tiny now, sneaking out from under the hood. All the air inside the car would be gone soon. He'd wanted to stop Rapp, not kill him!

Socko slogged into deeper water, his breath walloping in and out of his lungs. After nearly killing himself running away from the gang leader, he swam as hard as he could toward the sinister shape beneath the water.

He sucked in as deep a breath as he could and dove.

Afraid it was a trick, that Rapp was waiting to drown him, Socko came down over the windshield, nowhere near the open driver's side window.

The face behind the glass was an eerie green. Light fractured by the ripples on the surface scarred the face with a web of jagged white lines, but the face looked peaceful. Rapp was definitely unconscious. Always too cool to wear a seatbelt, Rapp must have hit his head.

The tables had turned. Now he was Rapp's worst nightmare—and his only hope.

Socko hooked the toe of his sneaker under the bumper and pulled himself over to the door. He grasped the handle and pushed the release. He yanked on the door as hard as he could, but it didn't budge.

Suddenly a hand was on top of his. He and Livvy pulled on the handle together. The door swung open slowly, like the door of a bank vault. It was only halfway open when a dancing field of tiny black stars clouded his vision. The hand on top of his let go and latched onto his shirt. He was flailing his arms when warm air hit his face. He sucked in a deep breath, making a horrible rasping sound. "Gotta go back!"

"No!" She held onto his T-shirt. "We need help!" she yelled.

He glanced around wildly. The scene on the surface had changed. Luke was running toward the pool. The Corrigans' baby blue Cadillac squealed to a stop and the doors flew open.

"The guy in the car is drowning!" Livvy yelled, letting go of Socko's shirt.

Socko dove again. He was barely under when he heard a loud splash and Luke was in the pool too, his shirt billowing as he pulled himself down through the water. He pointed at Socko, then up.

Socko was about to break for the surface when he saw Rapp. His legs were still in the car, but his upper body had spilled out. His hands and arms floated as if he were dancing. Funny way to die. The two words "funny" and "die" crashed into each other. It wasn't funny. And he couldn't let it happen. He swam over and grabbed Rapp's hands.

It took both Socko and Luke to bring Rapp to the surface. "Got him," said Luke. "I'll take it from here."

Socko shook the water out of his eyes. The scene had changed again. Livvy was being held by her mother. The rotating lights of a squad car strafed the water.

"Bring him here!" yelled the policeman at the edge of the pool—it took Socko a second to recognize Officer Fricke.

Luke dragged the limp body over to the kneeling officer, who grabbed Rapp's arms.

Socko couldn't take his eyes off Rapp's face as the officer hauled him out of the water. Mouth open, skin pale, he was barely recognizable. He lay still on the concrete. Officer Fricke felt for a pulse.

Too stunned and exhausted to pull himself out, Socko clung to the lip of the pool. He knew the officer wouldn't find a pulse. Rapp was dead. He pressed his forehead against the tile, his eyes squeezed shut.

"Socko! Socko!"

A gnarled hand was reaching for him. With the help of Uncle

Eddie, his great-grandfather had lowered himself to his arthritic knees. "Take my hand!" the General ordered.

"Great way to get yourself drowned too," said Uncle Eddie, offering Socko another hand.

Socko grasped both.

As he was lifted out of the water by the two old men, the weightlessness of floating receded. He was heavy again, sitting in a puddle on hot concrete.

"Goll-durn it, son! You trying to get yourself killed?" The General crushed Socko to his chest.

His wet face against his great-grandfather's sweater, Socko smelled old-man mustiness. He felt a cool hand on the back of his neck.

"Thank God, you're all right. Thank God." The General's voice shook with relief. "You about scared me to death! Lucky thing Eddie deserted his post and came to our place ASAP. We've been driving around looking for you and Livvy ever since."

"What do you mean deserted my post?" Uncle Eddie pushed to his feet. "I'm still on duty!" He picked up his flashlight and stood over Rapp just in case he needed subduing.

Luke was on his knees beside Officer Fricke. "You got a pulse yet?" he asked.

The officer didn't waste time answering. As Socko watched, he pinched Rapp's nose and breathed into his mouth.

Rapp would hate a guy doing that to him, but Socko guessed it didn't matter to Rapp anymore. Maybe nothing did.

Junebug hadn't gotten out of the car, and Socko saw her watching with no expression on her face like she was in shock.

"Come on," Luke urged. "Breathe!"

Socko's feet were still in the water. He wanted to slip below the surface and disappear, but his great-grandfather still had an arm around his shoulders. "I'm proud of you," the old man whispered. "You are one brave soldier."

Socko stared into the pool at his waterlogged shoes. The laces, both untied, floated lazily in the water. Behind him, he could hear the grunt of Officer Fricke working on Rapp, doing chest compressions. If this

232

was what being brave was like, it sucked.

Luke let out a sudden yell behind them.

When Socko turned, he saw that Rapp had rolled onto his side. As Officer Fricke sat him up, Rapp bent his knees and leaned forward. He puked a greenish liquid onto the concrete between his feet.

"Looks like he'll live." A bony hand rubbed Socko's back.

Officer Fricke got on the radio with the ambulance, trying to explain where they were.

"I'm taking this boy to the ER," the General said, squeezing Socko's shoulder.

"There'll be an ambulance here soon," the officer said. "And I need to question the kid."

"You know where he lives. 'Til then, you take care of the hoodlum. I'll take care of the hero."

Socko didn't get why he had to go to the hospital, but he was too tired to fight it, and it was still kind of hard to breathe.

Luke stood him on his feet. "You sure don't mess around when you take care of business!" He ducked under Socko's arm. "Go on, lean."

His weight supported by Luke, Socko was able to stagger to the car. He felt Rapp's eyes on him, but the tingle at the back of his neck was gone.

He wasn't scared anymore.

***

Socko sat in the back seat, embarrassed that after lowering him into the car Luke had had to help him lift his feet and get them inside too. But the old men were making their way toward the car even more slowly, the General leaning on Eddie Corrigan.

"You have the right to remain silent…" Officer Fricke said to Rapp as he took the handcuffs off his belt.

"He doesn't need to do that," Socko muttered.

Uncle Eddie lowered the General into the backseat beside Socko. Luke climbed in from the other side, putting Socko in the middle.

233

Uncle Eddie slid in behind the wheel. "Guess we took care of that boyfriend of yours!" he told Junebug, patting her knee.

"Hey, wait for me!" Livvy broke away from her mother. Her long hair and yellow dress were sticking to her, but Livvy didn't seem to notice. She grabbed the car door handle, then stopped. "Oh, Socko! You lost it! You lost Damien's hat."

Socko reached up, but his fingers found only the short bristly hair left by the General's buzz cut. Somewhere along the way the hat had blown off, been scraped off, or floated away. Whatever had happened, Damien's Superman lid was gone.

"Might be neither one of you will need it now," said the General, watching Officer Fricke pull Rapp to his feet. "I suspect that hoodlum will be going away for a while. Your friend Damien will have a chance to rethink his choices."

"Can he come for a visit?" Socko asked.

"So far everyone and their uncle has come for a visit, so why the heck not?" The General slapped the door, a signal to Eddie Corrigan to drive.

"Wait!" Livvy wrenched the door open and clambered over Luke's legs.

"No!" Socko groaned. Everything on him hurt, but he was too tired to fend her off when she sat in his lap. And maybe he didn't want to.

"Hey," said the General with a scowl. "I'd like to see a little daylight between you two!"

But Livvy wasn't going anywhere.

CROSSING JORDAN

"In this sensitive portrait of black-white relations in a changing neighborhood, Fogelin offers a tactful, evenhanded look at prejudice." — *USA Today*

*YALSA Best Books for Young Adults
*Notable Books for a Global Society (Honor Book)

ANNA CASEY'S PLACE IN THE WORLD

"Anna has inner pluck and outer charm: she's been through a lot, but knows what needs to be done. Evocative descriptions bubble up from a deep reality.... And places are found, if not the ones both kids thought they wanted." — *Booklist*

*Bank Street College of Education Best Children's Books of the Year

THE SORTA SISTERS

"With insight and compassion, Fogelin explores the complexities and rewards of friendship and family... A heartfelt story that shows the many factors that create family, friends, and home." — *Booklist*

*Florida Book Awards (gold medal, children's category)

THE BIG NOTHING

"Serious and humorous by turns, this seemingly simple story is actually quite complex but not weighty and will be enthusiastically embraced."
— *School Library Journal,* STARRED REVIEW

*Young Adult Top Forty, Pennsylvania School Librarians Association

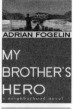

MY BROTHER'S HERO

"As in Adrian Fogelin's previous novels, CROSSING JORDAN and ANNA CASEY'S PLACE IN THE WORLD, this story has plenty of action, but it's the emotional drama, revealed in funny, realistic dialogue and spot-on descriptions, that distinguish the novel." — *Booklist*

SISTER SPIDER KNOWS ALL

"A Best of 2003 for Young Readers: Dead-on dialogue and strong, complex characters." — *The Washington Post*

*Parents' Choice Recommended Award

THE REAL QUESTION

"Fogelin delivers another smart tale... Fisher's delightfully telegraphed epiphanies, the funny, harrowing road trip, and a satisfying showdown with Dad yield a novel that may well appeal to teens of both sexes."
— *Publishers Weekly*

*Florida Book Awards (gold medal, young adult category)